C H A N D L E R
MORRISON
AMERICAN NARCISSUS
a   n o v e l

DEAD
SKY
PUBLISHING

For Sadie Hartmann

"Aphrodite's thirst was never quenched; it was cruel and dreamy. It was certainly the most splendid kind of thirst."

— ARTHUR RIMBAUD

Published by Dead Sky Publishing, LLC
Miami Beach, Florida
www.deadskypublishing.com

Photography by: Mark Maryanovich
Model: Alena Pokoptseva
Edited by Anna Kubik
Copyedited by Kristy Baptist
Formatting & Design by Apparatus Revolution, LLC

Paperback ISBN: 9781639511402
eBook ISBN: 9781639511808

CHANDLER
MORRISON
AMERICAN
NARCISSUS
a novel

ONE
ONLY LIES

ONLY LIES ARE SEXY.

Guys like Ryland Richter knew this. When the girl asked him what he did for a living, lying was the only option.

Nobody wanted the truth. They thought they did, these girls who all looked and talked the same. These girls—these *kids*—most of them at least a decade his junior, barely out of high school. What they wanted was to be told something inoffensive and life-affirming. Something that made them think, *Yes, I made the right choice in agreeing to go out with this guy.*

Ryland never told the truth—not when he was out with these girls, being asked this question. They didn't want to know he was a businessman, and the social strata of men with corner offices and expensive cufflinks represented, to them, something which needed to be torn down. Smashed. They didn't want to know he worked in the medical insurance industry. They didn't want to know his Mercedes-Maybach ran on gasoline paid for with money his team had refused to grant cancer-stricken grandmothers and mangled car crash victims based on whatever loophole they could find.

If he told them these things, it would lead to places he didn't want to go. They would find out through pointed questions that his voting history was streaked with red—more out of desire for self-preservation than any ideological grounds, but that wouldn't matter to them. His vested interest in his stock holdings and the accumulation of his possessions may as well have been a swastika carved into his forehead. And then they'd want to know his feelings about *the homeless* (he had none, save for a vague sense of disgust) and *immigration* (America had too many people as it was, especially here in Los Angeles, and more people meant fewer parking spaces), but he couldn't *say* any of *that*—if he did, they wouldn't sleep with him, and that was the only point of any of this—so instead he said...

"I'm a dog walker."

The girl smiled. Her lips hinted at something that might have been coyness. Playful skepticism. Her eyes scanned the quiet restaurant. Dark blue irises glinting in the candlelight. They stopped on the tuxedoed piano player with too-long fingers and a creepy grin before darting back to Ryland. "This is an awfully nice place to take a girl on a dog walker's budget. And your clothes, the car..."

Ryland sipped his champagne. Made a dismissive gesture with his hand. "I'm frugal," he said. When the girl raised an eyebrow, he added, "There's also, ah, family money."

The girl was somewhat satisfied but not all the way there yet.

"Enough for a few minor luxuries," Ryland went on, eyeing the waitress, trying to remember if he'd slept with her. "The car, the clothes, the condo in Brentwood." He returned his gaze to the girl. Gave her a small smile. "Nice restaurants for beautiful girls." He leaned back. "Most of the remainder goes to various charities."

He didn't give to any charities.

"I think it's imperative to assist the less fortunate in any way we can," said Ryland. "I see it as...an obligation." He could tell by the look on her face that he had hooked her.

The satisfaction he felt was coupled with disdain.

How greedily they all ate up this bullshit. They wanted men like him. It was in their biological code. They wanted someone who could *provide* for them, and had the trappings to prove it. But they also wanted a noble peasant, a martyr for *social justice*. They didn't realize they couldn't have both. There is no nobility in poverty. And thus, what they wound up with was guys like him, who could deceive them in the ways they wanted to be deceived.

Because the truth is ugly.

Only lies are sexy.

Later, Ryland left the sleeping girl in his bed and, clutching his phone, shut himself in the bathroom. He swallowed two Valium to help him come down off the coke. Sitting against the wall, he scrolled through the seventy-eight emails that had come in since he'd last checked it. None of them demanded immediate attention, which was disappointing.

He flipped to his voicemail. Nothing work-related, but one from Penny and another from Bruno. The sight of both these names dropped a weight of anxiety on his chest. He deleted both messages. He made a halfhearted promise to himself to call his brother back tomorrow, but Penny...he wasn't sure what he was going to do there.

Putting on his robe, he left the bathroom and exited the condo out the rear sliding glass door, walking the stone pathway to the lighted pool enclosed by a high wall of closely trimmed hedges.

The night was quiet and no one else was at the pool. Ryland reclined on one of the chaises and lit a cigarette. He opened his news app. The top story was about the fires in the Inland Empire. Indio had been almost completely overtaken. City officials in Thousand Palms were considering an evacuation. The origin of the blaze had been ruled as arson, but the governor had nevertheless pushed through a number of executive orders further tightening ecological restrictions. An emergency environmental coalition had been put together, and they began issuing fines to corporations not in compliance. Dozens of businesses had been forced to close.

Ryland's fellow executives had been lamenting things like this at length. They placed air-quotes around "the climate crisis." They complained that the governor was a precursor to a coming dystopia. And while Ryland nodded and muttered in feigned agreement, he didn't care all that much. Whether the planet burned up in ten years or in ten billion didn't feel like his concern.

"What are you doing out here?"

Ryland looked up. The girl he'd taken home with him stood several yards away. She was draped in his shirt. Her bedraggled hair pulled wildly away from her head.

"I...don't know," Ryland said. His eyes swept along the glittering pool water. Up to the hard, glassy black sky. "I guess I needed some air."

He thought of the deleted voicemail from Penny. A knot tightened around his rib cage. He could almost hear the bones creaking in protest. The knot moved to his left bicep, faint but pulsing, and he rubbed at it with kneading fingers.

"Come back to bed," the girl said. Her voice was thick with sleep. It wasn't becoming of her.

Ryland murmured his assent and gathered himself to his feet. He followed the girl to the dark condo. There was nothing else to do. Nowhere else to go.

TWO
FULLY GRADUATED

ARDEN COOVER GRADUATED from Berkeley with a bachelor's degree in philosophy, and found himself with no prospects and not much to do.

He spent the first couple weeks of the summer lazing around the pool house behind his parents' big Victorian in San Marino. He got stoned to the synthy pop mixes on the radio, swiping left on dating app profiles for girls with pictures that looked too professional. At some point, his father—once a successful movie director, now mostly retired and a "stay-at-home dad"—barged into the pool house to give him a lecture him about "the need for *action*, for *initiative*." He told him to find a job because he'd be cutting him off at the end of the summer. Arden could only look at him, unable to muster anything akin to emotion.

Near the end of the second week, Arden's high school friend, Baxter Kent, dropped by the house unannounced. Baxter was a tanned, blond surfer whose personality was little more than an Instagram reel of shirtless selfies and enormous bong rips. When he entered the pool house, Arden was lying stoned on the couch, staring at an episode of *Jersey Shore* with the sound turned off.

"Dude," said Baxter, picking Arden's bong up off the floor and sitting in a nearby armchair. "How long have you been back?" He checked the bowl before procuring a Bic from the pocket of his Bermuda shorts and taking a hit.

Arden's eyes didn't leave the wall-mounted flat-screen. "I don't know," he said. "Two weeks, I guess. I think."

"So, you're, like, what? Fully graduated now, or whatever?"

"Yeah," said Arden. "I'm *fully graduated.*"

"Sick," said Baxter, drawing out the *i*. He hit the bong again, scowled, and said, "Yikes, that's cashed." He stood and went to the window, looking out at the pool. Arden's bikini-clad sister, Tess, was reclined in a chaise longue with her face inclined to the sun. "God, your sister is so fucking hot. How old is she now?"

"Eighteen, I think. She just graduated high school."

"Nice." Again, he drew out the *i*. "You ever think about hitting that?"

"That's disgusting."

Baxter turned away from the window. His eyes wide with injured innocence. "Why? It's not like you're related. It's not like it's incest."

"Just because we're adopted doesn't mean I look at Tess as anything less than my sister. You fucking creep."

"Oh. Okay. So, like, can *I* fuck her?"

"You're impossible."

"Hey, that reminds me, what the fuck's up with your brother?"

Arden sat up and put his elbows on his knees. He rubbed his temples, wishing Baxter would leave. "He's not my brother," he explained. "He's my sister. I mean, um, *she's* my sister. She's doing the whole hormone replacement therapy thing." He paused, lit a cigarette, looking around for an ashtray. He found one in the drawer of the end table beside the couch. "Her name is Daffodil now."

Baxter mulled this over. "Uh, right, cool. But, like, isn't he—I mean, um, she—isn't she, like...three?"

"She's four."

"Oh, right," said Baxter, twisting his hands in front of him. "Yeah.

Four." He looked over his shoulder, out the window. "Uh, anyway. Does Tess have an iPorn page?"

"Jesus, dude. How should I know."

"Can you, like, find out?"

"I'm not going to ask my little sister if she has an iPorn page."

Baxter came back over to the armchair and asked for a cigarette. Arden tossed the pack to him. Baxter drew one out and lit it. He tilted his head back and blew smoke toward the ceiling. "So, like, what did you do in college?"

Arden thought about it, attempting to associate meaning or emotion with his hazy memories from the last four years. He took a desperate drag from his cigarette, as though it might fill the space inside him. "I don't know," he said at last. "College stuff, I guess."

"College stuff like...what?"

"A lot of acid." Arden looked at the faces and bodies moving on the TV screen. He tried to reconcile the notion that they were real people with actual lives, but he could not. He looked at Baxter, and he couldn't see him as a real person, either. Nobody had been real to him for some time. "Too much acid," he said.

"No such thing, bro," said Baxter. "You fuck a lot of girls?"

Arden shut his eyes. "Baxter," he said, "what are you even doing here?"

Baxter was amiable, relaxed. Arden's impatience didn't seem to register. "I don't know. Someone mentioned you were back. I thought I'd, you know, pop by, see what's hanging, what's shaking. Where's your hot mom? I was hoping she'd be here."

"She's not. Tess says she's never home. Some new job."

"Doing what?"

"I don't know. Something with medical insurance, I think."

"*She* should make an iPorn page. She wouldn't need a job." Baxter raised his hand for a high-five.

Arden blinked at Baxter's hand. "Baxter," he said again, hearing the exhaustion in his voice, "what are you doing."

Baxter lowered his hand, but his smile didn't falter. "Dude, you gotta get loose. You're way too tense." He nodded toward the bong. "It's probably that strain you're smoking. What you need is a good sativa, something to, you know, *invigorate* you. Let me know when you're free and we'll hit up the dispensary. My treat."

"Sure, whatever."

Baxter's eyes wandered to the TV. He squinted at it, as if he might find something of interest there. Finding none, he stood, crushing out his cigarette in the ashtray, and said, "I'm going to go talk to your hot sister, and then I gotta bounce up outta here. Hit me up, my dude."

"Yeah," said Arden, leaning back and shutting his eyes again. "Will do."

The energy inside the pool house remained the same after Baxter's departure. If not for the crushed-out cigarette in the ashtray, Arden could have pretended he'd never been there at all.

THREE
IMPERFECT

"WOW, THIS IS YOUR PLACE?" the girl from the dispensary said as Baxter let her into the sprawling foyer of his father's house in Arcadia, a short drive from Arden's. She took her shoes off and twirled around the wide hallway with her arms out, gazing at the high, arched ceiling.

"It's, uh, my dad's," said Baxter. He rubbed the back of his neck. "I stay here during the summer and live with my, um, my mom in Pasadena the rest of the year."

The girl turned to him. She had large eyes with irises like dollops of syrup. Her hair was long and tangled. "Is your dad *here*?" she asked, stepping closer to him.

Perspiration broke out on Baxter's temples and in the creases of his palms. He gave the girl a smile that he hoped came across as confident. "Ah, no. No, he's not. He's never here. He travels a lot for his job. I think he does something with, like, I don't know, finance or—"

The girl came closer, putting her hands on Baxter's biceps and pressing against him. She kissed him with a sloppy fervor that made his heart palpitate. "I don't give a fuck about your dad," she whispered in his ear.

Baxter stood at the foot of the bed. He examined the naked girl sprawled before him.

He tried not to see certain things, like the razor bumps dappled along her inner thighs, or the uneven stubble prickling her vagina. He tried to ignore the way one breast was somewhat disproportionate to the other, and appeared to hang an inch lower, just as he tried to ignore the three tiny hairs sprouting from the base of her right nipple. Her stomach distended slightly—not grossly, but enough for Baxter to be unable to ignore it. He also couldn't ignore how knobby her knees were, how *bulbous*, nor could he ignore how her labia resembled a wad of old roast beef.

His cock dangled useless and barely half-hard. If just one of the girl's glaring imperfections could be overlooked, he might have been able to conjure enough arousal to get hard enough to penetrate her, but in his current state this was an impossibility.

"What's wrong?" the girl asked. She propped herself up on her elbows, reading his face. Her stomach creased, forming a repulsive little pouch above the wretched folds of her genitals. The afternoon sun coming in through the wide window illuminated each flaw with nauseating precision.

You aren't perfect, he wanted to tell her. *I needed you to be perfect.*

She had *seemed* perfect, in the dim light of the dispensary, dressed in suggestive clothing that hinted at something sumptuous while concealing all that was unsightly. Baxter had ogled her from the other side of the counter. Had imagined what she might look like beneath her clothes. His fantasies had been tantalizing. Reality proved—as it so often did—to be a disappointment.

Baxter bit his lip and closed his eyes. He scrolled through his mental scrapbook of the Porn Girls, the ones with bodies tanned and toned and digitally tweaked to aesthetic perfection. The Porn Girls could get him hard in seconds. Could bring him to climax in under a minute. He suspected this girl, this *Real Girl*, would need to coax and tease him for hours to stimulate him to the point of ejaculation.

"Baxter? Are you okay?"

I don't think so. He wanted to tell her he was concerned—and not for the first time—pornography had ruined him. This was the sixth consecutive encounter with a Real Girl that was doomed to failure. In all, there had been dozens of such occurrences. Even when he could sustain an erection for long enough to go through with the act of copulation, the experience itself was unsatisfactory. He would either ejaculate too quickly, or his penis would grow soft inside the girl, forcing him to fake an orgasm that left him frustrated.

And afterward, the girls would *talk*. They would cuddle against him and prattle on about whatever nonsense bounced around in their skulls.

All he wanted in those instances was for them to leave. Those post-coital moments were perhaps the most exhausting aspect of the Porn Problem, because the Real Girls who managed to arouse him lost all allure as soon as the semen had been drained from him. Their bodies became so repugnantly human. Little gurgles emitted from their guts. Hot, pungent breath seeped from their lungs and pelted the side of his face.

"Baxter?" the girl said again. Her tone was tinged with agitation and a shadow of fear.

Baxter opened his eyes but did not look at her. He went to the window, looking out at the manicured backyard, the high wall of hedges, the lemon tree, the swimming pool. "I'm sorry," he said, and he was, but not for her. "You should go. I can't do anything for you."

"*What?*" the girl said. There was no longer any fear in her voice. There was only anger. Disgust. "What is that even supposed to *mean*?"

"You should go," Baxter said again.

"You *drove* me here, asshole."

"Yeah," Baxter said. "I don't know. Call a Lyft."

"Are you fucking *kidding* me right now?"

"No. I'm, um...I'm not kidding."

"Wow. *Wow*. Seriously, fuck you." He heard creaking bedsprings and fabric sliding over skin. "You rich assholes are all so fucked up." He heard padding footsteps on the carpet, down the hall, down the stairs. Heard the front door slam.

The worst thing, he realized, was that he would have to find a new dispensary.

FOUR
CHESS MOVES

"DO you remember the exact moment you fell in love with yourself?"

Tess Coover asked this as she came out onto the balcony of the mansion in the hills above Silver Lake. She wore the black La Perla negligee The Writer had made her put on. The Writer leaned shirtless and barefoot against the railing, so effortlessly sexy. His tousled brown hair with its flecks of gray. The taut muscles of his slim torso. He wore Persol sunglasses even though the sun had almost sunken beneath the metropolis sprawled out below them. A cigarette hung from his mouth. It had gone out. He looked up from the copy of his own novel he was holding open in his hands. Tess could sense his eyes appraising her body from behind the dark lenses of the sunglasses.

"Do you remember exactly when it happened?" Tess asked. "Or was it more of, like, a gradual thing?"

The Writer shut the book. He set it on the little glass table beside him. "CHANDLER EASTRIDGE" was emblazoned upon its cover in big, gold lettering that took up nearly half the available space. The title, *Barely on Fire*, was printed in a much smaller font, so small Tess wouldn't have been able to make it out if she didn't already know what it was. She supposed the title didn't matter.

Chandler reached into the pocket of his Armani jogging pants and took out a Zippo. It was customized with the cover artwork from his first novel, *Nothing but the Rain*. He relit his cigarette. Returned the lighter to his pocket. His movements were always calculated to appear casual. The smile that slowly broke out face was lazy and disarming. Tess looked away.

"You kids," he said. "You hate success. You want to make it into something it's not."

Tess glanced at him. "Something like narcissism? Because that's what it is. Maybe not all success, but with you, that's definitely what it is."

"There's something about seeing your work printed upon a bound page. Holding it in your hands. There's a magic to it. A mysticism. You spend all this time dreaming madly, trying to work it all out of your head. You slave over the right word, the perfect sentence, and all the while you're dreaming, dreaming. And then *this*—" he gestured at the book on the table "—is presented to you, your dream manifested into something tangible, something real." He grinned, shook his head. "You wouldn't understand."

"No, yeah, I get it," said Tess. "But how many times have you read it since the publisher sent it to you? Don't you get tired of mentally jerking yourself off?"

If he was bothered by this jab, he didn't show it. He smoked his cigarette and watched Tess with a patient kind of silence that made her feel both desired and disgusted.

She wondered how many other girls he'd made feel the same way, and moreover, how many of them had been during his time as a high school English teacher. She knew there'd been at least one, because she'd read his books—though she'd never admit that to him—and she didn't think he was that imaginative. The protagonists felt too much like him.

"Do you want to read it?" he asked. "It's my best one. It's a good place to start."

"I keep telling you. I don't really read fiction. Not even yours. Or *especially* not yours, whatever you like." In reality, she was looking forward to reading the new book. She'd loved everything he'd written —his books clarified some elusive, indistinct element of modern existence that other authors skirted around—but if he knew that, it would destroy their entire dynamic. Everything would collapse. Maybe that would be for the best, but Tess wasn't ready to pull that Jenga block yet. She wondered if she would ever be. A faint nausea swirled within her.

A half-empty highball sat on the edge of the railing. Tess went to it. Picked it up, knocked it back. She sat in the lone chair by the sliding glass door, ignoring the chill settling into the exposed parts of her body as the day's heat died.

"I could read it *to* you," The Writer said.

"Yeah, I bet you'd like that. And I suppose I'd need to complete the fantasy for you, suck your cock as you're reading, only pausing to tell you how brilliant you are."

His grin wasn't condescending, but it was close. "Your idea," he said. "Not mine."

Tess rolled her eyes. "Did you see that article about the top ten most toxic male authors?" she asked. "It came out yesterday, I think it was in *Vogue*. Like, 'Don't date a guy if he reads any of these writers,' or whatever."

The Writer frowned. Tess could tell she'd struck an elusive nerve. "I saw it," he said. "And it was *Teen Vogue*. Nobody reads that shit anyway."

"You were number three," said Tess with a wicked little smile. "You even beat out Franzen."

"I said I saw it."

"But in a *sense*, you're *basically* number one, because David Foster Wallace and Philip Roth are both dead."

"It doesn't mean anything. They're talking about me. Writing about me. The person who wrote that article—do you think they'll ever write anything about her? Anything at all? Can you even remember her name?"

"No. But I bet *you* do."

Something rare flashed across his face, a brief glimpse of untapped emotion, but it was gone quickly. "I don't," he said. "I haven't thought about it until now. People were saying that shit about me the minute my first book became a bestseller. Not even *people*—it's *kids*, you kids and your hatred of success. You can't stand it."

"Right, of *course*. Everyone is *jealous* of you. I know *I* am." She rolled her eyes again.

The easy smile returned to The Writer's face. "You don't need to be." He spread out his arms. "All of this could be yours. Just say the word."

"Yeah, sure, marry an eighteen-year-old fresh out of high school. That'll do wonders for your reputation."

"I don't give a damn about my reputation."

"Of all the lies you've told me, that might be the biggest one."

The corner of his mouth twitched. "I've never lied to you."

"Wow, look at you, breaking your own record left and right. Slow down, cowboy, don't hurt yourself."

"Such a charmer, always."

"What do you want to marry me for, anyway? I'm not even nice to you."

The Writer dragged from his cigarette before he asked, "Is this you fishing for compliments?"

"No. I honestly want to know. Why me? You could easily throw a ring on one of your zillions of little groupies. One who'd happily suck your ego's dick. I only suck your *real* dick, and probably not as often as you'd like. *Definitely* not as often as a groupie would."

"I don't sleep with my fans," The Writer said. When Tess gave him a look, he amended, "Okay, not anymore. They're not interesting. I know every word they're going to say before they even get the inclination to say it. You—" he pointed at her with the cigarette, jabbing the air with it "—you're different. I never know what's going to come out of your mouth."

"So, what, I'm unpredictable? That's your answer? You want to marry me because I'm unpredictable?"

The Writer turned away. He adjusted his sunglasses and placed his hands on the banister, watching the sun set on a dominion which, Tess thought, seemed more and more like his own. "You make everything so simple," he said.

"I'm only going off what you're giving me."

He blew smoke at the sky. "I give you everything."

"What about the three women you were married to before me? Were *they* unpredictable?"

"No. Hence their absence."

"If they weren't unpredictable, then why did you marry them?"

The lean muscles in The Writer's shoulders tightened. "Tess," he said. His voice was a warning. A blinking yellow caution sign. "Why are we talking about this. Why do they matter."

Tess extended her legs, crossed them. "You're asking me—your prospective bride—why your previous wives matter. Your *three* previous wives. Not very astute for someone who's supposed to be an expert on the human condition."

Rotating his body to face her, backlit by the fading light like an artist's ironic rendering of a biblical saint, The Writer said, "You're assigning significance to the quantity. Why? Three isn't that many."

"In what universe?"

"More than half of celebrity marriages end in divorce."

"Not making a great case for yourself, chief."

There was a harried exasperation in the tight-lipped smile he flashed at her. "See," he said, "right there. You're slippery. I think I have you in checkmate, and then you move a pawn and suddenly the tide of the whole match shifts."

Tess squinted at him. "We're talking," she said. "Not playing chess. I don't even know how to play chess."

"But you do. Every conversation between a man and a woman is a chess match."

"That sounds like a really...exhausting way to live."

"Not when you're accustomed to winning."

"What do you typically get when you win?"

"Whatever I want."

FIVE
DANCING SHADOWS AND FIRELIGHT

"YOU WORK TOO MUCH. You're always here."

Ryland glanced up from his computer screen. It had been a long time since he'd looked away from the spreadsheets and their endless rows of data. The office around him swam with floating integers and formulas, a hypnagogic hallucination as the dream world of Excel merged with reality.

He blinked, rubbed his eyes. Katrina Coover stood in the doorway, her face drawn into something resembling concern. She was his most recent hire, and he supposed that look was why he'd selected her from the pool of more qualified candidates—there was an alluring quality to the matronly nature she projected. At forty-two, she was only ten years his senior, but he could imagine her tucking him into bed, combing her fingers through his hair. Whispering him to sleep and shielding him from the evils of the world. Telling him everything would be okay. She could protect him. He supposed a therapist would have something to say about that. He did not have a therapist.

"I want to have everything buttoned up for Monday," Ryland

said. "Truman is going to look for any opening he can to shoot holes in our numbers, and—"

"There aren't any holes." Katrina's face broke into a smile that made Ryland nervous. She had an easy beauty; if there'd been work done, you couldn't tell. The blonde hair didn't appear to be a dye job. The three kids, she'd told him, were adopted, and thus her figure had been preserved. "I've been over it and over it," she assured him. "Truman won't find anything because there's nothing to find. Have you looked at the slides?"

Ryland minimized Excel and opened his inbox, started scrolling. The subject lines blurred together. He needed a drink, some blow. A cigarette at the very least.

"Did you send them? I haven't checked Outlook in—ah, never mind, here they are." A beat of silence as he scrolled. "These look good. Nicely done."

"Everything is ready. Go home, get some sleep. You have all weekend." She glanced at her watch. Ryland tried to make out the brand—Bulova, he was pretty sure. Classy, tasteful, not too flashy. "It's almost ten. There's hardly anyone else here. Even the cleaning people have left."

Ryland rubbed his eyes again. He rose to his feet and went to the floor-to-ceiling window, peering at the tiny beacons of slow head-lights moving along Olympic fifteen stories below. Up here, he was a god.

"I have some last-minute things to finish up," he told Katrina, not turning away from the window. "I'll be heading out soon. Go ahead, take off. Had I known you were still here I would have told you to go home hours ago." He watched the shape of her in the reflection of the glass.

"Are you sure? I can—"

"I'm sure, Katrina. Just because I don't have a life doesn't mean you shouldn't."

She smoothed her skirt, looking around as if there might be

something else for her to do. "All right, well, if you think of anything..."

"I won't." He turned to face her. "Turn off your phone. Don't check your inbox when you get home. Spend some time with your husband."

She made a face—it was barely perceptible but didn't escape Ryland's notice. She recovered, the smile returning. She thanked him, bade him goodnight, and vanished into the hallway.

Ryland waited a few moments before shutting the office door and locking it. He sat down on the leather couch against the wall and took his vial of coke from inside his suit coat, snorting two quick bumps off the little spoon affixed to the bottom of the cap.

His phone vibrated, and he frowned when he saw "PENNY" appear on the screen like an omen. He swiped "Ignore."

He still needed a cigarette, so he left his office and took the elevator down to the lobby, exiting out the south door into the court-yard. On the way, he passed a pale, creepy janitor who watched him with stabbing black eyes and a too-wide grin.

It was a warm night, made warmer by the tingling electricity dancing along the surface of his skin. He lit a Marlboro. The nicotine mixed with the coke to produce a pleasant hum in his veins and at the base of his skull.

The cigarette was down to its last few drags when Ryland noticed the silhouette of a girl watching him from one of the tables, away from the light. He was about to deposit the cigarette in one of the ashcans when she stood and walked toward him. Her heels resounded on the cement like gunfire. He knew she was attractive even before he could make out her features; she had that strut only certain girls do—poised, self-assured, that air of knowing she commanded attention.

She came to stand before him in the light, holding her cigarette elegantly away from her body, which was devastatingly thin but held enough shape so as not to appear sickly. Her long, night-black hair was glossy and well-kept and banded with blonde lowlights, and her young face—she couldn't have been much older than twenty-one or twenty-two—was meticulously made up. Ryland's eyes drifted to the faint stain of dark rouge lipstick on the filter of her cigarette.

"You're the big boss, right?" she asked. Her green eyes gleamed beneath the heavy black canopy of her long lashes. There was something within them that both excited and unnerved Ryland. A spark of mischief intermingled with something like madness.

Ryland gazed down at her; she was nearly a foot shorter. He hit his dying cigarette, surprised by how nervous he suddenly felt. "The big boss?" He forced a laugh. It sounded strained, and he winced. "I guess that depends what department you're in."

"Claims Adjustment," she said. Her voice possessed the same lighthearted lunacy her eyes did. "I'm new. Just started Monday."

"Well, ah, welcome. You made it a whole week. And, um, yes, I suppose that makes me the big boss."

Her eyes never left his. Never even blinked. "Pity," she said. She brought the cigarette to her lips. Held it there. Drew it away. The smoke hesitated with reluctant longing as it left her mouth.

Ryland swallowed. "Why is it...a pity?"

"Lots of reasons." The spark in her eyes bloomed into an emerald flame that jumped and quivered. "Mainly, I'd hate to have your job. Any corporate executive job like that. I'd hate it." She spoke quickly, but with measured precision. Like she was reading from a script.

"I don't mind it. I enjoy it, actually."

The corners of her lips pulled into an impish smile. Her teeth were small, childlike, impeccably straight. "Work will set you free."

"I don't know about that," Ryland said, feeling like he was missing something. "But, um. I mean, it pays well."

"I bet it does." A pause as she studied him. "You know," she said, "you look kind of like Robert Redford."

"You don't look old enough to know who Robert Redford is."

"I'm not." She said it like it was an admission. "But I liked that one movie he was in. Where he was a cowboy, or whatever."

"*Butch Cassidy and the Sundance Kid.*"

"Right. That one. He was the older guy, right?" Ryland frowned, and she added, "Kidding, I'm *kidding*, relax."

She came closer without seeming to move. Ryland could smell her perfume. Something expensive, but he couldn't identify it. He was aware of his elevating pulse and knew it had nothing to do with the coke. Those unblinking eyes fixed on his, searching, probing. A cough into his fist, a cleared throat, the shortening stub of his cigarette a heavy and foreign object between his fingers. The ground felt a long way down.

"You okay?" she said. It was phrased like a question, but it wasn't one. She knew what she was doing to him. The amusement in her face gave that away, but even that must have been intentional. "I really *was* kidding. I know who Paul Newman is, too. You don't look like him. Redford was better looking than Newman."

"Listen," Ryland said. The cigarette fell from his fingers. He didn't step on it. To move, to look away, to break the trance, her *spell*, whatever it was—this was out of the question. "Do you want to get a drink?"

The fire in her eyes jumped. Ryland could feel its heat on his face. "They frown on that kind of thing," she said. "You being you, me being me..." She lifted her eyes, waggled her head. Like it was all so trivial.

"They do," said Ryland.

"There's a boyfriend. At home, waiting. He wouldn't like it much if I told him I was going out for drinks with the big boss. I don't think he'd like it at all."

It occurred to Ryland for the first time that it was peculiar she was here so late, when all the other claims adjusters had left. But this was a minor detail, irrelevant, and so instead of inquiring about it, he asked, "Do you tell your boyfriend everything?"

She laughed, and it was in that laughter that whatever was wrong with her announced itself. It was a sound like sparks spitting from a tangle of frayed wires. It was the sound of someone coming apart. It was a sound that told Ryland to *RUN*...not as a warning, but a dare.

"They do say communication is the key to a healthy relationship," the girl said. The loose remnants of her harsh cackle still showed on her lips.

"Do you have a healthy relationship?"

"Nothing about me is healthy."

Run. RUN.

"What he doesn't know won't hurt him," said Ryland, feeling bolder.

The girl brought the cigarette to her full, dark lips. Her eyes considered him, or pretended to. The smoke curled around her face. Snakelike, sensuous. "You need some new lines," she said. She still hadn't blinked. The light of her eyes felt hot enough to burn Ryland to the ground, so far below. "I've heard them all."

"It's not always necessary to reinvent the wheel."

"You don't know anything about me," she said. "You don't even know my name."

"Isn't that why men ask women out for drinks? To find out the things they don't know?"

"No," she said. Her smile was wicked. "That's not why men ask women out for drinks. And it's Lyssi. Lyssi Rhodes." She pronounced "Lyssi" like it rhymed with "sissy."

"Lyssi," Ryland repeated, testing the name in his mouth. "What's that short for?"

Lyssi's devious grin grew, deepening her dimples. Ryland's heart fluttered. "Elysium," she said. "Like the afterlife. Like paradise."

"I like that. I don't think it's your real name, though."

She tilted her head to the side. "It's LA. Nothing here is real."

"I'm real."

The lunatic laughter again, abbreviated but no less terrifying. "Are you sure about that?" she asked, goading him with her eyes.

"Let me show you."

The laughter came once more, and with it, the dare.

Ryland remained rooted in place. Lyssi unslung her Prada purse from her shoulder, took out her phone. Its light cast a haunting glow upon her face. "Let me text Kyle," she said. Her thumbs tapped gracefully across the screen despite her long, scarlet nails. The unblinking eyes flicked to him after she'd returned the phone to her purse. She held up a finger. "One drink," she said. "Only one."

Ryland started to feel more at ease halfway into the third drink, as he listened to her talk in the dim, ambient light of The Edith lounge.

She was nineteen, an only child with erratic, drug-addicted parents to whom she didn't speak. She came from Millhaven, Ohio, just south of Cleveland. She'd moved here a year ago with the boyfriend—who was twenty-one—when he'd signed a semi-lucrative recording contract after his rap song, "Pussy Like a Porsche (Got Me Zoomin')," had gone viral. He'd recorded it on an iPhone in the basement of his parents' house.

Her interests included, but were not limited to: anime and manga, *The Real Housewives* series (all of them, but *Beverly Hills* was her favorite), Chandler Eastridge novels, the early albums from Marina and the Diamonds, makeup, manicures, Murakami (both Haruki and Ryu, though she preferred the latter), terrible horror movies from the eighties, *Children of Light* by Robert Stone (she reread it every autumn), shopping at the Beverly Center, all things Nintendo, and weed.

She didn't have a driver's license and had no interest in getting one; she Ubered everywhere. There was no real reason for her to have a job save for her growing boredom and the fact that Kyle, the boyfriend, was always having friends over to their apartment in Westwood, all of whom she hated.

She made a point of expressing her disgust with the medical insurance industry, but she'd gotten the position as a result of her connection with someone in the finance department—Ryland didn't ask what the connection was—so she'd set aside her scruples in favor of the short commute and excellent benefits.

Ryland heard all of this, and it registered enough to be filed away somewhere in his mind for later review, but in the moment her words themselves weren't all that relevant.

He was transfixed more by the shape of her mouth as it moved around the things she said. The way her eyes, alight with ceaseless promise, possessed their own self-sustained life force. By the intricacy of her mannerisms—the subtle tilting of her head; her small, expressive hands; the polite, dainty fashion in which she sipped her daiquiri; the twisting of a lock hair around her finger. The effect of the nearly three martinis Ryland had downed was negligible—it was Lyssi's mystifying essence on which he was growing drunk.

He couldn't shake the feeling it was all an act orchestrated for his benefit. That everything she did was a choreographed step in an elaborate dance of malicious seduction. He didn't care. He was in her grasp. Had surrendered to it.

It was when he'd finished the third martini that Ryland interrupted something she was saying about being a cheerleader in high school and suggested they "get out of here." The smile she gave him in response to this proposal appeared to signify a kind of victory within her.

She told him that Kyle was still expecting her. Ryland told her to make something up. This invited another smile much like the first, and she tapped out a text message before taking a final sip of her drink and saying, "You're the boss."

Ryland's condo was fifteen minutes away—a short drive, all things considered, but it felt much too long now. An urgency had arisen within him, a frantic desperation which required immediate satiation. They'd taken a Lyft to the lounge, and now they took one to the InterContinental on Avenue of the Stars. Ryland booked the room on his phone during the brisk three-minute drive as the car moved beneath the curved shadows of the palm trees. Lyssi sat close, her hand on his thigh, her lips on his neck.

In the room, she was upon him as soon as the door had closed. She kissed him like it would be her last act in life. Ryland had never particularly liked kissing—he saw it as a means to an end, an exhausting but necessary element of foreplay that he could have done without, but this was different. Her mouth locking with his, sucking his breath, the caress of her tongue along the backs of his teeth...her arms around his neck, her pelvis moving against his groin...it was everything. It was bigger than everything.

They undressed in an impassioned fury. The lights were dimmed, and Lyssi's white skin radiated a warm, candle-like glow. A butterfly-shaped piercing studded the navel set within her flat stomach. Her thigh-high stockings stayed on; everything else came off. She fell on her back upon the bed, legs parted in invitation, eyes pleading. Ryland stood helpless before her at the foot of the bed. He felt paralyzed by her beauty. The stillness of her repose, the arrangement of her body as she waited for him...she was like the subject of a painting, and she knew it.

Ryland stepped forward, fell to his knees. His hands ran up her legs, over her stomach, took hold of her breasts. He pressed his face between her legs, tasted her—another act he traditionally disliked, but which here felt natural, even pleasurable. Her narrow thighs pressed against his ears. The sharp acrylics on her nails scraped his scalp as her hands buried into his hair.

Her soft moans elevated into cries that were like music as she ground herself against his mouth. The taste of her flooded over his tongue, and then she pushed him away, pulled him to her. All at once he was inside her, her legs entwined around his waist as their bodies moved in tandem, her eyes wide and vulnerable, her arms splayed out beside her with handfuls of the bedsheets in her closed fists.

And...it wasn't like sex, not the kind Ryland was used to having.

It was a less physical feeling. More akin to what he felt when he looked out over the city from his office window after a successful meeting and a few quick bumps of blow. It was transcendent. Godlike.

It was how she looked at him as he moved atop her. All that madness in her eyes, that electric frenzy, the wicked and lunatic cunning...it was all gone, replaced with a tragic innocence, a *trust*, as though she had surrendered herself to him. Like she was a small, helpless animal in the palm of his hand, given over to his superior size, his dominance.

It made him want to weep, and he kissed her like she was the only thing he'd ever known in the world. When he came, he felt all that power drained away from him and returned to her, but that was good, too—it was *right*, it was *justified*, it *belonged* to her; she had only lent it to him, and that was okay...he couldn't live with all that power, not all the time.

He fell off her onto his side and pulled her to him, holding her body against his, afraid if he let go, she would drift away like smoke.

They may have slept for a while, coming in and out of a light half-haze, never disconnecting from each other. And then, there was more. All night, they did to each other everything Ryland could conjure in his mind, and a few things she suggested which he'd never so much as considered.

He convinced his coke dealer—at a steep additional expense—to deliver right to their room, and the two of them went through an eight-ball in a few hours, snorting long lines off each other's body. Ryland ordered a bottle of Dom Perignon from room service—the waiter who brought it up terrified him with his black eyes and too-wide grin that contained too many teeth, but he dismissed this as coke-fueled paranoia—and he and Lyssi became pleasantly drunk as they came down off the coke, feeding each other Valium and Xanax like they were exotic chocolates.

As the night edged into dawn, they lay together on the bed,

tangled in sheets dampened with perspiration and ejaculate, too exhausted for sex and too wired for sleep.

Ryland's fingers were tracing through Lyssi's sleek hair when she suddenly sat up, yawning, and stretching. Her eyes were leveled at him, her head cocked. "If you tell my boyfriend, I'll kill you," she said. It was uttered as a bland statement of fact, as casual as a comment on the weather. "I'll kill you in your sleep."

Ryland's resultant laughter died when Lyssi's face remained rigid and humorless. He propped himself up on his elbows, blinking at her. "Why would I tell your boyfriend? Why would I even...talk to him? I don't even know who he is."

"I know. I don't know. I just have to say it." She flashed a sweet smile, batted her eyelashes. "I need you to always remember that. If you ever try to interfere with my life in any way—*ever*—I will murder you. And I will get away with it."

"I wouldn't," Ryland said, dumbfounded. "I would never."

She got out of bed and went over to the window with a little skip in her step. She peered out the curtains, pushing them open with her fingers. Not looking at him, she said, "Don't get me wrong. He's annoying. He's *a child*. I hate almost every minute I spend with him. But he takes care of me. He's always taken care of me. And besides, I can't sleep alone. I *can't*."

Ryland had a preposterous urge to tell her she wouldn't have to sleep alone, she could sleep with him, but that was absurd. He had no desire to domesticate with anyone, much less a random girl—his *employee*, he reminded himself—he'd just met. Thus, he instead told her, "You don't have anything to worry about. That's not what this is."

She turned around and stared at him for a few long moments in that spooky, unblinking way of hers, and then she grinned and pounced onto the bed, lathering kisses upon his face. "Good," she said, snuggling up against him and laying her head on his chest. "Because if you did—if you ever betrayed me at all, in *any way*—I would ruin you. I'd ruin your whole life, and right when you thought things couldn't get any worse, that's when I'd kill you."

"You don't have anything to worry about," Ryland said again. He resumed stroking her hair and looked down at her peaceful, contented face, and he wondered to himself, *But...do I?*

SIX
THE MOST BEAUTIFUL THINGS

ARDEN WOKE early on Saturday morning, roused from a restless slumber by dreams of decrepit, reptilian humanoids feasting on obese guinea pigs, and of shallow trenches filled past capacity with the mangled corpses of people without faces.

He shuffled to the bathroom and did two lines of coke before downing his cocktail of prescribed pharmaceuticals—Lexapro and Cymbalta for the depression, Lamictal for mood stabilization, Neurontin for anxiety. He considered the bottles of Valium and Xanax and decided he didn't want them, not today, settling instead for a Vicodin, and then he brushed his teeth and showered before getting dressed and going outside.

Lighting a cigarette, he looked up at the purplish pre-dawn sky, watching the fading pale specks of the stars swirl and dance. They left orange trails in their wake. His eyes lowered to the water in the pool. It whispered to him, beckoning him into its silver depths. A crumpled beach towel on one of the chaises writhed as if in agony. Seeing it squirm like that filled him with such immense suffering he had to look away. He squeezed his eyes closed and sat on the pavement. When he opened them, everything had become still.

He got up and crept into the house through the back door. The angles and dimensions were wrong. He wasn't sure how long it had been since he'd been inside. He couldn't remember if he'd come in at all when he'd first gotten back, or if he'd gone straight to the pool house through the back gate. It felt like a dead place.

Arden tiptoed through the house and had almost made it to the foyer when he noticed the maid watching him from the kitchen. He couldn't tell if she was the same one they'd had when he'd left for college. He stopped, and the two of them regarded each other in silence. There was something like disapproval in her eyes. A hesitant kind of reproach. Arden looked away, ashamed of something he couldn't identify. He continued on his way and exited out the front door, getting into his Jaguar XF and backing out of the driveway.

He slowed as he passed the empty Tudor where the Riders had once lived. It had remained uninhabited since the family had disappeared before Arden had left for college. The daughter, Beatrice, had been a friend of Tess's during the short time the Riders had lived on their street, and Mrs. Rider had been a frequent guest at Katrina Coover's cocktail parties.

Something about the house unsettled Arden—the way it loomed dark and vacant on the otherwise quaint street was like a disfiguring tumor blighting the face of a runway model. The mystery around the circumstances of the family's disappearance had always struck Arden with a stab of dread. He gave one final appraisal of the house's black windows and untended lawn before speeding away.

He didn't know where he was going, only that he needed to move, to at least give himself the illusion he was an active participant in his life, in the world.

It was a lie, but it didn't matter.

He turned left onto Huntington and pressed the power button on his stereo. The end of an antidepressant advertisement gave way to something with a heavy drum beat. It sounded abrasive and mildly unpleasant, but after a few moments he was able to surrender to the music's mindless, almost comforting inauthenticity. There was familiarity there.

He took a joint from his center console and lit it, turning the music up. At a stoplight, he watched as a battalion of soldiers in red uniforms marched a small group of weeping citizens down the sidewalk. The soldiers' machine guns were trained on the civilians' backs. Somebody dressed as the Berkeley bear mascot was standing a safe distance away, watching the soldiers. Its yellow jersey was splattered with scarlet stains. One of the soldiers glanced at Arden. His eyes were small and cruel beneath the brim of his crimson cap. Arden looked away. The light turned green.

Some invisible force upon him lifted when he pulled onto the freeway and pushed down on the accelerator. The wide lanes were nearly empty beneath the pink-orange sky. He felt he could keep driving forever, until the road ran out and the world dissolved and everything terrible fell away into a black, howling abyss.

Arden spaced out for a while, lost in a slow trickle of memories that lacked substance or clarity. The road disappeared beneath his tires, swallowed by the cruel black nose of his car. The music floated in and out of his perception. He slowed only once, to maneuver around a tank blocking several lanes of the highway. More men in red uniforms stood around it, leaning against it and sitting atop it, smoking cigarettes and paying him no mind as he passed.

It hadn't occurred to him where he was going until he found himself in Malibu, turning into the driveway of his Aunt Judy's house. Judy was his father's younger half-sister, born from his grandfather's third marriage late in his life and only ten years older than Arden. Once an aspiring poet, she'd married a wealthy Jewish boy when Arden was in middle school. She now spent most of her time in a Valium haze by the pool, drinking champagne and staring at the ocean. Tess referred to her as "that gold digging drunk" and didn't associate with her.

Arden liked her because she never seemed to expect anything of him.

She answered the door in a Versace bikini top and matching pareo. A string of pearls hung around her neck, a crystal flute of pink champagne in her manicured hand. "Arden," she said, smiling. "I'd heard you were back. Come on in, I was about to go lie by the pool."

Arden glanced at the pale gray sky. "But there isn't any sun."

"It'll come out eventually. You know how it is out here by the ocean." She turned and went inside. "Do you want any champagne?" she called over her shoulder.

Arden followed her, closing the front door behind him. "No, thank you. It's, ah, a little early for me."

"Early? You're a college boy. It's never supposed to be too early for you."

"I'm not in college anymore," said Arden as the two of them stepped out onto the pool deck. Its perimeter was surrounded by a glass wall looking out at the beach. A low fog hung over the pitching waves. Judy took off her pareo and draped it over a chair before reclining in one of the chaises. Arden sat in the one next to her and lit two cigarettes. He gave one of them to Judy and asked, "Where is everyone?"

His aunt shrugged. "The help won't be here for another hour or so. Isaac is at the office. I think Grayden went with him, but I'm not sure. He might be upstairs, asleep."

"How old is he now?"

"Seven. He just turned seven." They were silent for a while, and then Judy asked, "So, what brings you out here so early in the morning?"

Arden pondered the question. He watched the hypnotic push and pull of the tide beneath the sinister fog. "I...don't really know," he said. "I couldn't sleep, and I needed to go...somewhere."

Judy sipped her champagne and took a short drag from her cigarette. "That's normal, I think. You're kind of in this weird limbo after college. What was it you majored in again?"

"Philosophy."

She gave him a wan smile. "Not a ton of career options with that one, but I guess you already know that. Who were some of your favorites?"

Arden blinked at her. "My favorite...what?"

"Philosophers, goofball."

"Oh. Right. Um. I don't know." He shut his eyes, trying to remember term papers he'd written, trying to attach significance to some of them, any of them. "Uh, Schopenhauer was cool, I guess. Cioran. And, um, Camus was...neat."

"Oof, kid. Bleak choices."

"Yeah. I guess." He considered this. "I don't know."

Judy looked at him. Her eyes were murky, far away. "Is something wrong?" she asked.

Arden's gaze shifted again to the ocean. He listened to the waves whispering their beckoning chant. They implored him to go to them, to disappear beneath them. "I think I did too much acid when I was at school."

Judy's laughter trailed off when she realized he wasn't joking. "What makes you say that?"

"I don't know. I feel...disconnected. Like there's nothing keeping me here in the world. I feel like I could float away if I'm not careful. And I don't know if that's from the drugs, or...everything else."

"What's 'everything else'?"

"You know. Life, or whatever. All of it. I can't find purpose in anything. You have to, like, assign meaning to things in order for them to have any. And it all seems like such a waste of time, a waste of energy. Why should I force things to mean something to me?"

"Wow," said Judy. "Those Berkeley professors really did a number on you. You hear the rumors about them, but Jesus."

"I don't even remember any of them."

Judy studied him with a concerned expression. "Are you dating anyone?" she asked.

"What does that have to do with anything?"

Judy took a deep breath, and then a long pull from the crystal flute. Arden caught, for the first time, the brief but distinct wave of ecstasy that washed over her face as she drank. "Things made the most sense to me when I was in love," she said.

Arden fought and failed to conceal the appalled incredulousness in his expression. "I mean, first of all, gross," he said. "Second of all, what about Uncle Isaac?"

"What about him?" The depths of desolation in Judy's eyes were so dark and unfathomable that a chill slithered through Arden's bones. He averted his gaze. "Listen," Judy said, "Isaac is a good man. I do love him. But I don't know that I'd be able to love him, to appreciate him, if it hadn't been for the guy I was *in* love with. He...he wasn't right for me, he wasn't the person I needed to be with, but he made everything make sense. Even now, I can think back to that time —that time when things made sense—and it, well, it helps me make sense of the way things are. Does *that* make sense?"

"Not really."

"It will. You probably haven't met her yet."

Arden thought of the girls he'd slept with over the past four years. He didn't think there'd been that many, and they hadn't meant anything to him. He had not assigned meaning to them. He couldn't remember their faces. Bodies pressed against his beneath dorm room sheets. He couldn't remember high school either.

"It will hurt," Judy went on, her voice solemn as she swirled the remnants of champagne at the bottom of her glass. She finished her cigarette and stubbed it out in the ashtray on the small glass table between them. "It always does when it's real. But it will be worth it. And when it's gone, and you've moved on, you'll come to miss the pain. Eventually you'll remember the pain and the pleasure the same way. It will taste the same in your dreams. You'll look back at the good times and the bad times and you won't be able to tell them apart. And that's how you'll know you had something beautiful."

"It doesn't sound beautiful," said Arden, crushing out his own cigarette. "It sounds very, very ugly."

Judy flashed a sad smile, but Arden had the feeling it wasn't for him. "The most beautiful things are often very ugly," she said.

SEVEN
FUCKING SHAMELESS

BAXTER WANDERED for what felt like a long time through his father's house. He was unsettled by the silence but too tense to put on music or a podcast. Everything was neat and clean, arranged by the maid he never saw. He fantasized she was a thin, buxom redhead who paraded around in miniskirts and thigh-high stockings, but he knew she probably was some frumpy Hispanic lady with sagging breasts and a leathery face.

He found himself standing in front of his father's study and pondered the closed door, trying to remember if he'd ever been inside.

It was most likely a nondescript room with a big desk and book-shelves filled with files and ledgers and Excel manuals, but he was bored, so he tried the knob. It was, as expected, locked. He turned and started to amble back down the hall, thinking he'd get stoned and watch some porn before lying by the pool, when he thought he heard something behind him. Something like footsteps, light but unmistakable. He spun around.

The locked doorknob was rattling. Baxter drew in a sharp breath and took a step back. He watched with mounting dread as the doorknob jerked left and right. He took another step back. The doorknob stopped rattling. There came a harsh *click* as the door unlocked, and swung open.

A girl stood in the doorway. She looked to be about Baxter's age, maybe a year or two younger. Her hair was long and auburn. She wore an expression of blank, dazed stupidity. Her vibrant blue eyes were quizzical, as was the way she held her head tilted to the side.

Baxter started to speak, to ask who she was and what she was doing here, but the words caught in his throat and died there as he continued to look at her.

There was something off about the way she looked. Something peculiar about how she was proportioned. She was tall, perhaps only an inch or two shorter than he was, with the long, slender neck of a supermodel. The swell of her breasts strained against the tight tank top that came halfway down her torso; they were, Baxter decided, *the perfect size*. Her stomach was hard, toned, and flat. Her hips tapered into an unnaturally narrow waist, and her cutoff jean shorts bared long, muscular legs. Her skin was a sun-kissed bronze, her lips full and luscious. Her dark eyelashes were thick and long but didn't look artificial.

She did not look like a *Real Girl*.

She looked better, in fact, than any Porn Girl Baxter had ever seen across his phone's screen.

The girl stepped forward. The curiosity in her face intensified. "Do you want me to suck your big, fat cock?" she asked. Her voice was high and airy. Slathered in saccharinity.

Baxter blinked. "Um," he said. "Um...what?"

The girl cocked her head to the other side. Her lips parted into a smile that made his heart skip. "Do you want to stick your cock inside me and fuck me like the dirty little slut I am?" She paused, and then added, "Daddy?"

Baxter coughed into his fist. "What...this...I don't..."

The girl ran her hands down her sides, gyrating her hips. "Oh,

Daddy, I want you to fuck me. I need it. I need your cock. I need to taste your cum in my mouth."

"Who *are* you?" Baxter breathed.

The girl smiled, tossed her hair. "I'm MechaHooker 6000, Daddy, but you can call me whatever you want. I'm your slut. I'm your whore, baby. I'm your bitch."

Running a hand through his hair, Baxter said, "You're, like...a robot?"

The girl blinked her huge eyes at him several times. Her smile faltered a little. Like she was trying to process his question. After a moment, she tossed her hair again and repeated, "I'm MechaHooker 6000, Daddy, but you can call me whatever you want. I'm your slut. I'm your whore, baby. I'm your bitch."

Baxter thought he might have seen something online a while ago about mechanical sex dolls, but they were not on the market yet. He wondered how and when his father had gotten one, and then was presented with the unpleasant image of his father fucking this girl, this *thing*.

He shook the thought away and then approached. She didn't move. She only kept smiling and blinking at him. He supposed it should have unnerved him, but it didn't.

When he was close enough to touch her, he reached out with a trembling hand. He ran his fingertips along the surface of her arm. It *felt* like skin, perhaps not completely, but it was so close the difference hardly registered.

"Oh, *yes*, baby. Touch me. Touch me *all over*."

"Jesus," Baxter muttered. He investigated the girl's face. She had no wrinkles, no pores, no blemishes whatsoever. "Jesus," he said again. "How much do you cost?"

Again, she appeared to be processing his question, running through complex algorithms far beyond his comprehension. The response selected by whatever computer whirred away inside her was, "I want you to come all over my tits, Daddy."

Baxter swallowed. He looked around the girl, this *MechaHooker*, and into his father's study. "Do me a favor and, uh, stay right here," Baxter said. "Don't go anywhere."

"I crave the taste of your load."

Baxter moved past her and into the study, where he began riffling through drawers. He found it easily enough—an instruction booklet, printed on glossy white paper with the manufacturer name (Shifuku—something even Baxter found a bit heavy-handed) and logo (a flower bearing absurd resemblance to female genitalia) emblazoned on the cover beneath "MECHAHOOKER 6000 – PROTOTYPE 3.1." He flipped through its contents, his palms sweating.

Designed for pleasure, the booklet said.

294 fully functioning erogenous zones.

Penetrable mouth, vagina, and anus.

Hassle-free self-cleaning system.

The illustrations left little to the imagination.

Baxter closed the booklet and set it on the desk, wiping his perspiring hands on his shorts.

The MechaHooker was standing where he'd left her, not moving. Something occurred to him, and he pulled his cell phone out of his pocket and called Dimitri, a tech geek with whom he and Arden had gone to high school and who now lived out in Yucca Valley, doing something in cyber security for the government. Baxter sometimes bought angel dust from him on occasions when his listless boredom became intolerable.

"Yes, yes, for certain, I've heard of these MechaHookers," Dimitri said after Baxter explained the scenario. "Shifuku is up-and-comer in tech game. Stocks trending upward every week. Has all of Silicon Valley sweating bullets. But MechaHooker is not on market yet. Many regulatory hoops left to jump through, last I hear. How did your father get one?"

"I don't know, he's always getting free shit from the Asian companies he works with. Stuff nobody else has even heard of." His eyes landed on the instruction booklet. "The manual says it's a prototype." He paused. "Look, the reason I'm calling you is—like, do you think it's, you know...safe? Like, to use?"

A pause on the other end of the phone. "Man. Your father has presumably been sticking his cock inside this, and you are going to fuck it?" Brief laughter, more like a snort. "Shameless, man. Fucking shameless."

"The manual says it's self-cleaning."

"Whatever, man. But sure, yes, probably it is safe. All of red tape nonsense is usually bullshit, anyway. If company gave him one, I am sure is fine. Let me know what is like." Another snort of laughter. "Anyway. Little birdy tells me Arden is back. Do me favor, ask him if he wants to buy party supplies. Have him give me call."

Baxter told him he would, hung up, and returned to the hallway where he'd left the MechaHooker. She blinked at him. Smiled. Baxter smiled back. Sheepish, childlike. Tentatively, he took the Mecha-Hooker's hand—it felt *so close* to human—and led her upstairs to his bedroom.

She moved her limbs to accommodate Baxter's clumsy removal of her clothes. He did not kiss her. As she stood naked before him, Baxter's eyes crawled over her body, hunting for imperfections. There were none. Not even the digitally modified Porn Girls looked as good as this.

There was brief disappointment when he first entered her—she wasn't as tight as he'd expected—but then her vaginal canal *constricted*, molding itself around his penis. The slick moisture within her increased, as well, as did the balmy heat, and she broke into loud moans, gasping, "Yeah, Daddy, your cock feels so huge inside my tight little pussy," and "Fuck, fuck, *fuck*, you're the *best*, you're a sex god, you're my *king*."

It was over in under fifteen seconds.

Collapsing off her, Baxter felt the customary wave of shame before he realized...she's a *robot*. She expected nothing. There was no standard to live up to. He was free.

He spent the rest of the afternoon and all night in bed with her.

When he wasn't fucking her, he was touching her, prodding her, licking her. As soon as he became sufficiently aroused, he was back inside her. They fucked in every position Baxter could think of, doing things he'd never dared ask a Real Girl to do. He smacked her around a bit, came wherever he pleased—inside her, in her mouth, on her face, her tits, her back, her stomach, her leg. He shrieked with the pleasure of it all. At some point, late into the night, he broke down in tears, sobbing with gratitude.

"I love you," he kept telling her. "I love you. I'm in love with you."

She always replied with something like, "Fuck me like the nasty little slut I am," and that was okay with Baxter.

All of it was okay with Baxter.

EIGHT
DON'T FUCK YOUR HEROES

THERE HAD BEEN a time when Tess had worshipped The Writer.

Don't meet your heroes, the saying went. *Don't fuck your heroes*, Tess thought, would have been more appropriate.

Their first encounter had happened nearly a year ago, in the waning days of summer before her senior year.

She'd been having drinks at the Chateau Marmont on a Friday night with Thom Valery, a popular YouTuber who'd recently moved to LA from London, and Sean Haldon, a podcaster with whom she occasionally slept. Thom was sixteen and Sean was nineteen. They were each worth somewhere north of twenty million dollars.

Thom was on his phone, swiping through girls' profiles on some dating app. "Fucking hell, mate," he said to Sean. He sipped his daiquiri and scowled at the images on the phone's screen. "Some of these American bints ought to be euthanized for looking the way they do. I thought California girls were supposed to be skinny. This app might as well be called Fat Cunts R Us." He showed a girl's photo to Sean, shaking his head. "Bloody disgusting. At what point do you look in the mirror and say to yourself, 'All right then, suppose I ought to stop eating now, shouldn't I?' Have some self-control, for fuck's sake. Respect yourself."

"Hot girls don't need to use dating apps," Sean said. He looked at Tess, grinning crookedly. "Take Tess, for instance. Tess, have you ever hooked up with a guy you met on a dating app?"

"No," Tess said. She sipped her martini. "I mainly swipe through them when I'm bored. I don't ever message anyone back."

"See, case and point," said Sean. "The only girls who use dating apps in earnest are the nasty ones."

"Eh, I don't know about all that. I've seen some right fit birds on here. They're far outnumbered by the ogres, for certain, but they're on here."

"Your 'fit birds' are just looking for Instagram followers," said Sean. He signaled to the passing waiter, a pale, lanky guy with too-white skin and too-long fingers who flashed an eerie grin at Tess as he listened to Sean's order.

"Fuck me," Thom said, grimacing at his phone. "Peep this one. Her cellulite has its own bloody cellulite." He held the phone out to Sean. "That's no girl. That's three hundred pounds of porpoise blubber."

Wincing at the image on the screen, Sean said, "What's wrong with its face?"

Thom took the phone back. He squinted at the girl's photo. "I think it's disfigured somehow. Maybe an accident?" He shook his head again. "You have to just kill yourself at that point, right? Even if you could lose the weight, you'd still look like you took a cheese grater to your face, wouldn't you?" He scrolled farther down the girl's profile and then began cackling. "Oh, mate, listen to this: 'I'm weirdly attracted to men who want to be my friend first and don't see me as a sex object,'" he read aloud. He and Sean both burst into boisterous laughter.

"I have some bad news for that poor bitch," Sean said.

"Imagine, she actually looked at herself in the mirror and was delusional enough to think, 'Right then, I think the boys of Southern

California would fancy a wee look at this.' And then she took a picture and uploaded it to this dreadful app, and *at no point* did she experience a moment of clarity sharp enough to realize what a rotten idea it was. Tess, doll, *look* at this fucking cow." He reached across the table, trying to show her his phone.

But Tess wasn't paying attention.

Her distracted gaze had landed on a party of three seated several tables away from them. Two of the men, both of nondescript appearance and dressed in business suits, could have been anyone. The third man was Chandler Eastridge. He stood out in his white Dolce & Gabbana blazer with its sequined black lapels, his tan skin, his eyes concealed behind Persol sunglasses. He was shaking the other men's hands, standing to leave, smiling with easy brilliance.

Her father being who he was, and her friends being who they were, Tess had met all manner of celebrity over the years. None of them impressed her. But Chandler Eastridge...that was different. She'd read all his books, to the point of obsession. An unfamiliar fluttering rose in her chest. A sensation both exciting and embarrassing.

If she didn't talk to him, she'd never forgive herself.

Tess rose from the table, ignoring the questions from her companions. Heart's "Magic Man" was playing over the sound system. She floated toward The Writer, positioning herself so she was dead center of his field of vision when he turned in her direction. An exaggerated toss of her hair had the desired effect when his eyes zeroed in on her.

He froze. She stopped before him, partially of her own volition but mostly because the smile he flashed was enough to petrify her muscles.

"*Well,*" he said.

He let the word lie there between them, coiling into itself like a rattlesnake. Tess felt him appraising her, knew he liked what he saw.

She moved her eyes up the length of him. He stood with statuesque self-possession. An air of royal dominance. She stopped at his eyes, hidden behind the black lenses of his sunglasses, where twin reflections of herself stared out at her.

"Isn't it kind of dark to be wearing sunglasses?" she said, determined to play it cool.

He took a step closer to her. The scent of his cologne was an intoxication. "Perhaps the fire in my eyes is so ravenous it would make unwitting girls fall tragically, hopelessly in love with me, and these shutters with which I board them is a kindness, a benevolent salvation they'll never come to appreciate."

"Wow. Some line." Looking back now, Tess could see the canned artifice of it, the slime-coated pretense. She supposed she'd seen it even then, but there'd been something soothing about his voice, about his command over his words. Combined with a hint of cajoling playfulness—the showy theatricality staged as an amusing parlor trick.

And then he took his sunglasses off, folding them with a subtle twirl of his wrist and stowing them in his jacket. He fixed his eyes on her. They were like sapphiric flames which burned with frigid intensity. Tess hated how they stirred her, the way they rendered her helpless and small, brimming with fragile innocence.

If he touches me, she thought, *I'll shatter.*

He smiled, those teeth so white, straightened with orthodontic precision. "See what I mean?" he said. He glanced over his shoulder at the businessmen, who stood frozen at straight-backed attention. Soldiers awaiting orders from their commanding officer. He dismissed them with a short nod, and they turned and departed in lockstep with one another. His blazing cold eyes returned to Tess.

Her heart seized. She put an unconscious hand to her breast. His eyes followed, lingered. An eyebrow lifted. "Were you looking for an autograph?" he asked. He gestured to her Prada purse. "Do you have my latest ferreted away in there, waiting for a maudlin inscription that'll make your friends swoon?" One side of his smile pulled wider. "Not you, though—you're not the swooning type."

Even in her captive state beneath his scalding arctic stare, Tess possessed enough wherewithal to recognize an opportunity for some semblance of equalization. She knew that what she said next would determine their entire dynamic. He had millions of fans. He was probably approached by them all the time. This was her one chance to be something else. To differentiate herself. So she said, "Your latest...what? Are you, like, some kind of...musician?"

A flash of rattled disbelief was there one moment and gone the next, but its shadow remained cast upon the faltered smile he summoned in a hasty attempt to recover. "I'm a *Writer*," he said, but the way he said it, the "a" may as well have been a "the." The "w," she supposed, was capitalized in his mind. And for all the countless hours she'd spent poring over the words pressed upon the pages of his works, every sentence that had ensnared her, each storyline that had swept her away...it was capitalized in her mind, as well.

"Oh," she said, feigning flippancy. "I'm not much of a reader."

"Well, forgive my presumption, then. It's only that, well...you approached me..." He trailed off. The glacial fire in his eyes pushed forth, goading her to explain herself.

She willed herself to look away, only to feel her gaze magnetized back into the cold light of his own. "I wanted to tell you I liked your jacket," she said. "It catches the eye."

"Mm," he murmured, as though something had been confirmed for him. "Yes, well. You can't go wrong with D&G."

Tess gave a short laugh. "No, I guess you can't."

He glanced around, as if casing the place. "A bit crowded here, don't you think? Terribly unintimate. Would it be too forward to suggest a drink at my house?"

Ann Wilson kept crooning from the speakers. The line in which the eponymous Magic Man says with a smile to *"come on home, girl,"* was timed as if The Writer had planned it. Tess would come to find that many things in his life worked this way. Like the universe was throwing him softball pitches down the center of the plate. He grinned and lifted his eyes toward the nearest speaker, as if in grateful acknowledgment, before returning them to Tess. "I have a fully stocked bar that puts the one here to shame," he said. "There's a dance floor. An old-fashioned jukebox. Really enriches the sense of atmosphere. Calls to mind memories of better times."

Tess put a hand on her hip. She forced her eyes upward and with the other hand extended a finger to tap her chin. "That *is* kind of forward," she said. "I don't even know your name." She lowered her eyes again to catch his reaction. That brief but unmistakable flare of affronted ego.

"It's Chandler," he said with only the slightest hint of terseness. His smile tightened. "Chandler Eastridge. There's enough about me online that you should be able to ascertain quite quickly that I'm not a murderer or rapist."

Narrowing her eyes and pursing her lips, Tess said, "No, I think I'll take your word for it. I like to live a little dangerously now and then."

He drove her through Hollywood and up into the hills of Silver Lake in his Bentley Continental. Reflections of the streetlights raced in tangled white ribbons over the gleaming black paint of the car's elongated hood.

Once inside the mansion, Tess was confronted with an enormous enlargement of a *Rolling Stone* cover on which The Writer had been featured. It hung in a gilded frame over the wide fireplace and bore the caption "LITERATURE'S LAST ROCK STAR."

Many of his possessions were testaments to his fame, like the whole house was a shrine to himself. Framed pictures of him with various celebrities and political figures, bookshelves lined with dozens of copies of his books, posters for his film adaptations, an eight-foot-tall statue of himself wearing a crown and holding a scepter. She commented on none of it, but she caught him smiling with self-satisfaction as he watched her take it all in.

They didn't go to the bar, and neither of them made mention of it. He went down on her in the dim light of the bedroom, tonguing her with learned precision, working into her the pleasure-maddening fingers of one hand as he caressed her breast with the other. When she came, it was with the kind of howling intensity which left her embarrassed, pried open, resenting herself. The Writer lifted his head from between her legs, his mouth glistening, and said, "You taste like such sweet tragedy."

Tess didn't know what to say to that.

He stood then, unbuttoning his shirt, peeling off both his leather pants and his Hugo Boss underwear in a single motion. Tess, her breath coming in short gasps, propped herself up on her elbows and looked at him. "Whoa," she said. "That's kind of a surprise."

He looked down at himself, smiling with faux coyness. "What?" he said.

"Don't pretend you don't know."

"But why is it a surprise?"

"In my experience, guys with big dick energy are usually compensating for, well...*not* having a big dick."

He laughed. "Honey," he said. "*Darling.* I have 'big dick energy' *because* I have a big dick."

"Shut up and come here."

He was gone when she awoke later. His clothes still lay discarded on the floor. Shivering in the air conditioning, she picked up his shirt and wrapped it around her chilled nakedness, fastening one of the top buttons. It draped over her like a dress, its cuffs hanging off her hands. She rolled the sleeves up as she padded into the hall. The faint sound of slow, plaintive jazz rose from somewhere indiscernible within the labyrinthine manor. She moved like a specter through the corridors, feeling empty, lost.

Here she was, in the domain of the man she'd idolized, and yet the emptiness inside her was bigger than ever. Like a growing sickness.

The sliding glass door leading into the backyard whirred open at her approach. She stepped out into the warm night. A light breeze teased her bed-mussed hair. Standing at the edge of the pool, her bare toes curling around its cement lip, she stared at the forlorn reflection of the moon shimmering on the surface of the water. A compulsion to jump in bloomed with sudden urgency within her. She shed The Writer's shirt, letting it crumple around her ankles like a shorn husk. Standing nude in the moonlight at the edge of the water, she broke its surface with the tips of her toes. The water bore all the warm solace of amniotic fluid, but she didn't wade into it. Instead, she stepped back, sitting on the concrete and drawing her knees to her chest. She tipped her head toward the sky, and let the tears fall.

No one came for her.

NINE
A HOSTAGE SITUATION

ARDEN WAS NURSING his third gin and tonic when he noticed her.

He was sitting in an otherwise empty booth in Guide Bar, a low-key spot on Franklin between Birds and La Poubelle. The clientele was sparse, even for a Sunday night. Arden had been watching a trio of drunk teenagers swaying on the dance floor when his bored, wandering eyes had landed on the girl sitting in a booth on the other side of the room. Her laptop was open in front of her. A martini perspired beside it on a napkin.

The way her face looked in the blue glow of the computer screen stirred something within him. It was the kind of face he could imagine speaking soft, kind words to him. Telling him everything would be okay. That he was safe.

Before he understood what he was doing, he had taken his half-empty drink and was walking to where she sat, sliding into the seat across from her. He set his drink on the table and started to speak, but his voice caught in his throat. He had to look down, stirring the drink with the swizzle stick so his hands would have something to do.

The girl looked up from her computer. "Um, hi?" she said. Her expression was at first annoyed, guarded, but as she appraised him and seemed to detect no immediate threat, it softened. The corner of her mouth pulled toward an amused smile. Arden realized she was older than he was, maybe late twenties or early thirties. There was something wizened and haunted in her eyes that was intimidating.

"Hey," said Arden, hating how dumb and flat it sounded. "I... don't really know what I'm, um, doing. I'm sorry. You just looked... you have a pleasant, um, aura, I guess."

The girl smiled a bit wider and closed her laptop. "What color is it?"

"What?"

"My aura. What color is it?"

"Oh. I don't know. I don't always see the colors. Only sometimes."

Her laugh was like birdsong. "Are you one of those new age hippie types? Into hemp and astrology, and all that?"

"No. I don't know anything about astrology."

"Well, that's a relief. You don't *look* like the type, but you never can tell these days."

"What type do I look like?"

She tilted her head to the side. The waves of her long black hair shifted like water. "Hard to say, exactly. There's something sort of tragic about you. A little bit lost."

Arden looked away. The kids on the dance floor were staring at their phones. "I just graduated college," he said, as if that explained everything. Maybe it did.

"Where did you go?" the girl asked. Arden was glad it wasn't preceded by a perfunctory congratulations.

"Berkeley. I majored in philosophy." Without thinking, he added, "I took a lot of classes on African American studies, though."

Raising an eyebrow, the girl said, "Is that supposed to impress me because I'm black?"

"African American," Arden corrected her before he could stop himself. And then, "Jesus, I'm sorry." He took a deep breath. "I mean, listen, there was a lot of....um, tension on campus. I get that it's like that everywhere, but especially there, it was..." He trailed off, sipped his drink. Took another breath. The girl watched him. "What I'm trying to say is, I don't know how to treat interactions... like this. Like, should I apologize? Is that how I should have started? I want to, you know, convey that I'm an ally, but I don't—"

The girl held up a hand. "Oh my God, stop, for real. Look, I appreciate all that, truly, but we can just be two people."

"Right," said Arden, looking at his drink. He twisted his hands in his lap. "Cool. I'm...sorry. For making it awkward, I mean."

"No, it's fine. It's kind of refreshing for someone to acknowledge it, I guess. People usually tiptoe around it. I feel like most of the people I talk to are walking on eggshells, and its bullshit. It shouldn't be like that. It's all part of some nefarious scheme to keep us divided, I think. Politics—it's nothing but theater. None of them care about any of us no matter what our skin color is. I just want people to be people."

"I don't think it's a scheme," said Arden. "It's an important—"

"Stop. Enough. We don't have to talk about it." She held her hand across the table. "I'm Rebecca."

Arden reciprocated the introduction, still overly conscious of his skin color and its implications. He went to take a nervous sip of his drink and found it empty. Blushing, he set it on the table and fiddled with the swizzle stick.

"I've not seen you here before," Rebecca said. "And I'm usually here a couple nights a week. I live right on Tamarind."

"I used to come here in high school," said Arden. "With friends." Even as he said the word "friends," it was a struggle to associate meaning with it. He couldn't recall their names, their faces. Had Baxter been among them? He couldn't be sure. "They never carded, so, you know. But this is the first time I've been here since I left."

"Feeling nostalgic?" Her smile was amiably wry.

"Something like that, I guess." He glanced at the pale man

behind the bar, who was grinning at him with a mouth too wide for his face. Arden shuddered and looked away.

"Nothing wrong with that," said Rebecca. "The first months after graduating college are...weird. It's like, *now what*? When you get home, you kind of float along looking for meaning, or a *sign*, something to point you in the right direction. You return to what's familiar, what's comfortable, because you don't know what else to do."

"What did you do?" Arden asked. And then, gesturing at her laptop, "And, like, what *do* you do?"

"I'm in public relations. Basically, I'm a glorified babysitter for people with too much money and too many Instagram followers. As for what I did after college—I don't know, I suppose I went to a lot of shitty parties and drank too much. I studied hard in college and took everything too seriously, so when I got out, I sort of let loose. It's not exactly something I'd recommend." She swallowed the last dregs of her martini. "In any event, my friend Ianthe introduced to me someone who introduced me to someone, and then all of a sudden I had a job." She met his gaze, and there was something in her eyes Arden couldn't decipher. "Sometimes—most times—you have to let things play out. It's usually better not to try and force it."

"If I'd let things play out tonight, I'd still be sulking on the other side of the room."

"How do you know I wouldn't have approached you?"

Arden raised a dubious eyebrow. "Would you have?"

"No," she admitted, "but only because I was working. Besides, there's a difference between forcing things and taking initiative."

"Was, um...was my initiative the right one to take?"

Rebecca stowed her laptop in her Vivienne Westwood shoulder bag and rose to her feet. "Well, Arden, why don't you walk home with me so you can...what is it the kids say these days? 'Fuck around and find out'?"

Arden blinked at her, taken aback by the frankness of the invitation. "Um...yeah. Yeah, that's...what they say."

Arden woke early again, sometime around five. The outline of Rebecca's body was visible beneath the sheets, but her face, turned down amid the pillows, was obscured by her long black hair. The shape of her rose and fell with the easy respiration of deep sleep.

Rising from the bed, Arden got dressed and tiptoed to the bathroom, wincing as each step brought a stab of pain into his temples and behind his eyes.

He flicked on the bathroom light and shut his eyes against the whiteness. When the thundering in his skull had slowed to a muted but persistent drumbeat, he reopened them and took the baggie of coke from his pocket.

Arden tapped an uneven line onto the edge of the sink and bent over to snort it with a rolled-up twenty. The instantaneous flash, that lightning-bolt *jolt* of electric clarity, eradicated the drums. He let out a contented breath and grinned madly at his reflection in the medicine cabinet mirror above the sink.

When he turned away, Rebecca was standing in the doorway wearing a gold Versace bathrobe, her arms folded across her chest. Arden held out the baggie to her. "Do you...want some?" he asked.

"No," she said. Her voice was soft but stern. "I do not *want some*, thank you." She turned on her heel and walked down the hall to the kitchen. After a moment, Arden followed. He sat at the table, staring at the vase of tiger lilies at the center of it. Rebecca had her back to him as she prepared the coffeemaker. "Would you like any?" she asked.

"No," he said. "Thanks."

"Are you a drug addict?" she asked, turning. Her empty coffee mug had a picture of Dumbo on it.

"Am I a...what, no, I'm not a drug addict." Arden stared at the cartoon elephant printed on her mug. Something about it made him sad. If he looked at it too long, it came alive and began to dance.

"So, you wake up at five in the morning to do coke because...why?"

"To take the edge off," Arden mumbled. "Listen, why is this such a thing to you? It's LA, everyone does coke."

Rebecca turned away from him again, filled her mug. When she sat down, she didn't meet his eyes. "When I was in high school," she said, "my friends and I got into drugs pretty heavily." She brought her mug to her lips, then set it down without taking a sip. "Some bad things happened."

"Bad things like...what? Like...rehab?"

"No. Not like rehab. Two of my best friends are dead because we were stupid, and experimented with stuff we had no business experimenting with. And my other friend...well, he would be better off dead."

"Oh. That's, um, pretty heavy."

"Yeah. It messed me up bad for a long time. That's why I went at my schoolwork so hard in college. I was trying to disappear into something."

"There are worse things to disappear into."

"Trust me, I know. Anyway, me and Ianthe—the friend I mentioned last night—we both swore off drugs after all that happened. We won't even smoke pot."

"No, yeah, that's understandable." Arden rubbed his perspiring palms on the legs of his jeans. "Look, I'm sorry I offered it to you. I was just trying to be—"

"Polite, I know, it's whatever. I don't care about that. It's just... listen, you can do whatever you want, obviously. But if you're going to go down that road, I don't want to watch. It's an ugly thing to witness firsthand. So, please, if that's how it's going to be, do me a favor and spare me from having to sit on the sidelines of your destruction."

Arden felt his heart seize up. She had again taken him by surprise; he'd assumed last night had been nothing more than a one-night stand, something to do on a Sunday evening, but her words here intimated the possibility of a future. Something that, up until this moment, his life had lacked. Fueled by coke-infused confidence, he reached across the table and took her hand, squeezed it. The smile he gave her was easy, languid. "It isn't like that," he said. "It's not anything you need to worry about."

Rebecca searched his eyes. "Don't take me hostage," she said. The fragile, injured innocence of her plea was a knife blade, pushed deep and twisted.

"I won't," he said, and he felt he meant it. "I won't."

TEN
A HARMLESS NOBODY

BAXTER'S TROUBLE had started with a girl in high school.

She was fifteen and had 68.1 million Instagram followers. Baxter had been one of them.

Celeste Ludovica. The name itself tasted of cherry-flavored promises when spoken. Her hair shone like golden hellfire, her olive skin radiated luster. The grid on her Instagram feed was populated with comedy bits, dance routines, and images of her sunning herself on various high-end beaches or lounging in the VIP sections of West Hollywood nightclubs.

The bits could be amusing, and she possessed a natural rhythm that made the dance routines hypnotic, but her fame hadn't been awarded her for *what* she was doing so much as how she *looked* doing it. The round, espresso-colored eyes welled up with faux innocence, the come-hither smile lined with teeth white as fentanyl...the bejeweled navel perforating the taut abdomen exposed by her cropped T-shirts, the smooth legs waxed and tanned to glossy perfection flashing beneath the swishing hem of her miniskirts. Boys and men craved her while their sisters and wives and mothers and daughters imitated her. Fashion brands plied her with endorsement deals. Her face appeared on billboards over Sunset and Melrose, rising over the hills of Hollywood and Silver Lake, advertising anything, everything.

At school, she was a pariah. *Untouchable* was the word applied to her in hushed murmurs when she strutted by. Her aloof confidence kept even the most glamorous of the popular girls at a distance. Most of the boys were too intimidated to approach her. This was worsened by the unceremonious manner in which she rejected any of the jocks dumb enough to try their luck at casual flirting, always bolstered by a battalion of bro-buddies watching with giddy eagerness from the sidelines.

Baxter first met her when he was a junior and she a sophomore. He'd been getting stoned with Arden under the bleachers while passing a bottle of Southern Comfort back and forth during the Homecoming game.

She materialized before him like a mirage. Something which produced a desperate yearning but could not be real. Baxter's mouth was already dry from the weed, the alcohol. At the sight of her, it became drier. Her clothes allowed for little speculation as to what they concealed. Baxter mumbled a few feeble words of greeting.

"I smelled your weed," Celeste said. She didn't so much as glance at Arden. "Can I have some? I'm crazy about the stuff." She giggled. It was a sound like windchimes. Baxter had heard it plenty in her Instagram videos, but never in real life. It was beautiful and sad, and it made him want to lie down and die.

Instead, he held out the half-smoked blunt. She came closer—so close—and took it, bringing it to her lips and pulling deeply, one eye closed, the other watching him with mischief. When she lowered the blunt, she held the smoke in for several long seconds before releasing it in a great, torrential cloud. She didn't cough. "My manager is all over me to lay off it," she said. "All the drugs. He says I'm getting spun out. It's becoming difficult to insure me, he says. And I'm like, what the fuck do I need insurance for, anyway? I'm a social media star, not a *movie* star. But I guess some brands are starting to get worried ever since the DUI scare. Hey, can I have some of that?" She indicated the bottle with an extended index finger, its pointed acrylic nail gleaming silver.

Baxter handed her the bottle. "I didn't know there was a DUI scare," he said.

She drained most of the bottle's remaining contents in four huge swallows. After handing the bottle to Baxter, she lifted her shirt to wipe her mouth, flashing the sun-freckled orbs of her breasts clasped tightly in a lacy blue bra. Baxter swallowed.

"I'm not old enough to have a license," Celeste said, letting her shirt fall back into place, not that it made much difference. "That was kind of the issue. Part of the issue. My lawyer got me out of it, kept the media quiet, but there were still some people who found out. Listen, you want to get out of here?"

Baxter looked at Arden. Arden shrugged and muttered something about having somewhere to be before wandering off.

Turning back to Celeste, Baxter tried to swallow again but couldn't. His voice hoarse, he said, "And go where?"

"Somewhere. Anywhere. I don't want to be here. I don't know why I came in the first place. You have a car, right?"

"Yeah, um...yeah. Totally."

"Great. Let's blow this popsicle stand." Baxter gave her a quizzical look, and she shrugged. "It's something my dad says. I'm thinking about bringing it back, getting it to catch on again. I don't know, maybe not."

In his red Mustang convertible, she connected her phone to the car's Bluetooth and put on an Avril Lavigne playlist. She'd let each track play for no more than a minute or so before skipping to the next one. Baxter put the top down and lit a cigarette. He tried to steel his nerves. The unattainable Celeste Ludovica, in his passenger seat. His caged heart railed against its confinement.

"Where am I going?" he asked her, measuring his words, keeping his tone casual.

"I told you," she said, not looking up from her phone, twirling a lock of hair around her finger. She crossed her legs. "Anywhere. It doesn't matter." Her voice was clear and unslurred, a surprise given how much liquor she'd consumed in such a short time.

Baxter headed in the direction of the coast, following the tidal pull of his blood. Before he reached the freeway, Celeste commanded him to stop at a 7-Eleven. She skipped inside and came out bearing a bag filled with liquor—peach schnapps, Jack Daniel's, Absolut, more Southern Comfort.

She opened the vodka and tilted the bottle back, guzzling it like it was water. "Do you have any more weed?" Baxter gestured at the center console. She opened it and squealed at the sight of the Ziploc bag stuffed with pre-rolled joints.

When they reached Malibu, Baxter parked the car at a McDonald's. The bottles clinked together in Celeste's 7-Eleven bag as the two of them ran across PCH. Baxter carried towels from his trunk. The night air was chilly, and the beach was dark and empty. As soon as Celeste's feet hit the sand, she set the bag down and took off in a mad run toward the water, stripping her clothes as she went. She was naked when she dove into the black waves. Baxter stood staring after her for a few moments, and then he took off his own clothes and ran into the ocean.

The icy water stung his skin. Celeste found him at once and clung to him. She wrapped her arms around his neck and her legs around his waist. He became aroused, his erection pressing against her groin, mere centimeters away from the point of entry. The slightest shift in position would allow—

"Well, now, cowboy, what's *that*?" Celeste whispered in his ear. She cackled and pushed away from him, swimming toward the shore. Dazed both from the cold and lust, Baxter followed. She reached the sand before him, and Baxter thought he saw her speaking with a tall, grinning man whose white skin seemed to glow in the darkness. But then a wave overtook him, and when he resurfaced Celeste was alone on the beach.

They toweled themselves off, shivering, and got dressed. Huddled together in the sand, they smoked and said little as Celeste took constant pulls from the various bottles, alternating between them.

Baxter took only occasional sips to warm himself from the night wind sweeping off the sea. He stared with unrestrained longing into Celeste's face, but she'd become sufficiently intoxicated as to hardly be aware of his presence. She was lost in some tormented reverie behind the coffee-brown pools of her eyes, which in her drunkenness had become sad and unfocused. When she could no longer sit upright and kept tumbling onto her side, Baxter suggested he take her to his house.

"My mom won't care," he said. "You can take my bed and I'll... um, I'll crash on the couch."

Sleepily shaking her head, her eyes half-closed, she murmured, "No, m' pa'ents urn't hum. M' house zz closer."

Baxter helped Celeste stumble off the beach, leaving the liquor bottles and the towels in the sand. By the time they reached the sidewalk, it became clear she'd lost most of her motor abilities, so he picked her up and carried her across the street. He placed her in the passenger seat of his car and, after failing for several minutes to translate her fragmented speech when she tried to give him her Bel Air address, he obtained it from the GPS app on her phone. She slept most of the way there, waking only when he needed her to punch in the code for the gate at the bottom of her driveway.

It took her six attempts before the gate slid open. Baxter parked at the top of the driveway and carried her up to the mansion's front door. He was relieved to find it unlocked. The brief slumber had cleared her speech enough she was able to direct him to her bedroom on the third floor, where he pulled back the sheets of her canopied bed and laid her within them. He started to leave, but she grabbed his wrist and brought his hand to her breast. "Don't go," she said, opening her eyes. He'd never seen such sadness before. "I want... fuck me."

Baxter pulled his hand away and took a step away from the bed. "Yeah, um...no," he said. "I'm...not gonna do that."

The sadness in her eyes clouded with a hazy indignation. She sat up and began pulling at her clothes. "Fuck me. Please. Just…please." Tears were running down her face as she struggled to pull her flimsy shirt over her head. She gave up and tore it down the middle, tossing the ruined garment to the floor. "Please," she repeated.

"No," Baxter said again, firmer this time.

She pouted at him with childish petulance. "Why *not*?"

"Because you're, like, super drunk. And I'm, like…super *not*. And, like, some people would call that, um…rape."

She made a sound signifying disgust, disbelief. "*People*. What *people*."

"People like me." He moved closer to the bed so he could pull the covers over her. There was a couch against the far wall of her room, and he jerked his thumb at it. "I'm gonna crash there so I can, you know…be here if you need me. Try to sleep."

"Fuck you," she muttered, turning away from him. Baxter shut out the lights before settling into the couch.

In the morning, she didn't apologize, and she didn't thank him. Baxter thought it was better that way. She woke before him, bringing him coffee in a to-go cup. "My mom will be home soon," she told him. "You should go." Even hung over and disheveled from drunken sleep, her radiance was astounding.

As he was leaving, Baxter stopped in her bedroom doorway. He turned. Celeste had climbed back into bed. "What is it?" she asked.

"It's just…" Baxter trailed off. He stared at the lush pink carpet. "Why me? Any guy there would have taken you anywhere you wanted to go last night. Even Arden, probably. So, like…why me?"

Celeste rolled over onto her side and shut her eyes. "You're a nobody," she said. "Nobodies are harmless. Only the somebodies can hurt you."

At home, Baxter collapsed on his bed and thumbed through Celeste's Instagram page. He tried to find some trace of the drunken mess he'd met last night, something which hinted at the turmoil beneath her poised and perfect exterior. There was nothing. The girl online gave no suggestion of the one who'd revealed herself to him on the beach, in her bedroom. Baxter's disappointment, his *shock*, was still setting in. He wanted to believe celesteludoXV4eva existed in the tangible world, and that the alcoholic wastrel who sometimes wore her skin was nothing more than a malignant phantom from whom he must save her.

Zooming in on a picture of her in a tiny blue bikini, he extracted his erect cock from his shorts and began to masturbate. Tears stung his eyes. He didn't wipe them away until he was finished.

Afterward, he called Arden and told him what had happened the previous night. "You should steer clear," Arden told him. "She's a disaster. You don't need that kind of drama."

In the halls of the school the following week, Celeste ignored Baxter as she always had. Her behavior offered no more betrayal of her secret demons than did her Instagram page. She showed up every day looking like candy, and she posted regularly to social media. Baxter resigned himself to the notion his night with her was a fluke, a one-time chance occurrence, and that he'd never get the chance to save her in the manner he'd fantasized he might. But then, late on Friday night, he received a text from a number he didn't recognize. *Take me somewhere*, it read. He didn't know how she'd gotten his number, didn't care. He left at once for her house, willfully heedless of Arden's warning.

Things transpired much as they had the first night. When Baxter deposited Celeste into her bed in the early hours of morning, she made the same drunken advances, and he gave her the same refusal. It happened that way the next night, and many nights after that. He never so much as kissed her.

Her nighttime behavior became erratic. She loped through crowded intersections, shouted at pedestrians, tried to take the wheel from Baxter or crawl into his lap while he was driving. More than once, he saw articles on Buzzfeed about Celeste's "downward spiral," and he even spotted himself in some of the paparazzi's photographs. He was always blurry and out of focus, but he was there. Arden knew they were spending more time together but said nothing.

It wasn't as though Baxter could tell her not to drink. Drinking was, he'd come to realize with dismay, an integral component of who she was outside of cyberspace. To rob her of it would reduce her to ash.

The subject was broached only once, and not by Baxter.

They were sitting on the grass in Echo Park late one Thursday night, smoking joints and sharing a bottle of Southern Comfort as they looked out at the mucky, reeking water. Nearby, a homeless man was talking to a dead crow on the ground while probing its fly-speckled corpse.

Celeste had drunk much more than Baxter, as usual, but she was a considerable way from the point of no return that she would reach as the night drew on. After taking a long pull from the bottle, she looked at it and said, "People are telling me I have *a problem*. Can you believe it?" She moved her eyes to Baxter, staring at him, imploring him to weigh in. Baxter tensed up. He hadn't imagined this conversation would occur. He wasn't prepared for it.

When he didn't answer, Celeste continued by saying, "Sometimes, *I* can believe it. I mean, I guess. Something happens, you know? When I drink. I need more right away. And the more I drink, the more I need. Not even *want*...I *need* it. It's like I'll fall into a million little pieces if I don't have more. There are plenty of times I *want* to stop. I'm just, like, 'Celeste, you've had enough, chill out.' But I can't. I have to keep going until everything turns black. The need only goes away when everything else does, too."

"That's, um, pretty intense," said Baxter. It was *too* intense. He didn't know how to handle it, what to say to her. He wanted her to be celesteludoXV4eva. Life was so much simpler in the tiles cascading down her Instagram page. Everything would be perfect if she could be the girl she made herself out to be on the internet.

"It's so stupid," Celeste said. "It's so unfair. If that's what it is—if I have *a problem*—I mean, what am I supposed to *do* with that? Go to rehab? Go to fucking AA meetings? I'm fucking *fifteen*. I want to *live*. I want to *do things*. I shouldn't have to give all that up because... because why? Because I, what, can't *control* my *drinking*? That's fucking dumb. Why can other people control it, and I can't? It's like I'm being punished. It doesn't make sense. I didn't *do* anything."

Speaking with great care, Baxter said, "Well, have you...I mean, you know, have you thought about trying to...slow down? Or maybe, like...just not...drink for a little bit?" He swallowed. His palms were sweaty. "I mean, you could still smoke, obviously. But if the problem starts when you drink, maybe just...don't start drinking?"

Celeste shook her head, like Baxter wasn't getting it. "It's not that easy. Because when I'm not drinking, I'm thinking about drinking. I can't think about anything else until I drink."

That can't be true, Baxter wanted to shout at her. *You can't tell me celesteludoXV4eva is thinking about drinking when she's dancing to old Frisk songs or having funny arguments with her brother.*

"Anyway, whatever, it doesn't matter," Celeste went on. "I mean, right? I'd get sober for...for what, exactly?"

"I don't know," Baxter said. He looked at the homeless man, who was plucking feathers from the dead bird's wings and putting them in his mouth. "I guess you could find lots of reasons. If you wanted to, I mean. Like, you said the other night that some of your endorsements have been canceled. So, there's that. And...health, also, I think. Things like that. Things for the future. I guess you'd get sober so you could have a better future."

Celeste turned her head to look at Baxter, and the expression on her face was like gazing down at a cavernous abyss right before you fall into it. "The future," she said. It was almost a question, but her voice was too flat. "What future. What future do any of us have." She brought the bottle to her lips and tipped it all the way back.

They never discussed it again. They kept hanging out, Celeste kept drinking, and Baxter kept tearfully masturbating to celesteludoXV4eva's pictures. Gradually, celesteludoXV4eva came to be replaced altogether by the booze-wild wretch that called itself Celeste. Her posts decreased in frequency. When she did post, it was often in the form of a drunken, incoherent rant about communists in the school administration or China's influence on American immigration policies. These were quickly deleted, but not before the media got their hands on them.

Celeste started hemorrhaging followers. Her manager locked her out of her social media accounts, but the damage was done. Halfway through the school year, she'd lost almost all of her contracts. People who had once avoided her out of intimidation, now avoided her out of shame and fear. Failure in Los Angeles carries with it the air of a contagious and terminal disease.

"You're the only friend I have," she told him one morning as he was leaving. He stayed over each night they went out while continuing to reject her advances. Many times, he'd help her to the bathroom and hold her hair back while she vomited. He hated every second of it. He often lamented how he'd at first thought he was getting a chance at a romance with celesteludoXV4eva, and instead he'd ended up as a glorified servant boy to her far less glamorous counterpart. He wasn't sure how that had happened.

"You have other friends," Baxter said, knowing it wasn't true. He fiddled with his keys. He wanted to get out of there. The bedroom reeked of stale alcohol and disappointment.

Celeste didn't acknowledge his lie. She took the bottle of Jim Beam from her nightstand and knocked back several swallows. "Hair of the dog," she said, in a tone that approached apology but didn't quite get there. Baxter tried to conceal the disgust from his face but wasn't sure he succeeded. "Anyway. They're talking about sending me somewhere. I guess you're the only person who'll miss me."

I won't miss you, Baxter thought bitterly. *I'd miss celesteludoXV4eva, but you killed her.* Because he couldn't say this aloud, he only said, "Yeah."

"Maybe things will be better when I get back." Even as she said it, Baxter could hear she didn't believe it. "Maybe everything…" She trailed off, unable to muster the energy to finish.

"I should get going," Baxter said, gesturing at the bedroom door behind him.

Now it was Celeste who only said, "Yeah." Baxter left.

He never saw her again. She was sent to an expensive rehab in upstate New York where, according to Buzzfeed—citing a source "close to the family"—she suffered a severe psychotic break while detoxing.

Her social media accounts disappeared, and she was apparently transferred to a psychiatric hospital before completing her stint at rehab. After that, all news of her ceased. Baxter scoured the internet for any updates on her condition, but there was nothing. He supposed she was wallowing away in a padded room, muttering to herself, shrieking garbled obscenities as the world moved on and she didn't.

And through all of it, what had he gained? Very little, save for the knowledge that Real Girls perhaps were not suited for him. He'd had occasional flings with surfer chicks and stoner girls, but he grew weary of them whenever they started displaying signs of emotional complexity requiring something from him. It became clear what he wanted was a pretty picture, and not much else. Something that wouldn't ask anything from him in return.

He turned to the internet.

He knew porn had begun, more or less, as videotape rentals with bad acting and cheesy writing, and that it had evolved into grainy, virus-prone internet videos. By the time he came to it near the end of his junior year, the internet's catalogue of high-definition and relatively safe clips had been in full-swing for years, providing him with an endless buffet of content. This had kept him sated for a long time, until the advent of iPorn when he was twenty-one.

iPorn evolved from the OnlyFans business model, with users signing up to deliver subscription-based pornographic content while pocketing a sizable portion of the proceeds. The gimmick came in that subscribers could upload images of themselves and, using deep-fake technology, insert themselves into the content creators' videos.

This was most commonly utilized by a seamless and convincing transposition of the subscriber's likeness over the likeness of one or more people having sex with the content creator in his or her (but mostly her) video.

With iPorn, you could watch yourself fuck anyone.

And the girls, they were flawless. It wasn't long before most of the industry's porn stars had migrated to the platform. The application's extensive editor suite allowed them to crop and airbrush themselves into digital goddesses. Baxter had never seen in person a girl who looked as good as the ones on iPorn, which is why more than $2,000 of his trust fund went to various subscription fees each month.

It had been everything he could have wanted in the beginning, at least from a porn perspective, but as time drew on it started to become a problem. The money wasn't an issue—there was a seemingly limitless amount of it, left to him by his late grandfather's real estate development fortune.

There was shame, though. The shame exceeded his funds. And there were times, such as the girl from the dispensary, when he tried to test the waters again with Real Girls, only to be thwarted by the impotent side effects of his addiction. For that's what it was, he knew—an addiction. He came to resent Celeste more and more as time went on, for it had been she who'd first presented him with the confounding chasm between virtuality and reality.

It hadn't, he rationalized, been the porn that had ruined him. Not really.

It had been celesteludoXV4eva.

ELEVEN
BEAUTIFUL AND DAMNED

THOSE FIRST NIGHTS. Those first nights were like poetry.

Ryland couldn't remember infatuation like this. Not ever in his life. The first kisses on warm evenings—in his car, at his condo, at Lyssi's place when the boyfriend wasn't around—they made him weak. Pressed against him, her arms around his neck, her breath in his mouth...there was such desperation, such rabidity. It electrified him. Jolted him alive. It showed him he'd been asleep before her. It showed him everything he'd been missing.

She always knew what he wanted and how to give it to him. She plied him with compliments that inflated his ego and eroded his most guarded insecurities. Before her, no girl had known how or when to say the things he needed them to say. He had a hidden fragility that Lyssi fortified into confidence and strength. Sexually, she was always one move ahead of him, knowing how he wanted to be touched before he had a chance to articulate it.

In return, anything *she* wanted, he gave to her.

He took her shopping, to expensive restaurants. They spent hours in Bloomingdale's, Saint Laurent, Gucci, Versace, Balenciaga, Dior. She danced with him in the dim, smoky light of discreet, speakeasy-style bars in Silver Lake and Atwater Village, floating in his arms as their feet tapped along the floor to the piano men's jubilant tunes. They got drunk on top-shelf champagne, stoned on the highest quality weed, high on the purest coke. And fucked like sweating beasts in captivity until exhaustion overtook them.

At the office, Lyssi was the picture of professionalism. She spared nary a glance in his direction on the rare occasions their paths crossed. She wouldn't text him during work hours. Outside of work, their text volleys were torrid and salacious—more so than Ryland was accustomed to even with the most fervid of his past trysts—but never when she was at the office. The way she fanned the mercurial flames of his ego in their off-hours made her at-work coldness all the more biting.

This level of prudence was necessary and appreciated, but Ryland ached for her attention. He longed for something as trivial as a smile, a surreptitious wink. When he was at his most stressed and coke-addled, he experienced dizzying urges to run to her cubicle and fall at her feet, hugging her calves to him and kissing her ankles.

She brought gifts to his condo—bottles of his favorite liquors, vintage cigarette lighters, the occasional necktie, and a growing collection of cutesy stuffed animals she would place atop his dresser, exclaiming over how much they "brightened up the place."

There were, however, *omens*.

She did not seem to experience intoxication in any sort of normal manner. It took Ryland several weeks to notice, as he was usually too blitzed himself to pay attention. But it was impossible to ignore once he realized it.

She guzzled the champagne like it was water and snorted enormous lines from which even he would have shied away. He lost track of how much weed she was smoking. And yet, she never lost her faculties. Her speech wasn't slurred. Her eyes were clear and bright. She kept up with their conversations without ever losing the thread or digressing into the kind of rambling tangents one comes to expect

from someone under the influence of any or all the substances she'd
ingested.

Then there was a night she didn't want to go anywhere so they
stayed in and ordered sushi. Already half-drunk on sake by the time
they'd finished eating, Ryland had accidentally walked in on her in
the bathroom. The acrid odor of vomit assaulted his sinuses. Lyssi
knelt hunched over the toilet. Her hair was tied back with a purple
ribbon, and her small body heaved as she retched. She'd extracted
her fingers from her throat and looked up at him. Her streaming eyes
burned with vitriol.

"*GET OUT,*" she'd screeched at him. Her sweat-slickened, pale
green cheeks bloomed with angry red blotches. Flustered, Ryland
backed out of the bathroom and closed the door behind him. He
absconded to the dining room to drink more sake. When she
emerged ten minutes later, her makeup had been fixed and her
extravagant hair fell freely upon her shoulders, the ribbon nowhere
in sight.

She smiled at him and made no mention of the incident, instead
straddling him in the chair and kissing him. Her breath tasted of
peppermint, and despite his straining, Ryland failed to locate any
traces of the sour flavor of bile. He could almost convince himself
he'd imagined the entire event, but after that night, he noticed she
excused herself to the bathroom after every meal.

Nothing about me is healthy.

And then there had been the Saturday night she slept over when
the boyfriend was spending a "weekend with the boys" in Tijuana.
Ryland had woken alone in his bed sometime around three AM. His
temples were pounding and his mouth was thick and dry. As he staggered toward the master bathroom for a glass of water, he noticed
the bedroom door was ajar. Leaning against the doorjamb, he
squinted into the dark hallway.

When his eyes adjusted, he saw Lyssi's silhouette sitting on the
floor, facing away from him. He went to her, feeling a mounting fear
he couldn't explain. He reached for her but stopped. She was whis-

pering to herself. Strings of nonsensical words tumbled from her mouth. Breathless, frenzied. One long, continuous hiss. Something foreign, something alien. Ryland withdrew his hand and retreated down the hallway. He shut the bedroom door and got into bed. In the morning, she was sleeping beside him when he woke. He never mentioned what he'd seen.

There were comments she made, too. Words spoken with a light lilt but hinting at something darker. Something serious. Sometimes she'd swear he was looking at another girl, and she'd say something like, "If you want her, tell me. Tell me and I'll kill myself. I'll kill myself so you can go be happy with her."

Penny's calls had been increasing in frequency, as well, and Ryland had to hastily swipe "Ignore" so as not to arouse suspicion— something he felt was absurd given the overall circumstances, but necessary. Especially since there were nights when Lyssi would cuddle up against him in bed and whisper, "Remember, don't ever betray me. If you betray me, I'll kill you. But first I'll make you wish you were dead. I'll take everything from you."

And, always, there was the laughter.

Laughter like worlds ending, like the earth's crust breaking open and birthing bloodthirsty, humanoid monstrosities. In Ryland's deepest slumber, that laughter accompanied nightmarish imagery that left him shaken and sweating upon waking. Perhaps the most unnerving element of the laughter was how it never reached her eyes. Not once. She could laugh and laugh until she was out of breath, but always her eyes remained cold and remote. They burned with emerald cheerlessness, both beautiful and damned.

None of this was enough to deter him from her. The things she said to him and the ease with which he could talk to her, the peaceful comfort of her proximity, the way she turned him into a god when they had sex...it made anything negative or distressing feel inconsequential. And despite Lyssi's jealous suspicions, Ryland was unable to look at other girls with any sort of sexual yearning. They all began to look like cheap imitations of her.

He was not without his own jealousies. Knowing she went home to another man—a *boy*, really—affected him in ways to which he was unaccustomed.

Many of the girls and women he slept with were in relationships of varying degrees of seriousness, but Ryland had never been bothered by this. He didn't care what they did when they left. He rarely thought about them.

Not so with Lyssi. He'd Googled Kyle Willard, aka K-Dolla Money, aka the boyfriend, and been unimpressed with what his nemesis brought to the table. He looked soft and boyish, about fifteen pounds overweight and with a round, infantile face which appeared alarmingly punchable. Ryland had never been a bully in school, but there was something weak and pathetic about the kid that made him want to steal his lunch money and stuff him in a trashcan. He supposed sleeping with his girlfriend was a greater triumph, but whenever Lyssi went home, leaving him in the cold confines of his solitude which not so long ago had been a solace, it felt a long way from victory.

He began to fear what she was doing to him.

TWELVE
THE EMPTY DISEASE

TESS ACCEPTED an invitation to meet her friends Megg and Vince at the Polo Lounge late one night, only agreeing because there wasn't anything better to do.

She brought Arden along as an afterthought, telling him it would be good for him to stop moping around the pool house. He looked strung out and kept his sunglasses on while checking his phone as the four of them sat at an outside table drinking gimlets and smoking cigarettes.

The only thing he'd said to Tess on the drive over was, "I don't know why you hang out with them." Tess had waited a long time before saying, "We went to high school together," as if it had been years ago. As if it explained anything.

"You *have* to cut that guy loose," Megg was insisting to Tess. "It's been, like, what? Almost a year that you've been with him? What are you still *doing* with him? We humored you in the beginning. We figured you were just having fun. But, like, enough is enough. I mean, a *writer*? Who reads *books* anymore? The guy is a *dinosaur*."

"She's right," said Vince, tapping a column ash from his imported Gauloise cigarette. "He's a relic from a dead era. He represents his generation's last gasp at holding a place in the upper echelons of society. It's all based on privilege, you know. Artistry? *Talent?* Please. Rewarding that kind of thing is rooted in a whole slew of systemic problems that are dying out." He rattled the ice in his drink, took a sip. "People like him are being replaced by people like me and Megg —influencers, streaming icons, social media stars, *et cetera*. It's how it should be. It levels the playing field. Talent is bred from privilege. What Megg and I do, *anyone* can do. We just had the gumption to do it."

"Right," Tess said. "Remind me again how much money your father had to shell out to make your first video go viral."

Vince ignored her. "And that's all without broaching the topic of his *subject matter*," he went on. "I've not read his books because, like, *come on*, but I've heard about them. Casual misogyny and light racism abound, from what I've been told."

"Did you see the article in *Vogue*?" Megg asked Tess.

"It was *Teen Vogue*," Tess muttered.

"It flat-out *says* you shouldn't date guys who *read* his books," Megg continued. "I think it goes *without* saying that the guy who *writes* them should *definitely* be off-limits."

"I guess it's a good thing I don't get my dating advice from fashion websites," said Tess.

Megg looked confused. "Where do you get it, then?"

"Besides," said Tess, "we're not dating. We're...I don't know." She finished her drink and signaled to the waiter for another before lighting a cigarette. "It's just...we're, you know, hanging out, I guess. It's not that deep."

The Writer's lighthearted, half-serious marriage proposal bubbled to the forefront of her mind, but she smothered the thought.

"You're *hanging out*?" Megg said. "You've been *hanging out* for the past *year*?"

Tess shrugged. "Whatever. He's good in bed. And it hasn't been a whole year yet. Anyway, I don't want to talk about him." The truth was, she didn't know why she was still with him. She couldn't locate if her disillusionment in the thing that was CHANDLER EASTRIDGE was because of who the man himself was, or something deeper than that. Something which had more to do with who *she* was.

Arden looked up from his phone. "Is anyone else worried about the fires? The ones out east, in the desert? The pictures on Instagram are pretty gnarly."

A still quiet passed among Tess and her friends before Vince said, "Well, yeah. Sure, of course we're worried."

"They're getting closer," said Arden. "People are saying they could reach LA soon if the state can't get them under control."

"I don't think it'll happen," said Megg. "They always seem to—"

She was interrupted by the arrival of Zelda, who sat in the empty chair between Tess and Megg and dropped her oversized Louis Vuitton purse onto the ground beside her. "God, I need a drink," she said.

Zelda waved the waiter over and ordered a Cosmopolitan, flashing her fake ID. "I just lived through *the most* stressful Lyft ride of my *life*. The bitch had *no idea* where she was going and kept trying to ask me for *fucking directions*, and I'm like, 'Lady, use your fucking GPS, I'm not going to do your job for you.' Like, for fuck's sake. And then she started yelling at me in, I don't know, Chinese or Japanese or Korean, or whatever, and I just *could not deal*. Thank God for Xanax or I would have *totally* popped off." The waiter arrived with her drink. She brought the glass to her lips. "Anyway," she said. "What are we talking about, what did I miss?"

"The fires," said Megg. "Whether or not they'll hit LA."

"They probably will," said Zelda. "This city's been asking for an infernal destruction for years."

"It's true," said Vince. "Yes, we've made great strides in our environmental policies, but it hasn't been enough. You can't half-ass these things. We're talking about the future of our planet."

"It has *nothing* to do with *the environment* and *everything* to do with our *crumbling infrastructure*," said Zelda. "Add to that the state-level restrictions on doing *fucking anything* in this hellhole, which

prevent companies from being able to make the necessary improve-
ments to—"

"Where'd you read that bullshit?" asked Vince, sneering a little.
"Fucking *Breitbart*? Christ, Z, Earth has become a goddamn *oven*,
and we—"

"I remember last winter as being particularly *freezing*," Zelda
said. "It didn't exactly reinforce the whole global warming idea."

"That's why it's been rebranded as *climate change*," Megg said.

"Correct," said Vince. "There are...variables. Nuances. Science is
all about course correction."

"Sometimes I think it's what this city needs," Arden said,
glancing at his phone. "Burn it all down. All of it."

"Easy there, Morrissey," said Megg.

Arden stared at her from behind his sunglasses, straight-faced,
saying nothing.

"Anyway." Megg forced a smile. "Subject change. I need everyone's opinion for a new video I'm thinking about doing. What's more
satisfying? Crunching dry leaves in your hand, or popping bubble
wrap?"

Tess watched in dejected disbelief as the others took the question
seriously enough to legitimize it with a response, all of them unani-
mously deciding bubble wrap was the correct answer. Even Arden
mumbled his agreement.

"Wait a second," said Vince, his face serious. "This actually ties
back to our previous conversation because we have to consider the
environmental factor as it pertains to bubble wrap. I'm changing my
answer to dry leaves."

Megg pondered this. "No, yeah, you're totally right.," she said. "I
can't believe I didn't think of that." Arden grunted in assent.

"The environment is fine," said Zelda. "I'm keeping my answer."

"Your ignorance is so boundless it's almost admirable," Vince
said, lifting his tone in mock reverence.

Arden's phone vibrated on the table. He snatched it and read
something on the screen. A warped funhouse version of its display

reflected on the lenses of his sunglasses. He glanced at Tess. "I have to go," he said, standing. "I'll get a Lyft."

"Where are you going? I can drive you, it's no big deal."

"No, it's fine." He looked at the others, who had launched into another argument about the environment. "Enjoy your, um, friends."

Tess couldn't tell if he was making fun of her, her friends, or both. Maybe he wasn't doing either. It was impossible to tell.

She had another drink and smoked a few of Vince's Gauloises, hardly aware of what was being discussed. When her drink was finished, she considered ordering another but decided against it, telling the others she was tired, and she'd see them around. They didn't try to coax her into staying. She hadn't expected them to.

It occurred to her as she left that she should have been drunk, but she felt dreadfully sober. When she got to her car—a white Audi A6 passed on to her from Arden—she took a joint out of her glove compartment and smoked it as she drove down Sunset, skipping through a playlist composed of Bat for Lashes, Calliope Laing, and Lana Del Rey.

She rolled her windows up as she entered Hollywood. Droves of homeless people lined the sidewalks on either side of the boulevard, standing around their tents, sitting on the curb, shouting profanities at the dark sky. She could feel eyes on her as she passed.

Tess found herself at Griffith Observatory for reasons she didn't understand, and then she was parking her car in the vacant lot and wandering across the wide lawn to the empty terrace. She leaned against the low wall and gazed down over the golden dusting of lights dappled across the black city beneath her. She could see the glow of the fires to the east. They simmered like a warm promise. Her eyes drifted to the general vicinity of where The Writer's house stood among the hills, and she tried to imagine what he might be doing. Tried to imagine what it might be like to care.

Just say the word, he'd said to her.

"Miss? Are you okay?"

She turned, startled; she'd thought she was alone. A man stood a few paces away, staring at her with glittering eyes a deep shade of onyx. He was dressed in a janitor's gray coveralls, but he didn't fit her preconceived notions of what a janitor should look like, and there was something familiar about him she couldn't place. Tall and lanky, he had the thin, angular face of a movie star and thick brown hair, a lock of which fell casually across his forehead. His skin was like polished ivory. Long-fingered hands wrapped around the yellow handle of a broom with an attached dustpan. He had white cowboy boots on his feet, made from some kind of reptile.

"Am I...okay?" she asked, confused, somewhat transfixed by his dark, probing eyes.

"You're crying," the janitor said. He smiled. For half a second it was a terrible smile, too huge and with too many teeth. Tess flinched and took a step backward, but then it shrunk and became friendly, pleasant, inviting. She felt inexplicably calmed.

"I...am?" she said, raising the fingers of her left hand to her face. She drew them away, saw them smudged with wet mascara. Her eyes returned to the janitor. "I wasn't facing you," she said. "How did you know?"

His smile widened. It wasn't enough to become the freakish grin Tess had thought she'd seen, but it was enough to erase some of the comfort she'd felt a moment prior. "I make it my business to know *everything*," he said. He had a voice like a spoonful of molasses. "Well, except calculus."

"But you're...a janitor."

He let out a short laugh that terminated so abruptly Tess didn't have time to decide if it was a nice sound, or a horrible one. "Matt Damon was *just a janitor* in *Good Will Hunting*," he said. He reached into the breast pocket of his coveralls and withdrew a pack of Dunhills, flicking it open and pulling one out with his teeth. He lit it with a snap of his long fingers.

Tess felt aware she should be unnerved by this, but the act seemed so commonplace she didn't give it much thought. The janitor held the pack out to her, raising his eyebrows. Tess looked at the red, square package, considering it before shaking her head.

"If you know everything," Tess said, "then why did you ask if I was okay?"

Curls of smoke unwound from the janitor's nostrils and seeped from between his grinning teeth. "Being polite, is all. I *know* you're not okay."

Tess glanced over her shoulder at the red-orange glow on the horizon. "I don't know where I'm going," she heard herself say. "I don't know where I'm supposed to go or what I'm supposed to do."

"Who says you have to *go* anywhere, *do* anything?"

"No one. Everyone. I don't know." She wiped her eyes again, took in a breath. "I mean, we're all supposed to do *something*, right? Isn't that the whole point? Like, of everything?" Some distant part of herself was aware of how absurd it was to be having this kind of conversation with a stranger, but somehow it felt natural. "We're all supposed to do something and find, I don't know, our *place*, or what-ever. I mean, right? We're always being told that there's more to life than *this*—" she gestured around with her arms "—and we have to go and find it in order to be...*happy*." She said the last word as if it tasted bad. "Whatever *this* is for any of us—and I guess it's different for *all* of us—it's supposed to be this thing that *isn't enough*. And it's not. It's *not* enough. So, we have to go find *more*, but more of *what*? And where *is* it? Where are we even supposed to *look*?"

"*Darling*," said the janitor, his voice slithering into Tess's ears, "I've been *everywhere*, and I can *assure* you there is *always* 'more.'" He drew air quotes around the word "more" with his spooky fingers. "Everywhere you can think of to go, anywhere you can look, you will certainly find *more*." He eyed her as he dragged from the cigarette. "But it is my humble opinion that *more* is ex*act*ly what's wrong with all of you. The desire for it, the pursuit of it...*that's* your problem."

He came to stand next to her and gestured at the urban expanse below them with the hand that wasn't holding the cigarette. "It's nebulous," he said. "It's unattainable. You can chase it, and you can *find* it, but you cannot pos*sess* it. The men who built the very ground upon which we stand were finding it all the time and trying to hold it in their hands. They built whole civilizations as they watched it slip through their fingers. It's the price of progress, yes, but it's also the weapon of your destruction. It destroys all of you." He grinned at her. "And I'd be lying if I said it isn't a *hell* of a good time watching you do it."

"You're talking about greed," Tess said, not looking at him, her voice hushed. "Capitalism, and all that."

"An understandable misconception, yes, but *no*, that's *not* what I'm talking about. Not *really*. You youngsters are always so *quick* to blame everything on capitalism, but that is a mere *symptom* of the true problem. It's not the actual *ailment*, and our *end*lessly charitable God upon His savage throne has my *ut*most gratitude for *that*."

Now Tess did look at him, and she asked, "Why?"

Grinning at her, the janitor said, "Because if capitalism *were* the source of the disease, I suspect it would be much easier to cure. And where would the fun be in such a prospect?"

"What is it, then? What's the disease?"

The janitor pinched out his cigarette with his thumb and forefinger and then flicked it over the edge of the terrace. "It's *inside* you," he said, pointing at her chest. Tess noticed his fingertip was unburnt, showing no sign of damage or smudging from the cigarette it had just extinguished. "It's inside *all* of you."

"What is? What's...inside me?"

"You tell me, girlfriend." His black eyes twinkled so brightly they seemed to glow.

Tess turned toward the gleaming cityscape below. She brought a hand to her chest and held it there. "It's...I don't know. It's a hole. A *void*. It's this huge emptiness. It's bigger than everything and I...I always feel like it's...like it's on the verge of swallowing me up." The hand she held upon her chest closed into a loose fist. Her heart pulsed beneath it, distant and apathetic. "And I guess I sort of...I guess I put things inside it to...to try and make it smaller, but it grows and grows." Tess looked over at the janitor. His face was so kind and benevolent it brought fresh, stinging tears to her eyes.

Her vision blurred, causing his image to warp into something leering and nightmarish. She shut her eyes and swiped at them with her hands, and when she reopened them, he looked as kind as he had before. "What do I do?" she asked him. "How do I make it smaller? How do I make it disappear?"

"Kiddo," he said, "you can't." He placed his hand on her shoulder, and even with the barrier of her clothes between her skin and his, it felt cold. He flashed a compassionate smile and withdrew his hand, and then he turned away and resumed sweeping the terrace, whistling a tune Tess at first had difficulty placing. The Beatles? No. The Rolling Stones.

She looked for a while at the city, at the millions of lives compressed into something which, from her vantage point, looked like nothing more than a child's toy set. When she turned around, the janitor was gone.

She went to her car and for a long time sat weeping in the empty parking for something profound that had been lost.

THIRTEEN
SUBJECTIVE REALITIES

SEX WITH REBECCA was like the first time. Like magic.

Not because of its quality—which *was* objectively high—but because Arden could not remember any of the sex he'd had in the past. There had been other girls, he knew—the exact quantity lost—but his memories had become limited to pre- and post-coital moments. The scent of a girl's moisturizer as he leaned in, the taste of her lip gloss, the feeling of damp fingertips beneath his shirt. After, the low voices talking about nothing, the sweat-stained sheets, the used condom floating in toilet water like something dead.

During the moments he spent inside Rebecca, Arden was often compelled to tell her he loved her. The bilious words rose to his lips in a spasmodic convulsion, threatening to spew out. He always swallowed them at the last moment.

He wondered if it was something about her specifically which aroused this impulse within him, or if he'd experienced similar urges with other girls. Had he ever actually uttered the phrase? Had it happened with someone else, and had he failed to choke down the words before they gushed from his mouth?

He wanted to call every girl he'd ever slept with and ask, "Did I ever tell you I loved you when we were in bed together?" This was an impossibility; their names were lost to him. He scrolled though the contacts in his phone, hoping one of the names would stir a spark of recognition within him, but they were hieroglyphs on a cave wall.

He told himself he wasn't foolish enough to believe he loved Rebecca. The impulsive desire to say the words didn't seem related to true emotion. When the sex had concluded, the urge—by then dissipated—felt absurd. He knew he liked her. But love? The idea was ill-defined. Foreign. He wasn't sure what it meant. If it was real. He wanted to believe it wasn't. A world without love was safer. More rational.

Rebecca's own feelings toward love were even more complicated, something she ascribed to her "untraditional" upbringing and the peculiar relationship between her parents.

"They never got married," she told him over dinner at Figaro one night. The dim dining room was sparsely attended, and the music was played low. She spoke in a hushed voice, leaning forward. The light from the candle in the center of the table glinted in her dark eyes. "They had this sort of hippie thing going on. What we'd call an 'open relationship' nowadays, but that was never how they referred to it. They never wanted to put a label on anything. But they were committed to each other, I guess. And they were basically in sync with how they raised me and my brothers. They just...they slept with a lot of different people. I mean, very openly. In front of us. Sex was never this taboo thing in our family. I guess it was kind of inappropriate in a lot of ways. I can't tell you how many times I saw my dad banging some girl or another. They never closed any doors. Ever. Sometimes they'd do it right on the couch while my brothers or I were watching TV."

"Whoa," said Arden.

Rebecca sipped her wine. Her eyes shifted away from Arden. "And then there was my mom, and her men." She paused. Her face was blank and inscrutable. Like she was reliving something.

"Look, not all of them were terrible. A lot of them were nice to me. But a lot of them also...you know. They did stuff with me. Starting when I was probably too young. You'd think it was the terrible ones, but it wasn't. Almost never. It was usually the nice ones. The ones I liked. I don't know if that made it better or not. Maybe it made it worse." She took another long sip of wine. "Whatever it was, my mom was cool with it. She didn't encourage it, exactly, but. It's not like she *dis*couraged it at all. These...these 'experiences,' she called them—she said they were healthy. That they *contributed* to my *development* as a *sexual being*. And that I should participate in whatever way I thought was appropriate."

"Whoa," said Arden again. He noticed someone at a nearby table was dressed as the Berkeley bear mascot, staring at him with its white-gloved hands clasped in its lap. Arden ignored it and asked Rebecca, "How old were you when this was going on? When did it start?"

Her eyes moved farther away from him. "Young," she said. "I was...I was very young. Probably too young to decide what was appropriate and what wasn't. But then again, who knows. It's not like anything magical happens when you turn eighteen, or even sixteen or thirteen. I think it happens at different times for different people, and even then, when it does happen, it's nothing mystical or earth-shattering. I think in some ways you have to learn your way through it."

"I, um...I don't think that's exactly...true. Not when you're a kid. Especially not when it's with adults."

"Better it be with adults than other kids who are just as confused and inept as you are."

Arden shook his head. "Rebecca," he said, exasperated. "What you're talking about...it isn't right."

"It's maybe not as bad as it sounds."

"I mean, um. It sounds pretty...it doesn't sound good."

"It's possible I was too young," she conceded, smiling and rolling her eyes. "But whatever. It doesn't matter."

And that was how they'd left it.

Still more complicated were her feelings toward him. Or, how Arden perceived them.

Whenever he thought he'd gotten closer to understanding how she felt about him, she did or said something to throw him off.

They'd been lying in bed together on an unusually cool and gloomy afternoon. The clouds purged rain that pattered against the windows. The two of them had just had a bout of what Arden thought had been particularly passionate sex. He'd felt close to her in a way which was all-consuming. Like they'd transcended something and arrived at a point where they could remain. Where nothing threatened them. The link Arden felt bonded them to one another seemed strengthened to the point of permanence. It was a good, safe feeling.

And then Rebecca had lit a cigarette and asked, "Do you ever think about leaving LA?"

It sounded like a harmless enough question at first. Arden said, "No, not really. Do you?"

"God, no. I'll never leave. With my career, it wouldn't make sense to be anywhere else. But you, you should consider it. I don't think LA is good for you."

Arden swallowed. "It's just a place," he said.

"Not a *good* place, though."

"People say that, but I don't see it. I don't think it matters where you live. Everywhere is just a section of land with people in it. Whatever significance you give it is basically imaginary."

Rebecca frowned, exhaled smoke. "I don't know," she said. "I've seen a side of this city that most people...well, I've seen some bad things, that's all."

"That's your experience, though. It's shaped your perception. If you remove your, you know, your subjective reality from the whole equation, all the meaning goes away."

"You can't remove your *subjective reality*," she said. Her tone was slightly mocking. "That's not possible. All you know is what you've experienced."

"That's not true. None of it is real." He thought of all the blank spaces in his memory. Everything he'd forgotten. The names and faces and encounters scrubbed from his brain. Maybe it had been the drugs, maybe it was disassociation. It didn't matter. "Everything can be erased," he said. "Nothing has to be anything you don't want it to be." He said this, but he doubted the words as they rolled over his tongue. Could he turn Rebecca into nothing? Could he make her something which didn't matter? "Why do you think LA is bad for me?" he asked.

"Oh, you know," she said. She tapped ash into a heart-shaped ashtray on the nightstand. "Generally, I think you're too nice. This isn't a town for nice people."

This puzzled Arden. He couldn't recall having ever given thought to whether he was a nice person. He wasn't sure there was such a thing. He thought people just were who they were. Everyone's agree-ability was subjective. Based on personal tastes, experiences. Your moral barometer. Things like that. "Nice" and "not nice" were too simple and unrealistic categories.

"And I think you could be really successful somewhere else," Rebecca went on. "Have a lot of fun. Like, you're a really attractive guy. But, I mean, guys like you are a dime a dozen out here. You could go to, like, Indiana or, I don't know, Oklahoma, or something, and you'd be a god to them. Farmers would probably bring you their beautiful virgin daughters on carts of roses."

"Jesus, Rebecca."

"I'm kidding, mostly. Not totally, though. Plus, it's expensive out here, and your philosophy degree doesn't exactly lend itself to the accumulation of untold riches. It wouldn't take nearly as much to live comfortably in, you know, one of those other states."

"That...doesn't matter to me," Arden said. "And I don't want to be a god to anyone. I'm starting to think you don't know me all that well. Too nice for LA? What does that even mean?"

"I don't know why you're hung up on *that*. I just think you're a lot more sensitive and romantic than you let on. I know you like all those grim philosophers who insist nothing means anything, or whatever, but honestly, that doesn't track. I think you *want* to believe nothing means anything, that it's all random and senseless, but you don't *really* believe that."

"What do I believe, then?"

"I don't know, but it certainly isn't *that*. I don't think *you* know what you believe, either."

Arden stared at the ceiling. "I just spent four years at a very expensive college. I'm supposed to have figured that out by now."

"Oh, please. If you get your whole belief system from college, you're doing something wrong. That's what they want—it's more an institution for brainwashing than anything. Honestly, you should have more questions after graduation than you did when you enrolled. That's how I see it. And for you, I think you'd be more likely to get answers if you went somewhere else. I don't think LA has that much to offer you."

Arden's palms were sweating beneath the sheets. He was thinking about the conversation they'd had about his drug use after their first night together. *Don't take me hostage*, she'd told him. He'd taken that as connotative of a future, one with both of them in it.

Now she was telling him to leave.

He wondered if there was someone else. Images flashed through his mind of Rebecca writhing on a bed with some asshole movie star in a Palisades mansion. She occupied that world. She was beautiful and had access to any number of Hollywood elites, men who had far more to offer her than he did. Shutting his eyes and listening to the rain, he told himself it didn't matter, that the world would move on irrespective of how things panned out between them. He knew this to be true, but the images wouldn't go away. They brought with them an overwhelming nausea.

"Arden? What are you thinking about?"

He opened his eyes and looked at her face, flushed and glazed with a light dew of perspiration. *I don't love her*, he thought, trying it on for size. *I don't know what love is, or who* she *is. I hardly know her at all. I don't love her.* But the words felt forced and hollow in his head. They weren't even in his mouth, but he could taste their sour tang of untruth.

Arden smiled sadly at her. "It doesn't matter."

FOURTEEN
THE MYTH OF LOS ANGELES

RYLAND TAGGED along with a few other junior executives to a party in the Hollywood Hills one night when Lyssi wasn't available.

No one appeared to know to whom the house belonged, and most of the several hundred guests seemed to have received vague invitations from people who "knew someone who knew the guy hosting it." Ryland lost the other executives upon arrival when they went to do ketamine with the DJ. People lounged around outside on the stone stairs leading up to the house, drinking and smoking. They congregated at the gazebo, or in the courtyard, or along the veranda atop a rock outcropping laced with vines. Inside the house, a crowd of people could be seen dancing through the floor-to-ceiling windows wrapped around the living room.

Wishing he were with Lyssi, Ryland grabbed a Pacifica from a nearby cooler and pushed through the interspersed clusters of bodies. He moved up to the deck alongside the house, where only a small handful of people stood talking over their drinks and joints and cigarettes.

He caught snippets as he passed by them: "—can be kind of two-faced, I *know*, but I'm a Sagittarius *with* a Capricorn rising, so—" and

"—it more of a chance than that, seriously. The first few episodes are kind of slow but once you get to, like, the eighth or ninth episode it *really* picks up and you—"

He moved along the guardrail to the end of the deck, where he had the most breathing room. Opening the beer with a Prozac-branded bottle opener on his keychain and then lighting a cigarette, he looked over his shoulder at the dark, sprawling hills below, dotted with orange and yellow lights. The silhouettes of tall palm trees swayed against the black backdrop of the sky. A red glow from the fires was visible to the east. To the south, downtown Los Angeles rose like a golden promise of something hateful and glittering.

His phone vibrated. He took it out of his pocket, hoping it was Lyssi, but the name across the top read "BRUNO."

Ryland frowned. It was almost three AM in Pennsylvania. He considered answering it, but ended up dragging his thumb across "Ignore," promising himself he'd call his brother back tomorrow. The phone returned to his pocket.

"Wow. I guess you could *maybe* look more bummed out, but I'm not sure how." The voice cut through the din of the party. Ryland turned his head in its direction. It belonged to a girl, early twenties, moderately pretty in a simple, unmade-up kind of way. She held a can of Modelo in one hand and a clove cigarette in the other. The darkness lent a haunting mysteriousness to her features, which Ryland knew wouldn't have been as impressive in the daylight.

"I'm doing my best Ben Affleck," Ryland said, his voice flat. He ashed his cigarette over the railing.

The girl emitted a raspy noise that might have been a snicker. "That's a good one," she said. She moved closer to him. The cigarette went to her lips, the ember blazing. She angled her head away to exhale the smoke and then fixed her gaze back on Ryland. "What are you doing here?" she asked.

Ryland gestured around them. "What's anybody doing here?"

"Not Ben Affleck-ing, for starters."

"I needed some air."

"You just got here."

"How do you know that?"

Even in the darkness, Ryland saw her eyes twinkle. "I've been watching you," she said, smiling a little. "You kind of stand out."

"Do I?"

"You do. You're not from here, are you?"

Frowning, Ryland said, "Where? LA? I've been here a while."

The girl nodded in a knowing way, like an assumption had been corroborated. "Sure, I bet. But you're not *from* here. You're from somewhere back east. Some small town nobody's heard of."

Ryland's frown deepened. "What makes you say that."

The cigarette returned to her lips as she eyed him. She opened the side of her mouth and let the smoke out in a quick, thin jet. "It's written all over you. The suit, the shoes, the watch. It's so in-your-face expensive. All you small-town boys who come here do the same thing. You get so enamored by the perceived glamour of what this town is supposed to represent, what you think it means to come here and make something of yourself. You wrap yourselves in tinsel. There's this sick romanticization of the idea of selling your soul to whatever this place is to you. You want everyone to know that *this* is who you are now, *this* is what you've become. You've subscribed to the myth of Los Angeles and pinned the receipt to your lapel."

Ryland took an absent pull from his beer as he looked at the girl, bemused. The tone she'd used when assessing him—though *diagnosing* him felt more accurate—was difficult to interpret. Was she being cruel, condescending? The still-present glint in her eye suggested it was all in good fun, but it was impossible to tell with certainty.

"Think about it," the girl went on, "because you're not. Right now, you're trying to figure out if I'm being playful, or if I'm just a bitch. It hasn't occurred to you to give any thought to what I said. You're not the introspective type, obviously—I can tell. Try to be, though, just for a minute."

Ryland opened his mouth to retort, but the girl held up a hand

and shushed him, telling him again to "*try it.*" Setting the beer on the railing, Ryland turned away from the girl and toward the city.

Had he subscribed to "the myth of Los Angeles"? Did he even know what that meant? And when people back home accused him of being "Californicated," of having turned into a stereotype, did he not feel a twinge of ugly pride? Had he not fantasized of sneering at them and telling them off? *You're right*, he'd imagined himself saying. *I'm nothing like you. I'm better than you, and if you're not jealous, it's only because you're too stupid to be.*

He sensed the girl's presence in his proximity. He glanced over and saw she'd come to stand beside him. "You're thinking about it," she said.

Ryland watched a police helicopter roving the air in lazy circles somewhere far below. Its searchlight jerked erratically. He rubbed at a faint pain in his left arm. "Who are you?" he asked the girl. "What's your angle here?"

"My angle? I don't have an angle."

"It's LA. Everyone has an angle." Even as he said the words, they sounded hollow, unoriginal, like he'd heard them somewhere or read them in a book.

"Yeah, no, I don't think that's true," she said. "Not any more than it is of anywhere else. And if it *is* true, well." She dragged from her cigarette, casting a sly glance at Ryland. "If it's true, it's only because people like *you*—people who believe that—come here and perpetuate it. It's part of the myth. You think LA is something specific, something shrouded in black magic. What none of you ever figure out is that it's *just* a *place*. It's a bunch of buildings and roads and houses. A truth like that, though...it's bitter. Too bitter for you to swallow. You come here for glamour, for that sexy darkness that oozes from old noir movies. The facts don't fit the narrative, so you write your *own* narrative and scrawl it up and down the sidewalks, on the side of every apartment building, over the windows of all the shops and along the walls of all the hotel lobbies. It's like some shared fanfiction that you all keep adding to, but what you don't realize is that you're using invisible ink, and the only reason *you* all can see it is because you're wearing those stupid decoder glasses you get out of a cereal box."

"Wow. And you got all that from how I'm dressed?"

She smiled at him in a surprisingly friendly way for someone who was telling him he was a phony. "You're not as special as you think," she said.

FIFTEEN
SMALL, DEAD ANIMALS

"I USED TO KILL SMALL ANIMALS," Baxter told the MechaHooker. She sat naked on the bed, blinking at him, listening but not comprehending. That was fine with Baxter. It was preferred. "Like, you know, cats and squirrels, and whatnot. Hamsters, mice. Never dogs, but I don't know why."

"I want to choke on your dick," the MechaHooker said.

"I don't know why I did it at all," Baxter went on. "Any of them. I don't know why I did it." He was lying on his side atop the covers. He drew his knees close to his chest and reached out to the Mecha-Hooker, putting his hand on her bare thigh. The almost-skin was warm beneath his palm.

"I was huffing a lot of glue back then. And paint, and stuff. I'm not sure if it's related. I didn't *want* to kill them. I *hated* killing them." He could feel his face growing hot and tingly, the pressure building in his sinuses as the flood of tears grew imminent. "They were so helpless. And they made the saddest little noises when they were in pain. I tried not to make them suffer. I didn't want—" His voice broke as the first sob came. A stinging pall blurred his vision. "I didn't want them to be in pain. I didn't want to do it at all, but I especially didn't want them to be in pain. I wanted it to be over as fast as possible."

"Come suck on my tits," the MechaHooker said. "Titty-fuck me, Daddy. Put your dick between my big, juicy tits and cover me in cum."

"I've never told anyone about this," said Baxter, closing his eyes, feeling the tears slide down his face. "It's not like I ever could. It's too fucked up. I tried to tell Arden once. I thought he might get it because I always thought he was sort of lonely and lost in, like, ways that were maybe similar to mine. But in the end, I couldn't. He wouldn't understand. I know that because *I* don't understand. And I just want to know...I want to know why I did it. Why I *had* to do it. It was only, like, for six months or so during my senior year of high school and I've never done it since then, but I want to know why I did it at all."

"Your cock is so huge. It's the biggest I've ever seen."

"And then I'd leave them, like, in people's driveways, you know? Or in their front yards? Just random houses in random parts of the city. Sometimes I'd hit the same house a few times in a row. I kept checking the internet to see if people were reporting it, but I never found anything."

"Your dick is gonna feel so good and big in my tight little asshole."

"They never belonged to anyone, I don't think. I caught the cats and squirrels with a butterfly net. The cats were strays. I'm pretty sure. And the hamsters and mice, a few gerbils—I got those from the pet store. They just let you buy them. You can go in and buy them, and they don't ask questions. There's no, like, waiting period, or anything like that. And I'd cry the whole way home, listening to them scurry around in the little cardboard carrier they give you. *I didn't want to hurt them.* I just...I can't, you know, stress that enough. But it was like I *had* to. And I wonder...why did I feel like that? Why did I feel like I had to do it when I hated it so much?"

"Suck on my fat titties, you nasty fuck."

"But whenever I think back to that time, and I think about all those dead animals, all I can remember is just...just all this sadness and anger. And *helplessness*. I felt so helpless against everything the world is, like it was going to swallow me up because I'm *nothing*, because I mean nothing just like everything else means nothing, and everyone is just *okay* with that, but I'm *not*. I wasn't. And the noises they made. Did I mention that? And how they looked when I put them in front of people's houses, all stiff and dead, like they'd never been alive to begin with. I remember all that shit, but it doesn't *tell* me anything, you know? It doesn't explain anything. Like, it's not like I feel any different now. I don't feel any better about anything. I just...one day I just couldn't stand killing them anymore, so I stopped. I've never wanted to do it again. But there has to be a reason, right? There must have been something that made me do it. I mean...right?"

"Stir up my guts with your huge flesh pole."

Despite himself and the tears stinging his eyes, Baxter realized he was hard. Sobbing quietly, he pulled the MechaHooker to him. "Make me better," he whimpered. "Make everything all better."

SIXTEEN
THE CLOSEST THING TO HELL

RYLAND TREKKED into the burning desert after finally answering one of Penny's calls, and because of this he fancied himself a decent person.

To make the drive on a rare Saturday when he wasn't at the office made him even better. He hadn't seen her in over a year, and the way he saw things, he bore no moral obligation to take her call, much less drive out to Desert Hot Springs—a city that was dangerously close to the fires, no less—on one of his few days off. He was doing this, he reasoned, *because* he was a decent person. Maybe not a good one—he wasn't delusional—but a decent one.

He frowned when his GPS signaled him to turn into the parking lot of a dilapidated, four-story apartment building across the street from a 7-Eleven. He parked and got out, dropping his cigarette to the shimmering blacktop and crushing it beneath the toe of his Tom Ford loafer.

A sickened sense of dread filled his stomach as he looked up at the crumbling stucco building etched against the smoldering red sky. Bars lined the first-floor windows. An overflowing Dumpster sat askance alongside its west wall. A pair of mangy dogs fought over something on the far side of the parking lot.

Ryland texted Penny, *I'm here.*

Inside, the halls were pasted with peeling wallpaper. The carpeted floors reeking and spotted. He didn't trust the elevator, so he took the stairs to the fourth floor, stepping over a filthy litterbox on the third-floor landing. A few moments after knocking on the door to 404, he heard five locks unlatch before it swung open.

Ryland stared at Penny for a few terrible moments before looking away. Her blonde hair was greasy and unwashed. It hung in tangled clumps around her gaunt face. She couldn't have weighed more than ninety pounds, and her tattered, oversized tank top draped over her skeletal frame like a tent. Her lips were chapped and burnt. There were open sores up and down her bony arms. The vacancy in her eyes was the closest thing to hell Ryland had ever seen.

"Jesus, Pen," he breathed.

"Get in, get in, don't just stand there." She grabbed his arm and yanked him inside with surprising strength. Her head poked into the hallway, darting left and right before she slammed the door shut and refastened the locks.

Ryland looked around at the scattered clothes, the ratty furniture, the ancient takeout boxes with their gatherings of flies. The burnt pipe on the table. The blackened sheet of tin foil. The syringe in a jar of bleach. Penny caught his eyes lingering on the needle in the jar and said, "I don't know why I bother with the bleach anymore. Old habits, I guess."

"Huh?" said Ryland. He was lightheaded.

"Sit down, sit down, please." She scurried to the armchair and unloaded a pile of crumpled laundry from its seat. Gesturing at it, she flashed a feeble attempt at a smile.

"I'll, um...I think I'll stand," Ryland said.

Penny's eyes narrowed. "Why's that? Is my furniture not good enough for your Armani-clad ass?"

"Hey, whoa," said Ryland, holding up his hands. "I mean, Christ, Penny. It's Valentino."

"Valentino," she repeated. "Right. Of course." She looked like she might cry. "Anyway, whatever, do what you want."

Sighing, gritting his teeth, Ryland went to the chair and sat in it.

"Let me get you something to drink," Penny said, hurrying toward the kitchen.

"No, please, nothing," Ryland said too quickly. "I'm...not thirsty."

Penny stopped, looking at him with swimming eyes. She nodded in a way that made her bear more than passing resemblance to a rodent. That, Ryland decided—the erosion of her beauty—was the most tragic part of all this. She had once been ravishing.

"I'm glad you came," Penny said, sitting on the couch and folding her legs beneath her. She fidgeted with her fingers. "I didn't think you would."

Ryland didn't know how to respond to that, so after a short pause he said, "It's...been a long time." He took his cigarettes from inside his blazer and lit one, then offered the pack to Penny. She took three, tucking one behind each ear and lighting the third with a torch lighter on the coffee table.

"You look good," Penny said. "Glad to see you're still doing well for yourself."

"I do okay."

Her grin was bitter. "You do okay," she said, sucking hard on the cigarette.

"Why did you call me out here, Penny." Ryland was startled by the flat, hollow weariness of his voice. He'd intended to sound concerned, sympathetic. He cleared his throat and tried again. "What is it you need?" A little better.

Penny chewed the nail on her left ring finger. "I have to tell you something. I wanted to do it in person."

"Well, I'm here."

She drew in a haggard breath that rasped in her throat. Ashing the cigarette in a can of Diet Pepsi beside the pipe on the coffee table, she looked into Ryland's eyes before dropping them, shutting them. A tear streaked through the sheen of sweat and unwashed grime on her face, then another. "I'm sick," she said. "I'm going to die."

Ryland's cigarette hand stopped halfway to his mouth. He lowered it. "I don't understand. Sick how? With what?"

Penny held out her track-marked arms. "What do you think."

Ryland looked over at the window. The curtains were closed. A sliver of scarlet sunlight sliced through the small opening between them. "I don't understand," he repeated. "I didn't think people got that shit anymore."

"Well, they do." She sniffed, wiped her face. More tears came. "I wouldn't have even known. It's a long story, but basically I ended up in the hospital—someone took me, I wouldn't have gone myself—and it was for something else, something unrelated, but they tested me when they saw the needle marks, and *voila*."

Ryland glanced at her. He tried to see the girl he'd once loved, but there was no trace of her in the apparition sitting across from him. He felt nothing, and this absence of feeling stirred only an obscure pang deep within him, buried so deep it hardly registered. "Isn't there something they can do?" he asked. "Some sort of...treatment?"

She shook her head. "No. It's too late. Too advanced. There's no hope for me."

"There's no hope for anyone," Ryland muttered.

"Anyway, I thought you should know. I'm not sure what I expected. I know you don't care about me anymore. There are lots of days when I'm not sure you ever did."

"I did. I...do."

She glared at him with her big, washed-out eyes, murky with toxic tears. "It's because of you I am where I am, doing what I'm doing." She hit the cigarette, moving her head to the side but keeping her eyes on him. "You know that, don't you? Do you ever think about that?"

"Come on, Pen. That isn't fair."

"Really. Tell me why it *isn't fair*."

Ryland suddenly felt exhausted. This had been a mistake. There was nothing for him here. "I should be going," he said, starting to stand.

"*ANSWER THE QUESTION.*"

Flinching, Ryland lowered himself back into the chair. He held his cigarette up to his face. His hand was steady. "I didn't make you follow me out here to California. I didn't ask you to. And I certainly didn't make you get mixed up with those deadbeat thugs. The smack, the crank—all that shit—that was all you. You did this to yourself."

Penny put her face in her hands. Her shoulders hitched with silent sobs. Ryland watched her for a long time.

When at last Penny looked up, she said, "You were so different in Pennsylvania. I don't know who you are anymore. I don't know what happened to you." She wiped mucus from her nose with the back of her hand. "You used to be a nice person. You were happy. *We* were happy."

Ryland's eyes went to the bar of light between the cheap curtains. He could see himself with Penny, years ago.

He could see himself holding her hand as they walked among fallen leaves on a brisk autumnal afternoon. He could see them together at the county fair, her upturned face illuminated by the flashing lights of the Ferris wheel, and he could see himself as he took her chin in his hand and pulled her mouth to his. He could see her in the passenger seat of his ancient Crown Victoria, his hand on her thigh as she sang along to the radio. He could see her as she had once been, and himself as *he* had once been, but they might as well have been strangers.

"You should have never taken that promotion," Penny whispered. "You should have never moved to Los Angeles."

"You told me to take it."

"I know. I was wrong."

Ryland leaned forward and dropped his cigarette into the can of

Diet Pepsi. He rose to his feet. "I'm going to use your bathroom," he said.

"Down the hall," Penny said, not looking at him. "First door on the left."

He went into the bathroom and wiped down the sink with a wet bundle of toilet paper before doing a line of coke off its edge.

After a moment of consideration, he did another. Uplifted, he flushed the toilet, ran the sink for a few moments, and stepped back out. He stopped in the hallway when he noticed a dog watching him from Penny's bedroom. It was small—some kind of chihuahua/terrier mix, by the looks of it—and it was curled up and trembling in a pink dog bed on the floor. Ryland walked into the bedroom and knelt down in front of it.

Its ears dropped back, and it whined softly. Its tremors grew more intense as he drew closer. Ryland extended his hand and placed it atop the dog's head, gently stroking it. Its high-pitched whine increased in pitch, and Ryland realized a puddle of runny shit was spreading beneath it. He retracted his hand and looked at the dog. After a while, its trembling subsided somewhat, and it put its head down and shut its eyes, opening them every few moments to see if he was still there.

When Ryland stood, he was startled to find his eyes had become damp. He wiped them with perturbed agitation and took his Gucci sunglasses out of his jacket pocket, putting them on and returning to the living room. "I have to get going," he told Penny.

"Of course. You're a busy guy." She didn't look at him, didn't stand. "The next time you see me, I'll be dead."

"I hope that isn't the case," said Ryland. His voice again sounded distant, empty. He glanced down the hall. The dog had peeked its head out of the bedroom and was staring at him. Its ears were perked up. He felt something foreign and uncomfortable in his chest, and he swallowed and turned toward the door. "Good luck, Penny," he said. He went to the door and set about unlatching the five locks.

"*Everything is your fault,*" Penny called after him as he was shutting the door behind him. He didn't look back, didn't stop. He did a couple bumps off his keys when he was in his car, but they didn't help. The image of the dog, scared and shivering, was burned into his brain. He peeled out of the parking lot and drove too fast.

He didn't start to feel better until the hazy outline of the city became visible in the distance.

SEVENTEEN
EACH SEPARATE MISFORTUNE

ARDEN WAS LOST in a Valium slumber on the pool house couch when his phone rang. He opened his eyes and sat up, hoping it was Rebecca, though it was only late afternoon, and he wasn't expecting her call until nightfall.

He picked up his phone and stared at the screen, not recognizing the number. He debated letting the call go unanswered but slid his thumb across the "Answer" bar instead. He muttered a garbled greeting.

"Arden? It's Zelda. Tess gave me your number."

Arden rubbed his eyes and lit a cigarette, trying to picture which one Zelda was. He couldn't. All his sister's friends looked the same. "Hey," he said. "Tess, um, isn't here. I don't know where she is."

A beat of silence. Muffled speech in the background. "I know. I'm calling you. If I needed her, I would have called her. I *did* call her to get your number."

"Um. Right. Why do you...need me?"

Arden detected a trace of annoyed reluctance in Zelda's sigh. "I'm shooting some footage on Skid Row for a short documentary, and... look, *I'm* not worried about it, but my camera girl would feel more comfortable if we had a guy with us. To, like, act as a *deterrent*, or whatever."

"A deterrent for...what?"

"I don't even know." Zelda sighed again. "*Rape*, or something. I guess." She lowered her voice. "But trust me, *no one* is going to rape *this* girl. You'll know what I mean when you see her."

"Wow. Jesus." Arden ran his hand through his hair. "What am I going to do? I mean, if something...*happens*, I'm not—"

"Look, nothing is going to *happen*. You'll just be there as a formality."

"Can't you pay someone to do this kind of thing?"

"I *did*, but there was...an issue. Last-minute cancellation. I can't book anyone else on this short of notice. But listen, if you're looking for money—"

"I don't need money." Arden was exhausted. "What's this documentary even about?"

"Does it matter?"

"I...guess not. I just—"

"Whatever, it's called *Third World LA*. It's about the wealth gap in Los Angeles. The focus is on how the political factions in charge don't give a shit about minorities, despite all their posturing."

"I don't...think that's true. Isn't it kind of irresponsible to, um, propagate something like that? And you shouldn't say *minorities*."

"What difference does it make? I'm not asking you to back the fucking thing. You're just going along to make sure we don't get raped."

"You said you weren't going to get raped."

"We're *not* going to get raped. Christ. Will you do it or not?"

Arden looked at the ashtray on the coffee table, his thoughts wandering to Rebecca. "Yeah," he said. "Yeah, I'll do it. Do I need to, like, bring anything?"

"Do you have a gun?"

"What?"

"A joke, relax. We'll pick you up in a half hour."

Arden got up and staggered to the bathroom to splash water on his face. After a short minute of deliberation, he palmed two Xanax and popped them into his mouth. He relished the bitterness as he chewed them. He then went to the couch to smoke half a joint before walking outside and into the house.

His father was sitting with Daffodil at the dining room table, quizzing her with arithmetic flash cards. They paid him no mind as he made his way to the front of the house, exiting out the front door. He walked to the end of the driveway to sit on the curb and smoke cigarettes in the hot sun while he waited.

Zelda arrived in a black Porsche Cayenne. She pulled up to the curb and rolled the window down, telling him to get in front. He did as instructed, glancing in the back seat at the girl with the camera equipment. She was mousy and bespectacled, maybe eighteen or nineteen, about forty pounds overweight.

"Arden, Louanne, Louanne, Arden," said Zelda. The Porsche jetted forward.

"Hey," Arden muttered to Louanne. To Zelda, he asked, "Can I smoke in here?"

"Yeah, whatever. Give me one."

"You're so skinny," Louanne told Arden. "Everyone here is so skinny. You all look like models."

"Louanne is new in town," Zelda explained, exasperated. She pulled onto Huntington. A group of red-clad soldiers were beating a woman with truncheons outside a Chevron station.

"I wish I could be skinny," said Louanne.

"You *can* be skinny," said Zelda, rolling her eyes. "It's quite easy. It's the easiest thing in the world."

"For you, maybe."

"You're never going to make it here looking like you do," Zelda told her. She glared with disdain at the girl in the rearview mirror. "You're talented, but lots of people are talented. You have to at least look somewhat fuckable if you want to get noticed."

"I'm behind the camera, not in front of it. I don't see why it matters. Besides, *you* noticed me."

"I'm not a man. I don't have any clout. What we're doing here, it isn't shit. It's to get *me* noticed. That's all. It's not going to get you anywhere. Not when you look like *that*."

"Beauty isn't everything," Louanne murmured.

"Beauty is the only commodity that matters," Zelda said. She looked at Arden. "Speaking of which, have you seen Corrine? She's totally let herself go. *All* that girl had was her looks. The *one* thing she had to do was keep up her appearance, and she would have been set. She's turned into a complete *cow*. Fat, terrible hair, no tan. The whole nine. I saw her in Erewhon the other day and she wasn't even wearing *makeup*. Pathetic."

"I don't know who Corrine is."

"You went to high school with her." And then, "Didn't you two used to *date*? For, like, *a while*?"

Arden stared out the window. "I don't know," he said, sighing. "Maybe. I can't remember."

"Tess said you went to prom together."

"Maybe," Arden said again. "I...really can't remember. High school was a long time ago."

A look of vague concern passed over Zelda's face. "Four years isn't that long, Arden." Her voice had lost some of its edge.

"It is, though. It's...a very long time. It's a whole eternity."

There was nothing else for anyone to say the rest of the drive. As they neared the city, Arden gazed out the windshield at the towering spires rising into the smog. They kept warping and changing colors, twisting around each other like snakes in a pit. He tried to remember the last time he'd been downtown. Actually, he wasn't certain he'd ever been to Skid Row. A dim, faraway anxiety began to form somewhere deep within his chest. He lit another cigarette and wished he'd brought more Xanax.

They parked on 6th Street. Zelda and Louanne got out of the car, but Arden remained frozen inside. Trash and filth were everywhere.

Both sides of the street were crowded with makeshift tents constructed from dirty blue tarpaulin and torn garbage bags. Homeless men and women wandered in wild-eyed stupors, tripping over refuse and bumping into one another. Many lay stretched out in the middle of the street; the few cars that passed through simply drove around them. The surrounding buildings stood in various stages of disrepair, pocked with shattered windows and jutting rebar, the paint on their surfaces peeling away in curled strips.

Arden's door opened, and he jumped. Zelda stared at him. "Are you coming?" she asked.

Arden unbuckled his seatbelt and got out, assaulted by the acrid odor of warm garbage and melting feces. A man with an ace of spades playing card glued to his forehead jostled past him, muttering to himself in a language Arden didn't recognize. He was followed by the Berkeley bear mascot, lumbering along in its red-stained jersey. It carried in its white-gloved hand a birdcage with several dead parakeets inside it.

"It's jarring, I know," said Zelda. She shut the door of the Porsche and locked it. Arden noticed a naked woman crouched in the middle of the intersection of 6th and San Julian, holding a crack pipe to her lips as an intermittent stream of diarrhea spattered onto the pavement beneath her.

"How long has it been like this?" Arden asked.

"It keeps getting worse." She pointed at a sign hanging askew from a nearby building. The sign proclaimed the neighborhood to be the precinct of CONGRESSMAN CHARLES SCHAEFFER, D. "He's the problem," said Zelda. "They're all the problem."

Arden watched Louanne setting up her camera on its tripod. She trained its lens on a man pulling an unconscious woman from a tent by her ankles and then climbing atop her, licking her face, chewing on her neck. "I...I don't think that's the case," said Arden. "I mean, it's the rent crisis, right? The rent is what drives these people out of their homes. The landlords are the problem, not the politicians."

"The *rent crisis*? Don't be stupid. Do you think these people couldn't make rent one month, so they said to themselves, 'Guess I have no choice but to go live on Skid Row'? Is that *really* how you think things transpired with *any* of them?"

A few yards away, a man was beating his head against the side of a building, grunting a garbled line of gibberish. Near him, a weeping woman sat amid a pile of split-open trash bags and stabbed at her emaciated arm with an empty syringe. A small child ran by, stuffing pieces of cellophane in his mouth as he went.

"Well...yeah," said Arden. "I mean, what else would it be?"

"If you really care, I'll tell you sometime. I'll tell you all about the long list of nefarious schemes used by the California political regime to keep these people exactly where they are."

Arden looked at her. "Do *you* really care?" he asked. "Come on, Zelda. You can't tell me you give a shit about these people. What got them here, what keeps them here, any of it—none of it matters to you any more than..." He trailed off, gesturing at Louanne and her camera. "Any more than however it pertains to this little project."

"So what? What does that have to do with anything?"

Arden thought about it. "Nothing, I guess."

"Exactly. Just because I don't have any personal stake in these people's plight, that doesn't make the circumstances surrounding their plight any less true. So, like I said, if you ever want to know what's *really* going on, you let me know. But you won't because you don't care about these animals any more than I do. You'll go home today, and you'll forget all about them. You'll go back to wallowing in whatever first world problems are making you depressed, because that's what we do. The same can be said for the people who will watch this film. They'll cry their crocodile tears and shake their fists and clutch their pearls, but at the end of the day, it won't affect their lives in the slightest."

"Then...what's the point? Why bother making a film like this?"

"*Because*, Arden," said Zelda, not exactly condescending, but almost. "Hypocrisy sells. People love it. They eat it up." She turned away and went over to Louanne, telling her to point the camera at a girl of about seven who was fellating a boy of roughly the same age. Arden lit another cigarette, unsure of what had happened to his last one, and tried to tell himself that none of this mattered, that it was only a small increment of time in his life that would soon be over. He attempted to recall a passage from Schopenhauer or Camus, something that would reinforce the comforting, cosmic irrelevance of everything. But his thoughts kept turning to Rebecca, of how it felt to be next to her, inside her, and it became more and more difficult for him to believe that life was without meaning.

At home that night, freshly showered and stoned in the pool house with the lights dimmed and The Eagles playing low on the stereo, it was easy for Arden to disassociate himself from what he'd seen that afternoon.

The filth, the squalor, the crime—it all felt far away, a dream, something that had happened to someone else. Zelda's words echoed—*You'll go home today, and you'll forget all about them...because that's what we do*—and it was an easy enough task to push them down, lock them away.

He lit a cigarette and opened Instagram. He typed "Corrine" into the search bar above his list of followers and tapped on the profile for someone named Corrine Dalloway. Her most recent post was from two years ago. It was a professional-looking, black-and-white picture of her smoking a clove cigarette outside the entrance to the Louis Vuitton store on Rodeo. She was striking, but he didn't recognize her.

He scrolled further down her page, stopping suddenly on one, also in black and white, in which she and a boy, both dressed in formal attire, stood holding hands, looking at each other and laughing beneath the Pasadena bridge. Arden brought the phone closer to his face, squinting at it. The boy was unmistakably him, but he could not remember having posed for it or having ever seen this girl. His relaxed face, the easy laughter, the casual calmness of his posture—he couldn't remember having felt like that. The date beneath the photo indicated it had been uploaded five years ago.

There were more pictures with him in them—dozens more. On the beach, at the Malibu pier, at restaurants like La Scala and The Henry, Birds and Dan Tana's. There was a video of him and Corrine singing gaily to Blondie in the cockpit of what was now his sister's Audi. Another of him reclined on a huge bed in a bedroom he didn't recognize, blowing a succession of smoke rings while London Grammar played in the background. He remembered none of it. Yet here was evidence of his participation in a life foreign to him.

His phone vibrated. Rebecca's name appeared at the top of the screen. When Arden answered, Rebecca was quiet for a moment, and then she asked him what was wrong. She said it sounded like he was crying.

Arden touched his face. His fingers came away damp. He cleared his throat and said, "No, no. I'm...not. I'm fine. I'm just...tired."

"Oh. Well, if you don't want to come over tonight, that's—"

"No, really, I'm fine. Give me, like, a half hour."

He did two lines before leaving. They blasted the unremembered images from his brain. He reopened Instagram when he got into his car, selecting the "block" option on Corrine's profile.

By the time he was on the freeway his life felt a little more like his own.

EIGHTEEN
NARCISSUS ASCENDED

TESS SAT across from The Writer in the back of the limousine on the way to Vroman's for a book signing celebrating the release of *Barely on Fire*. He was dressed in tight, black leather pants and a Nirvana T-shirt beneath a Hugo Boss tuxedo jacket, sporting sunglasses. She wore a red dress from Hervé Léger. The Writer had picked it out for her based on its low hemline and the way the revealing bodice accentuated her cleavage.

"I don't usually bring guests to these things," The Writer was saying. "So many of my fans are women. *Young* women. Girls your age. Younger. It's beneficial if they think I'm available. It enriches the fantasy."

"Whose fantasy?" said Tess. "Theirs, or yours?"

The Writer looked away. He lit a cigarette. "Rebecca tried to talk me out of it. I told her I want to marry you, and she tried to talk me out of that, too."

Tess examined her nails. "Who's Rebecca again?"

"My publicist."

"Kind of weird for a publicist to give relationship advice, isn't it? Isn't that a little personal? A little not-her-business?"

"I'm a public figure." There was a haughtiness in his tone. A lion's pride. "Nothing about me is personal. Everything about me is everyone's business."

"The way you relish in that is disturbing. It's unnatural."

He smiled. Tess hated how perfect his teeth were. The way the casual carelessness of his relaxed expression melted into the movie-star features of his face.

The limo pulled into the packed parking lot of the enormous bookstore. Flashbulbs burst outside the tinted windows. Tess pressed her face to the glass, looking at the crowds of people. She saw that The Writer hadn't been exaggerating—many of them were, in fact, girls her age and younger, most of them attractive and done up like little Lolita wannabes.

She glanced at The Writer. Could practically smell the heavy odor of smug self-satisfaction wafting off him. She felt disgusted with herself. The revulsion came from the knowledge she had once been not so unlike the other girls outside the car, and, perhaps, wasn't as far removed from them as she might like to think. She, too, had been enamored with The Writer's words the first time they had washed over her. And for as much as the man himself ground on her sensibilities, there was no denying the effect of his wry, laconic detachment, his distinguished gentleman's handsomeness, his methodical, almost scientific sexual mastery. Even his relaxed arrogance, though at times enraging, had a certain charm.

"Not a bad turnout," The Writer said. He grinned to himself as he peered out at the crowd. The din of their excited clamor was audible even from within the sealed confines of the limousine. "It's nothing compared to the European crowds, though. France and Germany, especially."

"Is it always like this?" Tess asked. "You'd think they were here to see Taylor Swift."

"For me, yes, it's always like this." He took a vial of coke from inside his jacket and did a few quick bumps. Tess wasn't sure she felt like getting high, but she did the line he offered her. "Events like this don't really happen for authors anymore," The Writer went on. He sniffed and rubbed his nose. Checked his reflection in a pocket mirror. "Not of this magnitude. The celebritization of the literati is a dying thing. I'm the last of my kind, in a sense. There's a few left who can draw decent crowds, but nothing like this."

"Wow. I'm such a lucky girl."

"You truly have no idea."

An entourage of identical-looking men in black suits waited for them at the curb near the path leading up to the entrance, separated from the crowd by a barrier of red velvet rope. "Who are they?" Tess asked. "The FBI?"

"Bodyguards," The Writer answered. One of the men opened the door once the car came to a stop. The Writer exited first, turning to the crowd and waving, flashing a grin that sent them into a roaring frenzy. He leaned inside the car and offered his hand to Tess, still wearing the grin. She took it and allowed herself to be helped onto the curb, wincing against the flashing white lights of the cameras. The bodyguards whisked them inside and locked the doors behind them. Tess let out a breath. She relished the quiet of the bookstore, which had closed early for the occasion.

They were greeted by a beautiful girl in a shimmering silver dress. She was holding an iPad and had an earpiece affixed to her ear. The Writer introduced her as Rebecca, his publicist. Tess detected the specter of disapproval in her eyes when she shook her hand.

One of the bookstore employees appeared with a tray of champagne flutes. The Writer took two, handing one of them to Tess. "When are you letting the horde in?" The Writer asked Rebecca.

Rebecca tapped the iPad's home button, glanced at the time. "Fifteen minutes, on the nose. We've got you all set up over there." She motioned to a wide table behind which sat a plush chair fashioned to look like a king's throne.

On one side of the table was a blown-up print of the new book's cover, and on the other side was a cardboard cutout of The Writer himself. Displays with Chandler's books—he had nine, but

Barely on Fire was featured most prominently—were set up everywhere.

A boy was standing at one of the displays. He was leafing through a paperback copy of *Sickness and Health*, Chandler's third novel. Given the unexpectedness of his presence there, it took Tess a moment to realize the boy was her brother. "Arden?" she heard herself say.

Arden turned, saw her, and put the book back. He came over. "Hey," he said to Tess, not acknowledging The Writer. He looked tired, strung out.

Tess suddenly felt uncomfortable and exposed in her short, revealing dress. "What are you doing here?" she asked Arden.

Arden put his hands in the pockets of his jeans and looked around. "Hanging out, I guess," he said. "I came with Rebecca. We're, um..." He trailed off, looked to Rebecca for help.

"Friends," Rebecca finished for him.

Tess caught Arden's disappointed wince. Chandler cleared his throat. Arden finally looked at him, raising an eyebrow. "You're the writer?" he said.

It was hard to tell because he was still wearing his sunglasses, but Tess could sense Chandler's agitation. "Yes," he said. "I'm *The Writer*."

Arden studied him with his drawn, washed-out eyes. "Cool," he said. "I mean, I don't really read fiction. I saw that article in *Vogue*, though. You were number two, right?"

"It was *Teen Vogue*. And I was number three."

"You should get in position," Rebecca said to The Writer. She took his arm and led him over to the signing table. Tess looked at Arden. He raised his shoulders, palms out, and then ambled away.

Rebecca returned to Tess, brushing a lock of hair from her eye. "You can go wherever," she told her. "Just stay somewhere behind the table. It's going to get a little claustrophobic on this side." She paused, touched a finger to the button on her earpiece, listening for a few moments and then saying, "No, not yet. I'll tell you when." She pressed the button again and said to Tess, "Can I get you anything? Some water? Something from the catering table in the back?"

"No, nothing," Tess said. "I'm fine." She sipped her champagne and looked at Rebecca. "How long have you been sleeping with my brother?"

Rebecca's face showed no sign of reaction. "Not long," she said. "We're having fun." Almost as an afterthought, she added, "He's a nice boy."

"He likes you. A lot."

"He told you that?"

"No. He didn't have to."

Tess could see her considering this, weighing something in her mind. "He's a nice boy," she said again, albeit with more distance. "You should stand back, over there somewhere. I think I'm going to let them in a few minutes early. They're getting restless."

It went on for hours. Tess watched from off to the side. She sat in a chair Rebecca had fetched for her, growing buzzed on champagne. She'd never seen The Writer interact with fans before, and she was surprised by how he comported himself. She'd expected him to be aloof, standoffish, brusque; instead, he was courteous and patient, feigning humility at the showers of compliments rained upon him, cracking jokes that had everyone in earshot cackling their syco-phantic laughter.

He declined at least a half a dozen requests to "Oh my God, *please* sign my tits,"—Tess suspected this level of restraint hadn't always been present—and he pretended to be delighted whenever a twenty-something boy or girl produced a manuscript for him to "critique, if you get the chance—I'm sure you're really busy." These manuscripts he handed to Rebecca, who carried them away to some unknown location. Tess later asked where they went, to which The Writer replied, "The trash."

Watching so many young people fawn over The Writer, Tess was struck by the implausibility of it all. She couldn't imagine any of them sitting down to *read* a *novel*, much less the high-brow literary fare Chandler produced. *Barely on Fire* was itself nearly 700 pages long. There were soapy, crowd-pleasing elements present in all his work—love triangles, extramarital affairs, murder, melodrama, explosive plot twists—and she guessed that had something to do with their wide appeal, but they were also steeped in complex language and often featured avant-garde structural decisions. His previous novel, *Dreams of Silence Lost*, was famous for having more footnotes than *Infinite Jest*. She couldn't help but wonder how much the author photo in the backs of the books contributed to the fanaticism, but as she listened to the besotted praise gushing from the mouths of The Writer's admirers, it became clear they were just as taken with the books themselves as they were with the scribe.

But...was it so hard to believe? When she thought about it, she supposed not. She herself had been a sophomore in high school when she'd picked up *Nothing but the Rain*, and she'd voraciously consumed the rest of his books within several months. Now, as she watched these girls bubbling over with their giddiness, she could recall having felt a similar emotion when she'd noticed him at the Chateau Marmont nearly a year ago.

How disappointed these girls would be, how *crushed*, if they knew how he looked at them—as dollar signs, at most, little more than additional adornments for his already gargantuan ego. They, like everyone else in his life, were mere objects floating through his self-contained ecosystem, present—and only on a temporary basis —strictly because he allowed them to be. Once they disappeared from his field of vision, they would cease to exist. The world, for him, had been reduced to the limited confines of his perception.

He had written many great works, at least three which could be called masterpieces, but his greatest achievement was the creation of the fictitious universe in which he had taken up permanent residence. It was one where he was God, and where its denizens' lives mattered solely in respect to how they pertained to his own.

When she grew sick of it all, Tess wandered away from the commotion and browsed the fiction aisles. So many names, so many titles...so many countless, toiled hours behind innumerable keyboards, and so few of them would amount to much more than a single, unnoticed slot on the shelf. So many eyes had and would continue to slide unseeing over their spines. Did *her* writer deserve all the success these soon-to-be-remaindered ones would never have?

The door to the employee break room was open. The room was empty, and the catering table Rebecca had mentioned remained largely untouched. Several unopened bottles of champagne floated in melting ice within a large steel bucket. Tess opened one of them and sat on the ancient, lint-speckled couch against the wall. She drank straight from the bottle, thinking about questions that didn't have answers, until she fell into a restless doze.

When she stirred sometime later, she stood and brushed herself off before staggering in a haze to the front of the store. The crowd had emptied out, and the bookstore employees were tidying up, tearing down the displays. Arden sat behind one of the registers with his feet on the counter. His nose was buried in *Sickness and Health*. The Writer was still at his signing table, but he'd taken off his sunglasses. He was talking with Rebecca and another girl whom Tess took to be the final straggler from the legions of fans.

As Tess drew nearer, something about this girl unnerved her. She was beautiful in a poisonous sort of way, with hair black as cancer swirled with ribbons of gold, and huge green eyes that devoured everything they fell upon. She was short, and perhaps too thin, but with enough figure to be flaunted by her tight black minidress.

"Tess," The Writer said, smiling. "This is Lyssi. Rebecca's firm represents her boyfriend. He's some kind of...what did you say, a *musician*?" He said this with an oversaturation of condescending irony.

"He's a rapper," the girl said. She didn't appear fazed by Chandler's disdain for her partner's profession. Her eyes landed on Tess, and Tess felt her blood go cold.

There was a haunted emptiness in the way she looked at her. A lost, forlorn lunacy. Tess at once pictured a rabid, whimpering dog wandering an empty stretch of road at night. Snarling. Barking at ghosts. "He's nowhere near as talented as *your* boyfriend," Lyssi said to her. She grinned at Chandler. Tess flinched at the word "boyfriend" and thought about correcting her before realizing she didn't know if there was a more accurate word for whatever he was to her.

"I...haven't read any of his books," Tess said.

"Oh, you *have* to." She hugged her copy of *Barely on Fire* to her chest. Like a young girl with a teddy bear. "There's nobody better."

"That's what everyone keeps telling me. Chandler included."

Chandler, Lyssi, and Rebecca all laughed. Lyssi's laughter rose above the others', high and shrill. Untethered. In Tess's experience, crazy girls who had mastered the mask of sanity could somehow never manage to disguise the psychosis in their laughter. They could talk and act like anyone else, but the veneer cracked as soon as they laughed, if only for a second.

Rebecca sighed and looked around, her hands on her hips. "Well," she said, "we should get out of here so the staff can close up shop. Do you guys want to go somewhere and get drinks?"

Tess could see The Writer considering it, his eyes locked with Lyssi's, but he must have noticed something in Tess's face when he looked at her because he said, "We'll take a raincheck. I think Tess has probably had enough for one night."

"Go ahead," Tess said. "I can take a Lyft home." She realized she was baiting him but wasn't sure why. She was reasonably certain she didn't care one way or the other.

"Yeah, come *on*," Lyssi urged The Writer. "I have so many things I need to ask you." There was nothing subtle about the way she looked at him.

"Another time," The Writer said. "Rebecca can set something up. Bring the rapper." Establish distance for Tess's benefit by offering Rebecca as the intermediary. Invite the boyfriend to draw an imaginary line in the sand—also for Tess's benefit—while referring to him as *the rapper* to maintain his show of superiority; that piece was for *Lyssi's* benefit, and translated to, "Your boyfriend means nothing to me, and I could oust him without lifting a finger." Classic Chandler. Tess read him like he was one of his own books. It was so transparent.

Not looking at Tess, Lyssi said, "Oh, no, I wouldn't do that to you. He's obnoxious. He's a drag."

"Nonsense, all of Rebecca's other clients are family to me by default." He hated all of them, Tess knew, but he also hated his family, so this technically wasn't a lie. "I'll have her send me some of his songs." This *was* a lie—The Writer only listened to concert symphonies and smooth jazz. The Nirvana T-shirt was nothing more than a costume.

Lyssi made a face and rolled her eyes. "Oh, God, they're terrible, don't subject yourself to that. I'll let you and the pretty lady get going, though. Thanks so much for the lovely inscription in the book." Her eyes flicked to Tess. A fiery green defiance blazed within them. She said goodbye to Rebecca and strutted out of the store, walking with elegant, straight-backed poise. Her strides were long and confident, with just enough swing in her hips to be noticeable without being exaggerated. The Writer watched her until she was gone.

In the back of the limousine, Tess said to him, "You should have gone with her."

NINETEEN
LOST SOULS, LOST ILLUSIONS

ARDEN STOPPED at Baxter's to pick up some coke because his dealer wasn't answering his texts. As he sat on the couch in the palatial living room, watching Baxter scoop a couple handfuls of coke from a ceramic bowl into a Ziploc baggie, Arden wondered if the dealer was dead, if perhaps the soldiers in the red uniforms had gotten to him.

"Don't worry about that, dude," Baxter said when Arden took out his wallet. "It's my dad's, anyway. Plus, I don't do that much of it anymore. Not ever since you went away to school, I guess." He handed Arden the baggie, who thanked him and stuffed it into his hip pocket.

"You know," Baxter went on, "I'm glad you're here. There's something I want you to see. Something I've, ah, been meaning to...show you." He scratched the back of his neck, grinned a goofy smile. He was like a human cocker spaniel. Arden wondered if he'd always been like that. He tried to remember what he'd been like in high school but couldn't.

"Okay," Arden said. "But, um, I don't have a ton of time."

"Yeah, no, don't worry, it won't take long. Stay right there." He disappeared down the hallway.

Arden checked for texts from Rebecca. There were none. He considered texting her something, a short *thinking of you* or *hope you're having a great day*, but decided against it. He felt nauseated.

Baxter had a girl with him when he returned. She was tall, with an agonizingly beautiful face, and dressed only in a bra and panties. The impossible, Barbie-doll proportions of her body lent her a surreal quality somewhere between arousing and freakish.

Arden stood to introduce himself, but the words stopped on their way out of his throat. He looked closer at the girl, squinting. His eyes shifted to Baxter. Baxter beamed.

"Baxter," Arden said, eyeing the girl with suspicion. "Is she...?"

"Yeah, dude. Totally fake." He spoke with the pride of a new father. "She's basically a walking sex doll. They're not on the market yet. She's a prototype. I'm guessing my dad got her through one of his, like, business contracts with China or Japan, or whatever. They're always giving him free tech shit."

"So, she's...your dad's? She's your dad's sex doll?"

"Yeah, I found her in his study."

"So, like, he...fucks her? It, whatever."

Baxter gazed in admiration at the robot girl. "I mean, I don't know, I guess. But she has a self-cleaning mechanism and—"

"Wait. You've *also* been fucking it?"

"Dude. I know what you're thinking. But, *seriously*, it's unlike anything you can imagine. It's so much better than real sex. I don't know if I'll ever fuck a real girl again."

Arden sat down, rubbed his eyes, his temples. "Jesus," he muttered. He looked up, staring at the thing. It smiled at him in a way that was so natural it was terrifying. "What are you going to do when your dad comes home?"

Baxter's smile faltered. "I haven't figured that out yet," he said. "Maybe, like, he'll let me keep her."

Arden asked, "Does it talk?"

The proud smile returning, Baxter said, "Oh yeah, dude, she talks." He squeezed the thing's hand and said, "MechaHooker, say something."

The robot looked from Baxter to Arden and back to Baxter. Its smile widened. "One of you boys should fuck my whore mouth while the other one fucks my sloppy wet pussy," it said. The cadence and rhythm of its speech sounded eerily, convincingly human.

"She can recognize the presence of more than one user," Baxter boasted, like he was reading from the manual.

"User?" said Arden.

Baxter ignored him. "She only speaks in, like, sex talk, so her vocabulary is kind of limited, you know? But what she says changes depending on the situation and the different things I'm doing to her, so it's—"

"Christ, Bax, that's enough."

"I'd let you take her for a spin, but..." He trailed off, shifting on his feet. "Well, you know. I guess I've gotten kind of possessive of her."

"That's...definitely not a problem." Arden got off the couch. "Listen, I really do have to get going."

Suddenly anxious, Baxter said, "Hey, like, don't mention this to anyone, cool? Like I said, she's not even on the market yet, so it's kind of—"

"Who would I say anything to? I don't really talk to anyone."

"No, yeah, I know. But, like...I don't know. Your sister, or whatever. Or anyone we went to high school with."

"I'm not going to say anything to my sister. And I haven't seen anyone from high school since I've been back." He remembered Corrine Dalloway's Instagram profile. The nausea returned, intensified.

"Okay. Cool." Baxter shifted again. Ran his hands through his hair. "Let's hang soon. Hit me up."

"Sure. Thanks again for the blow." Arden looked at the robot and said, "Um. Nice...meeting you."

"Come stab my pussy with your fat cock," the robot answered. Baxter laughed.

"Wow," said Arden, shaking his head. "See you later, man."

A deep and profound sadness came over Arden as he drove home. He was struck with sudden images of himself and Baxter as children, playing on playgrounds and in sandboxes. Running through sprinklers. Hunched in front of the television with video game controllers in their hands. The memories were an unwelcome shock. Had he even known Baxter that long? Were the memories real? He supposed he felt *something* for Baxter—some kind of kinship, a familiarity that pierced through his perma-haze. But even that was fading. Each time he saw Baxter, or spoke to him, whatever connection they'd once had felt more strained and tenuous.

He looked at the fat baggie of coke in his passenger seat. Saw the sky changing colors and distorting, the lines on the road peeling off and jumping in place. He thought of Baxter with his mechanized sex doll, pilfered from his father. Flashed on a strange and obscure vision of Baxter screaming as he lifted his face from a bag full of glue, and then another of a dead squirrel lying stiff and sundried in a hot driveway. Dreams? Memories? Hallucinations? He didn't know.

"What happened to us," he said aloud. "What happened."

TWENTY
SEPARATE BEDROOMS

TESS STARTED HANGING around The Writer's house more and more. She figured it was an attempt to see what it would be like living there. A halfhearted trial run, a casual dipping of her toe in dark waters.

She hadn't been giving serious thought to his flippant marriage proposal—in fact, she tried to think about it as little as possible—but it occupied a cumbersome amount of space within her mind. It floated like a phantom on the edges of every conversation she had with Chandler, rarely spoken of but always present.

Incidentally, The Writer had begun working on a new novel. He spent many hours locked in his study. On the occasions he and Tess were in the same room together, he was distant and preoccupied, often agitated and ill-tempered.

Even the sex suffered somewhat. He was usually attentive in a way that could be mistaken for selflessness if you didn't understand him like Tess did, and in some ways this was still the case, but now there was something mechanical and distracted about the way he handled her in the bedroom. She stopped having orgasms.

Tess spent most of her time alone. She wandered around the gaudy, oversized fortress of a house, getting lost in its hallways and discovering new rooms she'd never seen before. Sometimes, she'd run into members of the cleaning staff that came three times a week —most of them (save for the gardeners) young women dressed like French maids, and all of them Caucasian—and they always looked at her with a sad, confounding pity. They never said anything.

She frittered entire days away stoned and nude by the pool, getting drunk on whatever expensive liquor she'd filched from The Writer's bar that morning. She read *Barely on Fire*—on her Kindle, lest he catch her reading it—and was annoyed to find that it was, indeed, his best. Its conclusion left her breathless and filled with melancholic longing. For a few moments as she lay beneath the sun in the wide, opulent backyard enclosed by its perimeter of towering hedges, she could almost convince herself that she *did* love The Writer, and perhaps a life with him was something she could come to tolerate and, more abstractly, enjoy.

One evening, when the sun was in the final stretch of its descent into the horizon, The Writer came out into the yard clutching a tumbler of brandy and trailing cigarette smoke. He wore Bermuda shorts and a button-down Hermès shirt open at the throat, the sleeves rolled up. His feet were bare, his sunglasses on. He walked around the pool and sat in the chaise longue beside Tess, kicking his feet up and reclining.

Tess could sense the tension within him. "How's the book coming?" she asked. He swiveled his head in her direction. His expression was unmoving. She could feel his eyes appraising her nakedness, but she detected no lust; he was like a man at a museum passively gazing at a Renaissance painting.

"It's coming," he said, looking away. He took his sunglasses off and put them atop his head, leaning back and shutting his eyes. The drink went to his lips. The cigarette followed. "You've been here a lot lately."

She considered her words, cycling through several possible replies before deciding on, "That makes one of us."

He opened one eye. It scrutinized her before shutting again. "This book," he said, "it requires a high degree of attention. Lots of moving parts. If I seem detached, that's why."

"You always seem detached. But, yes, I'd say you're more detached than usual. You haven't managed to make me come all week."

He snorted. "Apologies for that, your majesty. The detachment is part of my process. It's something you'll have to get used to if we're going to get married." It was the first time he'd mentioned the subject of marriage since the book signing at Vroman's.

Tess looked at the pool water. It shimmered like white gold in the setting sun. She had an urge to throw herself into it, sink to the bottom, and scream. "You haven't gotten me a ring."

"I'll get you a ring when I know what your answer is. You can pick it out."

"How romantic."

"Go fuck a poet if you're looking for romance."

"We should talk logistics. Like, what exactly would it look like? Me being married to you, living here. All that."

The Writer tossed back the rest of his drink and took a final drag from his cigarette before dropping it into the empty glass. It hissed as it was extinguished by the sticky dampness remaining within it. "Within reason, it would look like whatever you'd want it to look like," he said. He sounded annoyed. "Pick a room and I'll convert it into a bedroom for you. I'll buy you a car. You can have access to my limousine service. No pets, though, that's a firm rule. And you'll—"

"Hang on a second. We're going to—"

"Okay, fine, you can get a hamster. *Maybe.* I'll have to think about it. But absolutely no dogs or cats."

"No, I don't want any pets. But...we're going to sleep in separate bedrooms?"

He looked at her, bemused. "Of course we are. Domesticity kills sexual attraction faster than anything else."

Tess was pretty sure that was a line from one of his novels, though she couldn't remember which one. "We don't sleep in separate bedrooms now."

"That's because you're still new enough to be exciting to me, and until recently you only spent two or three nights a week here, so the risk associated with bed-sharing remains relatively low for the time being. It helps that you have the rare quality of being an attractive sleeper—like something exquisite and dead. You know, if you were to die young, you'd look so beautiful in a casket. Like such sweet tragedy."

"Jesus, Chandler. What the fuck."

"What? It's a compliment. You should feel grateful, because how you look when you sleep is the primary reason I'm *able* to sleep with you. Not to mention you're almost as attractive without makeup as you are with it—a most unusual trait, I should add—so waking up beside you isn't unpleasant. But you'll notice I use a different bathroom whenever you're here. Sexual partners should never be exposed to one another's bathroom habits."

"You really have everything figured out, don't you."

"I do," he said, shutting his eyes again. His grin was small but triumphant.

Something about that grin infuriated Tess. Such a snide display of superiority was commonplace for him—a *Chandlerism*, as Tess privately referred to these gestures—but she was unable to pinpoint when they'd stopped being endearing and instead began to grate on her nerves.

"Has everything always been easy for you?" she blurted before giving herself the chance to map out the direction in which this would steer the conversation.

The Writer reopened his eyes. He seemed put off that she was still there. "I don't know what you mean by that," he said.

"Like, did you ever struggle? With anything? Was anything ever *difficult* for you?"

"Not sure what you're playing at here. You know I started out as a high school teacher. You know this about me."

"For, what, two years? Weren't you, like, twenty-four when your first book blew up? And you had family money, right? You were never hard out for cash, even before you started getting published. And I'm guessing student loans were never a factor."

"Your family has far more money than mine ever did. I was never *poor* if that's what you're asking, but I wasn't rich, either. Not like you are. I've earned everything I have."

"Struggling is about more than just money. I mean, did you ever bomb a test? Did you ever strike out with a girl you liked? Have you ever not known what the exact right thing to say was?"

He squinted at her, his apparent agitation growing. "What are you trying to get at? If you're asking me if I was ever a loser, the answer is no. The younger generations have created this idea of the Noble Failure, this concept that there's dignity in being soft, broken. *Weak.* Weakness is not a desirable trait, Tess. At least, it's not supposed to be. If you want weakness, I'd again invite you to go fuck a poet."

"I don't think failure and weakness are the same thing."

The Writer shut his eyes once more. He leaned back and lit another cigarette. "I sincerely hope you're only saying that in an attempt to get a rise out of me," he said. He grimaced, sniffed. "I can smell the fires. They're getting closer."

Tess reached over and took his cigarettes. She lit one for herself. "I don't smell anything," she said.

Tess went home that night, needing a break from The Writer. It was after ten, but her mother's BMW wasn't in the driveway, and neither was Arden's Jaguar.

She found her father sitting alone in the dimly lit dining room. He was scrolling on his phone and nursing a cognac. His eyes lifted from the screen when she entered. The lenses of his glasses were cast in reflected blue light.

"Where have you been?" he asked. There was no admonishment in his tone; he was only filling the silence. He wasn't looking for an answer, so she didn't give him one. She poured herself a glass of wine and sat across from him at the table in a feeble show of politeness. She couldn't remember the last time she'd had a real conversation with her father. When she asked where her mother was, he shrugged and said, "Work, I guess. I see less and less of her ever since she started that new job." He set his phone facedown on the table and asked how she was.

"Great," she answered, noncommittal. "Really great."

He sipped his drink and studied her. "I read online that you were seen at some book thing with Chandler Eastridge," he said. "'Daughter of Film Director Jared Coover Spotted with Literary Megastar,' or something to that effect."

"You shouldn't believe everything you read online."

"There were pictures."

"Oh. Well, I guess that proves that, then."

He studied her some more. "You're an adult, you can do what you want. I know that. It's a bit surprising, though. I wouldn't have thought he was your type."

"Do you know him?"

He made a so-so gesture with his hand. "I've met him a few times over the years. The first time would have been...God, before you were born, I think, or at least not long after. He was a kid, probably not even thirty yet. Warner Brothers was producing the adaptation of one of his novels. I can't remember the name of it. That weird genre experiment he did. I think it was his second or third book."

"*Dangerous Ideals*," Tess said. It was his second book, a noirish, hyper-surrealistic techno-thriller set in dystopian Seattle. Tess liked it the least among his oeuvre, and it was his worst-reviewed work, but that hadn't stopped it from selling millions of copies. The movie bore resemblance to the source material only in its broadest strokes, but it had been a huge hit and won something like six Oscars.

"Right, that one," said her father. "Very strange book. I never understood it. In any case, a friend of mine—well, a former friend— was the DP and had invited me to the set. Chandler was there, but he wasn't involved with the production in any way. The rumor was that his contract stipulated he be allowed on set whenever he pleased, probably so he could bask in the perceived glory of it. That's what he was doing when I was there, at least. Getting high with the cast, yukking it up with the director, flirting with every girl in sight— everyone from the PAs to the lead actress. Benny, the DP, told me he slept with dozens of them."

"Why are you telling me this?"

Her father took a pensive swallow from his tumbler and looked at the ceiling. "I'm not sure. Thinking out loud." His eyes returned to her. "Is it serious?"

Tess thought it was appropriate the way the question was phrased as though he were asking about an illness. "I don't know," she said, not exactly lying. "I don't really know what it is."

"Does he treat you right? Is he good to you?"

You're almost as attractive without makeup as you are with it.

You're still new enough to be exciting to me.

You'd look so beautiful in a casket.

"Yeah," Tess said. She didn't meet her father's gaze. "Yeah, he treats me fine."

"Well, that's what's important." He shifted in his seat, rubbed his jaw. This type of parenting was outside his comfort zone, Tess knew. It was like watching an ant writhe under a sun-glared magnifying glass. In an act of mercy, she bade him goodnight and took her wine upstairs, shutting herself in her bedroom.

She took *Nothing but the Rain* from her bookshelf and settled into the armchair beside her window. As she flipped through the pages, her eyes fell on passages she'd highlighted and underlined. There were so many of them. She tried to conjure within herself the girl she'd been, not three years ago, when she'd dragged the highlighter's tip across the words. Would that girl have swooned at the notion of becoming the author's betrothed? Would she have succumbed to the schoolyard giddiness she'd seen in the girls at the book signing? She didn't think so. She couldn't recall ever being faced with the prospect of unattainability. Nothing—at least, nothing tangible—had ever seemed beyond reach. Everything had always felt possible of possessing.

She thought of her earlier conversation with The Writer when she'd challenged him on the ease with which he navigated his own life.

She had never failed a test. High marks in school had always been achievable with a minimal expenditure of effort. *She* had never been rejected by a boy—or girl, for that matter—she'd liked. Unrequited love, unreciprocated lust—these were things she'd read about in countless novels but never tasted for herself. *She* tended to know the right thing to say in any given situation.

But for all these qualities, life had never felt *easy* to her. Her ability to attain things had never made existence any less bewildering. She supposed that was what she resented most about The Writer. He was more like her than she was willing to admit, but he'd made it work for him in a way she hadn't.

She was *jealous* of him, and that was more infuriating than even his most narcissistic qualities.

Closing the book, she stood and looked out her window at the pool water shimmering like oil beneath the night sky. The hedges enclosing the backyard—not as tall as The Writer's, but formidable all the same—reminded her of prison walls.

She sipped her wine and stared at the dark windows of the pool house, thinking about Arden. Something had happened to him in his years away. The essence of him had been lost. The drugs, she figured, were partly to blame—maybe even mostly—but not entirely. Drugs were always a symptom of a larger affliction. She didn't know what Arden's affliction *was*, but she suspected he was well beyond the point of recovery.

With a shiver, she wondered if she were all that different.

TWENTY-ONE
WATER OF THE WOMB

"WHY DON'T you ever talk about your family?" Lyssi asked Ryland one Saturday as they lay on a beach in Ventura they had driven to that morning because Lyssi wanted to "get out of the city for a little while."

Ryland sat up. He looked at Lyssi, stretched on her towel in a skimpy Saint Laurent bikini. The beads of perspiration on her skin glistened like rhinestones in the sun. Lighting a cigarette, he pushed his hair back and gazed down the long, mostly empty stretch of beach. He stared at the almost transparent blue shadows of the mountains in the distance. "There's not much to talk about," he said. "I'm not close with any of them."

"Do you have siblings?"

"A brother. Bruno. He's older." He thought of the multiple missed calls, making another mental note to return them. "He lives back in Pennsylvania. Married, two kids. We're...he and I are very different. He's just so...*loud*. Everything he does, he does in excess."

"What about your parents?"

"They're in Pennsylvania, too. They, um...they don't like me all that much. Not anymore. They're disappointed with some of the paths I've chosen. The decisions I've made."

Lyssi sat up, and she gingerly took the cigarette from Ryland. She closed her eyes and dragged from it, tipping her head backward to let the smoke unfurl above her. She opened her eyes to watch it dissipate in the light wind, and then she gave the cigarette back.

"What do you mean by that? What could you have done to make your own parents dislike you?"

Ryland hesitated. Out in the surf, the black dorsal fins of dolphins pierced the surface of the water, slick and gleaming in the harsh sunlight. "It's...you know, it's a culmination of things. My dad owns a pretty successful landscaping business that he'd originally wanted Bruno to take over. But Bruno went into investment banking, so then it was supposed to be me who took the reins. When I didn't, I guess that was strike one. Strike two was accepting the promotion that brought me out to Los Angeles. They're both hardcore Catholics and they think LA is some kind of Sodom and Gomorrah. They're convinced it's...I don't know, *infected* me, somehow. And strike three..." He trailed off, flashing on the image of Penny's husk standing in the doorway to her decrepit apartment.

Bringing the cigarette to his lips, he noted a slight tremor in his hand. "There was...a girl. Back in Pennsylvania. Penny. Pennsylvania Penny. That's what people out here called her." He gave a short, humorless laugh. "She was kind of your typical all-American girl, the type your parents want you to marry. The type *my* parents wanted *me* to marry, at least. She followed me to LA maybe a year and a half after I'd left Pennsylvania, but by then it was...too late. I was different, she was different. Things had changed."

"What happened to her? Where is she now?" Lyssi's voice was tipped with a knife's point. Ryland noted this small expression of jealousy with what he realized was an inappropriate degree of satisfaction.

"She's out in the desert. Alone." He swallowed. "Things fell apart between us pretty quickly when she came out here. And then she got caught up in drugs—the bad kind, the kind that kill you." He paused and watched the waves roll into themselves. "My parents blame me for what's become of her. So do her parents. So does she."

"Do *you* blame yourself?"

"No," he said, and it wasn't a lie. "No, I don't." After a moment, he added, "I can't." Somehow, those two additional words blunted the edge of his stated denial. They made him sound less cold, as though he had chosen this stance with reluctance.

"Well, that's good. You're right, of course—you *can't* blame yourself. There's no reason to, anyway."

Ryland had a feeling she was only placating him; she had no stake in this one way or another, and he didn't think she cared much about his morality, at least as it pertained to matters which didn't concern her. Still, her validation—however conciliatory—sparked a surge of affection for her. He leaned over and kissed her, tasting the brackish sea breeze on her lips. When he pulled away, the charming smile on her face was enough to make him forget about Penny almost altogether.

The frequency of Bruno's calls increased over the next week. Ryland dodged all of them. He deleted the voicemails without listening to them. *I'll call him back*, he kept telling himself. *He can wait.*

Then, when lying in bed and half-watching some ridiculous anime show with Lyssi one night, his mother called. He looked at the phone vibrating on the nightstand, the name BARBARA lit up on the screen. His mother never called.

"I...think I have to take this," Ryland said. Lyssi nodded. There was a cold suspicion in her eyes. Ryland grabbed the phone and carried it out into the hallway, closing the bedroom door behind him. He slid his thumb across the phone's screen and lifted it to his ear.

"Who was it?" Lyssi asked when Ryland came back into the bedroom, phone held at his side. He sat in the armchair by the window and ran his hands through his hair. "Ry, who was it?" Lyssi asked again. She paused the TV show. "You look terrible."

"My mom," Ryland said. He rubbed a light ache in his left arm. "It was my mom."

Lyssi's eyes narrowed. "You said you don't talk to your mom. *Literally* you *just* told me this, like, less than a week ago."

"I don't. Not...not under normal circumstances."

"Well, then why did—"

"My brother. Bruno. Bruno is dead."

She was off the bed and across the room, in his lap, stroking his face, his hair, speaking to him as a mother would a child. Though Ryland was distracted and numbed by the news, he had enough awareness to detect something like wicked glee in her eyes. Like she was deriving some deranged pleasure from what she assumed was a tragedy.

"He was overweight," Ryland said. "He had a bad heart. High blood pressure, and all that. It isn't exactly shocking." His gaze drifted to the family of stuffed animals Lyssi had arranged on his dresser. They looked nightmarish. Their glassy black eyes stared over the rumpled bed.

"Were you guys ever close?" Lyssi asked, still petting him. "You didn't say. You only mentioned he was some sort of banker guy. And that you two were really different. You never said anything more about him."

"Yeah, no, we were never close. It isn't contentious, or anything. He's just a—it's like I said, he's different. We're not at all alike." He realized something and winced a little. "Weren't," he corrected himself. "We weren't at all alike."

"Oh, baby." Lyssi pulled her to him. She pressed the side of his face to her chest. Her nails gently raked over his scalp. Ryland closed his eyes. He was ashamed of the comfort he took in the sensation.

"I have to go back," he murmured. "For the funeral. It's this weekend."

"Shh," Lyssi said. "You don't have to go anywhere right this second." She got up and pulled him to the bed. "Let your little Lyssi-loo make you feel all better."

As she went down on him, Ryland's eyes kept moving to the stuffed animals on the dresser. They were watching him. Judging him for some unknown indiscretion of which only they were cognizant. He could almost hear them whispering.

TWENTY-TWO
IN THE CEMETERY OF THE HEAVENS

SEVERAL MONTHS AGO, The Writer had been needed on set in Palm Springs to provide consultation for the miniseries adaptation of his fifth novel, *Victims of Love*.

The dates overlapped with Tess's spring break, so he offered to take her along. "I'll be working the whole time," he'd told her with a weariness she assumed was exaggerated; she couldn't imagine whatever "consultation" was required from him would be grueling business. "You'll have to entertain yourself. But the studio is putting me up at the Renaissance, so that shouldn't be terribly difficult."

Her friends were going to the usual places—Miami, Cancun, Vegas, Cabo. Her initial plan had been to do the same, but The Writer's offer was more appealing than getting wasted on an over-crowded beach for the fourth spring break in a row.

This was how she wound up in the passenger seat of his Bentley, watching the outside temperature display climb as the car raced along the dry roads into the desert.

When they drew near to the hotel after driving for the better part of two hours, she looked out at the forest of windmills with their languorous blades gleaming molten white in the fierceness of the setting sun. Most of them spun listlessly, but some stood inert. Something about these still shapes—were they broken, or simply shut down?—caused a formless, indefinite sadness to well up within her. She had to look away.

For the first couple days, Tess spent most of her time lying by the pool with her earphones in. She floated in a trancelike delirium, high on Valium and margaritas.

She rarely saw The Writer; he left early and got in late. He would leave packets of coke for her on the nightstand, and pills in unmarked bottles—party favors, she supposed, from wherever he was going after shooting had wrapped for the day.

On the third night, she woke from an inebriated slumber sometime after one AM, stretched on the bed in her bikini, with no recollection of lying down. The Writer wasn't there, and she discovered a text from him on her phone informing her he wouldn't be back until the following night. Whatever the implications were, it didn't faze her. She got out of bed and did some of the coke. It shattered the icy shards of frosted tequila clinging to her brain.

Pulling shorts and a tank top over her bathing suit, she left the room to wander down the wide, maze-like hallways. They continued endlessly, deviated by occasional bends that gave way to passages which would have been identical if not for the different posters of various vintage cars hanging from the walls.

Tess reached the elevators in their glass corridor that jutted away from the hotel and paused for a while to look out at the fearsome black bulk of the mountains rising over the basin of the valley. She imagined creatures living among the dark rocks, unspeakable monstrosities peering at her. They called to her in voices she felt but could not hear. A chilled shudder skittered down her spine, and she turned away, summoning one of the elevators and riding it to the first floor.

She walked beneath the high ceilings of the deserted lobby and over to the bar. It was empty save for the bartender and a tired-looking man in white jeans and an oxblood leather jacket. Tess took a seat two stools away from him and ordered a martini. The bartender—corpse-pale, with black eyes and long, freakish fingers—flashed her with a knowing glance but didn't card her.

As Tess drew her first sip from the cocktail once it was placed before her, the man in the leather jacket looked at her, staring for several seconds and then dropping his gaze. He smiled to himself and shook his head.

"What?" Tess asked, emboldened by the coke.

"Nothing," the man said, still smiling and shaking his head. "I'm sorry." He was youngish, maybe mid-twenties, with a handsome, lightly stubbled face and brushed-back blond hair. A stray lock of it hung curled against his tanned forehead. "It's just, you see it happen in the movies, you know? Guy is sitting alone at the bar; beautiful woman sits down next to him. You don't think it happens in real life."

Tess was thrown off kilter—she couldn't recall anyone ever referring to her as a *beautiful woman*. Beautiful *girl*, yes—though it was more frequently "hot girl," or "sexy young lady" or, usually when she had their dick in her mouth, "delicious little bitch"—but never *woman*.

Recovering, she said, "Well, you know. Life imitates art, or whatever."

The smile he gave her was sad. "No," he said. "No, it doesn't."

His name was Logan Taylor. A director, he was here helming a lengthy shoot for a Netflix miniseries based on Norman Mailer's *The Deer Park*. Before this, he'd directed a number of stylish music videos —"Do people even watch music videos anymore?" Tess had asked, and he'd told her no, they don't.

The adaptation of *The Deer Park* was Logan's first time working with actual, legitimate actors. He lamented the experience at length to Tess. "'Would my character really *say* this?'" he mocked in a whiny voice. "Or, 'I'm really struggling with my character's motivation here.' It's pathetic. All the action, all the dialogue—the screenwriter took all of it right from the novel. If they truly cared about *motivation*, they'd read the fucking book. But good luck getting an actor to read anything that isn't formatted like a script or a press release."

He had an undeniable arrogance about him, but it wasn't as showy or grandiose as The Writer's. Tess liked the way he looked at her. It was different from the way The Writer looked at her. There was a reverence in Logan's eyes when they were upon Tess. A subdued and patient amazement. The Writer looked at her like something to own. Something to eat.

They sat talking until well past three—Logan spoke far more than Tess, but she didn't mind. He had a pleasant voice lacking in pretense or affectation. In combination with the gin and vermouth, it had a way of lulling her into a pleasing state of dazed hypnosis. The substance of whatever he was saying didn't matter; Tess was content to float on the musical timbre of the flexing and contracting of his vocal cords. She nodded and smiled in the right places, murmuring what few words were necessary to keep him going.

It was still hot outside, where they shared a cigarette beneath the awning over the front entrance. Logan smoked Pall Malls, which Tess found odd and amusingly pedestrian. When she told him this, he laughed, and then he kissed her. She allowed it because she liked how he had tossed aside the cigarette and, without asking permission, closed the distance between them so he could seize hold of her, pressing his liquor-tanged mouth to hers. Most males were always asking for that sacred word of consent before taking any such action. "*Can I kiss you?*" they'd ask, and it sounded so pathetic. She often responded with, "I don't know, *can* you?"

Even The Writer hadn't first kissed her until she'd been splayed naked on his bed, at which point consent was a forgone conclusion. *This* was what she wanted—a daring display of boldness, a willingness to take a risky leap from a precipitous ledge.

She'd intended to allow it only for a few seconds before pulling away, citing *someone else*, but she found herself falling into it for reasons not known to her. She pressed against Logan and draped her arms around his neck. She felt weightless. Swept away. Plummeting.

In the elevator, they were upon each other again. Kissing and sucking, biting and pulling. The heat rising within Tess felt strong enough to ignite. Logan's hands on her skin were like flame-reddened coals. Her desire was a painful, physical thirst threatening to consume her if not soon sated.

Stripped bare on the bed in the director's darkened suite, Tess experienced this new man's naked proximity in and around her body with a kind of shock. She'd not had sex with anyone but The Writer since she'd begun seeing him. Variations presented themselves at once.

Gone was the director's polite manner; he made love with a ferocity so violent Tess felt absurdly like it was a conscious act of defiance against The Writer's gentle attentiveness. The first minute or two was thrilling in its newness, but then he was pulling her hair too hard, gripping her neck too tightly, thrusting into her with too much force. She became frightened, and she contemplated telling him to stop in a brief flight of fancy, but of course she couldn't. It would turn into something else if she told him to stop. She could only lie there and wait for it to be over.

She dressed in silence while Logan lay spent and self-satisfied. He watched her with eyes once again kind and reverential. They made plans to meet at the bar the next night, but Tess knew she wouldn't go.

Except, it seemed, she *did* go. After a lost day stoned and drunk by the pool, there came a curtain of opaque blackness, and then she was awakening on sweat-soggy sheets amid a tangle of warm limbs. She freed herself and stood at the foot of the bed, gazing at the naked bodies sleeping upon it. On either side of the director lay a blonde girl. One of them might have been fourteen. The other couldn't have been older than eleven.

Riding the elevator up to The Writer's floor, fragments of obscene images flashed in Tess's mind. She lied to herself and reasoned they were false memories; she never would have agreed to the horrible things—*evil* things—she saw herself engaged in amid these grotesque snapshots burning in her brain. She told herself this, but she didn't believe it. When she let herself into The Writer's room —he still had not returned, a kindness granted from a God in which she didn't believe—she had to rush to the bathroom so she could vomit into the toilet. Liquor and pills came up, but the images remained inside her.

She wept herself to sleep that night.

Three days later, when it was time for her to leave, she rode the elevator down to the lobby to wait for the Lyft The Writer had paid to take her back to Los Angeles. The elevator stopped at the third floor, and the doors slid open. The director stepped inside, wearing shorts and a T-shirt, a beach towel draped over his shoulder. His eyes were hidden behind Vuarnet sunglasses. He didn't acknowledge her, or even look at her. The doors opened again at the first floor, and he wordlessly went out to the pool as if she hadn't been there. She let out a breath.

It didn't happen. None of it happened. I got too drunk and did too many drugs, and I dreamt all of it.

But then she saw the two blonde girls sitting at a table in the dining area near the bar. Their faces were solemn, and their youth was more horrific in the daytime. The older one locked eyes with her, and she whispered something to the younger one, who turned her head to look at Tess. The spooky bartender grinned at her with too many teeth. Tess rushed outside and dropped her duffel bag on the pavement so she could dry-heave into a bush.

On the ride home, she vowed she'd never again go to Palm Springs. She told herself something sinister lurked out there in the desert. A black disease which had taken root and flourished in its necrotic potency. But as the spires of downtown Los Angeles came into view, she wondered with mounting fear if the disease had been metastasizing inside her all along.

TWENTY-THREE
BREATHING SMOKE

THE ROW of surfboards hanging in the garage filled Baxter with something like sadness. Surfing had once given him such pleasure, such peace. It felt like that had been a long time ago. Sometime before the Porn Problem. He still surfed on a regular basis—at least once a week—but it didn't hit the same way it once did. The emptiness he felt as he smoked his joint and gazed upon the boards' polished surfaces was so wide and so vacant, he thought he might fall into it.

He crushed out the joint and went inside. After running four miles on his father's treadmill, he spent thirty minutes lifting weights. The endorphin rush was pleasant but fleeting. When he stood naked and sweating in front of the mirror, staring with hollow passivity at the contours of his muscles, he wondered what the point was. For whom was he staying in shape? Who was there to impress?

Once he'd showered, he went to his bedroom to check on the MechaHooker. She sat on his bed, her legs stretched out in front of her. She spread them when he entered. "I want to feel your sex cream drip out of my hot pussy," she said.

Baxter lit a cigarette. "You don't care whether I'm hot or not," he said. "You'd still fuck me even if I wasn't jacked. Is that what love is?"

"Let me guzzle your salty sperm."

"I just feel like I've lost a piece of myself. Maybe this is all there is, and that's fine. It's better than fine." He breathed smoke. "But I keep wondering if there's something I'm missing. Like, you're the answer. I know you're the answer. But I don't know if I ever knew what the question was, you know?"

"I love being your wet slut."

Baxter shut the door. He went downstairs and out to the back-yard. The sky was pink and the air smelled like fire. Sitting in one of the chairs by the pool, he called Arden. There was no answer. He thought for a moment, smoking in silence and inhaling the campfire scent, and then he called the Coovers' landline. Katrina Coover picked up on the third ring.

"Baxter," she said. "It's been such a long time. How've you been? Are you still surfing?"

He was picturing her naked and he hated himself for it. "Uh, yeah. Yeah, um, I'm great, Mrs. Coover. I'm...still surfing. How, um. How are...you?"

"For the last time, please, you can call me Katrina. I mean, my God. You're practically family."

"Yeah. Yeah, I'm sorry. It's just, you know. It's been a long time, and." He coughed. "It's just been a while. Um, is Arden around?"

The sound of water running. A clatter of dishes, and then the water shut off. "I haven't seen him today. I don't see much of him, to be honest. I can go check the pool house if you—"

"No, no, it's fine. I just...well, can I ask you something?" He was still trying to will his brain to put clothes on the image of Katrina he had in his head.

A short but noticeable pause. "Sure," she said. "Of course. What is it?"

Baxter could hear the trepidation in her voice. It made him self-conscious and ashamed. "Well, I...I was wondering if..." He coughed again. Cleared his throat. "When me and Arden were kids, did you ever...like, did you ever think about what would happen to us?"

A longer pause. More trepidation in her voice when she answered, "I'm not totally sure I know what you mean."

"Right. I'm sorry. I guess what I'm asking is...well, did we turn out the way you thought we would? The way you'd...I don't know, hoped?"

The silence echoed like a condemnation. When at last she spoke, Baxter felt like something had been severed. "I still don't think I understand," Katrina said. Her voice was distant and cautious. "I never had any sort of...*plan* for my children. I know some parents do. I guess I just figured Arden and Tess—and now Daffodil—would do what they were going to do. And they have."

"What about me?" Baxter shut his eyes. His cigarette had gone out. He let it fall from his fingers.

"Well..." She drew the word out. "I haven't seen you in so long. I don't know what you're doing these days. But, I mean, that doesn't really matter. I'm sure you've found your way. I always knew you would."

"Did I seem...lost? When you knew me. When I was a kid. Was I lost?"

"Not...not any more lost than everyone else is, I suppose. I'm sorry, Baxter, I just don't know what you're trying to ask me."

"Are other people lost? Are you?"

"Sure. Yeah. Everyone is a little bit lost." There was an edge of agitation in her voice now. "But we find our way. And then we get lost again. It's a cycle."

"What if time is running out? What if the ones who are lost aren't going to have enough time to find their way before things end?"

"Before *what* ends, Baxter?"

He took in a deep inhalation of the smoky air. "Everything," he said.

"Well, then, I guess it won't matter, will it?"

"No," Baxter said. He opened his eyes. "I guess it won't matter." He looked at the pink sky. "I'm sorry for troubling you, Mrs. Coover. I'll let you go."

"It's no trouble," she said, but Baxter could hear the relief in her tone. "I'll tell Arden you called."

When he'd hung up, Baxter took off his clothes and dove into the pool. He let himself sink to the bottom. The water surged up his nostrils and purged his sinuses of the smoky smell.

It returned as soon as he resurfaced.

Back inside, he wept into the MechaHooker's lap.

TWENTY-FOUR
BACK EAST

RYLAND DIDN'T MIND air travel, but returning to Pennsylvania filled him with such sour dread that the only recourse was to take two Valium and remain inebriated for the duration of the flight.

He was on his second drink by the time the plane lifted off the runway. Sinking into his first-class seat, his earphones in to discourage the passenger beside him from attempting to engage him, he stared with heavy-lidded eyes out the window and watched Los Angeles shrink beneath him. He could see the fires to the east. It looked like they were close to the city. Like they were getting closer.

Walking toward baggage claim some five hours later in a drunken haze—the only way he knew how to handle the Philadelphia airport—he found he had enough lucidity to be struck by how unpleasant everyone looked. They were tired, sallow, overweight. Their faces bore menacing scowls. People jostled into one another, cursing under their breath or barking into cell phones. Ryland spotted only three girls who were remotely fuckable, and they clearly weren't locals.

He texted Lyssi to tell her he'd landed as he waited at the

baggage carousel. She responded with a nude photo—feet stockinged in thigh-highs, one hand between her legs and the other cupping her breast—captioned with *miss u* and a string of heart emojis. Too drunk to be aroused, he replied with several kissing face emojis and put his phone in his pocket. He watched his Louis Vuitton suitcase move toward him on the trundling black track.

The Uber ride to the Cold Spring Falls Marriott—the only decent hotel in Ryland's hometown—lasted over an hour. It was made longer than normal by the heavy rain sweeping across the freeway as the driver's Lexus made its way north. Ryland took another Valium about fifteen minutes in, and soon the silver-gray water streaking up the windshield became calming and hypnotic. Even the jagged branches of lightning spiderwebbed across the dark afternoon sky were soothingly apocalyptic.

The rain had slowed to a drizzle when the Lexus dropped him off in front of the Marriott. As he got out of the car, he became unnerved by the oppressive quiet. Without the steady, mechanical thrum of urban civilization to which Ryland's body had become accustomed, nature's whispering breath was the only sound—the soft patter of scattered raindrops, the rustle of wind in the trees.

Mandy, the girl at the front desk, had been there for what Ryland thought was too long a time. She'd been standing in the same place the first time he'd stayed at the hotel five years ago, a little over one year after he'd moved to LA.

Twenty-five and built like a cheerleader, spray-tanned and fake-lashed and emanating bright-eyed cheer and youthful sexuality, she had come to Ryland's room four consecutive nights after her shift and fucked him with memorable vigor and expertise. Now, at thirty, she was unrecognizable. Pale and bloated, with a bleary, blotchy face. Her once-sleek auburn hair had gone frizzy. There was nothing left of the girl whose expired pleasures Ryland had long ago known so intimately. He noticed a cheap wedding ring on her finger that explained it all. There were probably children, at least two. A beer-guzzling husband who beat her. A ramshackle house somewhere rural, away from uppity, suburban Cold Spring Falls' high property taxes.

As he checked in, his gaze met her sunken, washed-out eyes only long enough to see the despair there, the hopeless tragedy of the dead-end life. He looked away.

This is what happens to all of them. They get stuck here in these small towns and it warps them into haggard beasts. He thought of Penny, dying in her dilapidated apartment as the heroin and meth ate away at her brain, her body. He decided she'd been doomed either way. There was some consolation in that.

After leaving his suitcase and sport coat in his room and swallowing two Xanax, he went down to the dim, empty hotel bar. He sat nursing a scotch with his earphones in, thinking of his dead brother. He thought he'd feel guiltier about the calls he'd ignored and not returned, but his conscience was satisfied with the justification that he'd "been busy."

It had been several years since he'd seen him in person; their paths had crossed in Vegas one summer, and Ryland had tagged along as Bruno bopped from brothel to strip club to brothel. Ryland, who disliked both brothels and strip clubs, had gotten drunker as the night carried on. He had vague memories of doing a lot of coke in what now seemed like an unusually high number of chromium bathrooms. He remembered Bruno strutting up the neon-bathed boulevards, surprisingly dexterous in his gait for someone of such considerable height and girth. He'd kept bellowing "TITTY CITY" at the sky, his tremendous arms spread wide. Ryland had skulked behind him, trying not to appear associated with him.

"Money and minge," Bruno used to say to him, leering from his wide, bearded face. "That's all that fucking matters." He'd sip his beer, he'd hit his cigarette, and he'd say, "*Minge*, man, I said it. I know you youngsters like the cue-ball pussies these days but fuck all that. I don't want no bald beaver swallowing up my cock. I don't

want to go down on some shaved snatch, some tweezed twat. *No.*"
He'd bang his fist on the table then. "Bruno Boy needs a nice, pillowy
muff bush. I want to be coughing up cunty pubeballs for *days*."

Ryland finished his drink and paid the bartender, tipping too
much, and then he went to his room and had a bottle of Cristal sent
up. The waiter who brought it was a spooky-looking fellow with too-
white skin and black eyes and fingers that were too long. For half of a
fear-frozen moment, Ryland was certain he'd seen him somewhere
before, that his presence here was both ominous and impossible, but
he was drunk enough to lose the thread of what must be a false
memory. He tipped the creepy waiter before shutting the door in his
face.

Retreating to the bed, Ryland proceeded to drink himself into a
cloudy sleep.

The warm rain was light but persistent the next morning at the
cemetery. Black umbrellas canopied the sparse mourners like rotting
mushroom caps.

Ryland stood hung over and shaky, away from everyone, huddled
beneath his own umbrella. The tapping of raindrops atop the canvas
above his head was deafening, and the Valium/Vicodin/vodka cocktail was doing little to help. He tried to focus on the priest's solemn
sermon, tried to locate something in the words that would stir some
semblance of emotion, but the address was garbled into something
foreign and unintelligible by the rain's torment.

His parents stood close to the grave, crowded together. Their
stern faces were more suggestive of anger and disappointment than
of sorrow. Neither of them had said a word to him since his arrival.
He couldn't decide if he was hurt or relieved.

When the priest had finished his spiel, Bruno's coffin was

lowered into its grave plot. For a moment, Ryland felt a curious sensation of frantic helplessness as he watched his brother sink into the earth. He imagined Bruno grinning next to him, his big hands in the pockets of his pinstriped pants. "One last hole, little bro," the ghost said with a greasy chortle.

Bruno's widow, Christiane, appeared before Ryland as the mourners began to scatter to their vehicles. Christiane was a small, mousy woman who had been pretty a long time ago but now bore signs of weathering in her face and frailty in her figure. She was only, Ryland thought, somewhere in her early forties, but her marriage to Bruno had aged her. "Hello, Ryland," she said. Ryland's nephews—Michael, fifteen, and Daniel, eleven—stood on either side of her in ill-fitting suits.

"Christiane," Ryland said. He peered out from beneath his umbrella at the gray sky. "My, um...deepest condolences."

"Thank you," she said with a tight smile. "You lost someone, too, you know."

Ryland couldn't disguise the confused expression on his face as his intoxicant-addled brain spun, trying to recall to whom she might be referring. It took him several painful moments to realize they were talking about the same person. "Um, right," he said. He coughed into his fist. "I know he and I weren't that close but I...you know, I...loved him."

Christiane regarded him with an amused pity before telling her sons, "Boys, go catch Grandma and Grandpa and ask if you can ride with them to the restaurant. I want to talk with your uncle." Ryland tensed up as his nephews turned and jogged through the rain to catch up with their grandparents, who were nearly at the parking lot. Christiane leveled her eyes at Ryland and said, "You were planning on coming to lunch, right?"

"Uh, yeah. Yeah, I remember my mom mentioning something about that." He had not planned on attending. He wanted only to go back to his hotel and crawl into bed with a bottle of gin.

"I noticed you didn't drive here. Come on, I'll save you the Uber fare." Ryland would have paid exorbitant sums of money to avoid whatever conversation he was about to endure, but his head hurt too badly for him to come up with a plausible excuse.

He followed Christiane to the parking lot. She'd driven Bruno's white Maserati Quattroporte, explaining, "I thought he would have liked that—he loved this damned car more than anything. I think, though, I'm going to sell it. It's so gauche. Michael will be disappointed—he gets his learner's permit soon—but no teenage boy needs a car like this."

Ryland gave a grunt of agreement as they got into the car. Christiane pressed the ignition button with a brittle-looking finger. The stereo stayed silent. As they pulled out of the parking lot, Ryland said, "You, um...you wanted to talk to me about something?"

With a short, terse nod, Christiane said, "Bruno talked about you quite a bit these last few months. He said he'd been trying to call you."

Ryland gripped the sides of the leather seat and looked out the window. "Right," he said. "Yeah, I know. I've just been...busy." In a gesture of bitter capitulation, he added, "It's not an excuse."

"I'm not admonishing you, Ryland. That's not what this is."

"What is it, then?" There was more brusqueness in his voice than he'd intended. It had been, he realized, more than thirty-six hours since his last dose of cocaine. He could feel the razor-cut agitation sawing into his jangled nerves.

Slowing to a halt before a stoplight at an empty intersection, her fingers fidgeting atop the steering wheel, Christiane said, "The last year or so with Bruno was...well, it was better. He didn't whore around as much. He drank less, went out with his work pals more infrequently. He hardly ever hit me anymore. Even the pot—and you know how he loved pot—even that tapered to a degree. He was more present. Did more with the boys, lost some weight, stopped working on weekends. It was a good year for us. Almost like it was in the beginning."

"That's, ah, really great. I'm...glad to hear it."

The light turned green. Water jetted sideways as the car cruised forward.

"Ryland," Christiane said. "Listen to me. It was like he knew he was running out of time. There was a night, maybe eight months ago, when he took me to dinner downtown. It was such a surprise. I couldn't remember the last time he'd taken me out. And when we got back that night, I caught him crying. Not *weeping*, of course, you know he'd never do that. But he had these great big tears in his eyes, and he was trembling, and he said, 'I wasted it all, Christy. I thought it was what I wanted, but it was all a waste.'"

Ryland felt a fetid disdain for his brother then, irked near to the point of sickness at the cliché he'd apparently become. The happy hedonist turned penitent paragon in the face of his impending twilight. It was all so typical. He'd never particularly liked his brother, but in that moment, picturing him crying over his "wasted" life, he liked him less than ever. For all Bruno's faults, his crassness and his tactless vulgarity, Ryland had at least admired the unapologetic manner in which he conducted his sordid affairs.

"I don't know why you're telling me this," Ryland told Christiane. Exhaustion was settling into his bones and constricting around his joints.

"I think you do."

"No, really. I mean, what is this? Some kind of intervention? Am I supposed to burst into tears and tell you you're right, I need to change my ways, that whatever *light* you think your husband saw in his last few months has come for me and swept me into its arms? Let me tell you something. Bruno didn't *change*. He didn't experience some grand *epiphany*. He was a middle-aged man with a bad heart and high blood pressure and cholesterol levels through the goddamn *roof*, and he started to get skittish the more he felt his mortality. There's nothing special about it. It happens to guys like him all the time."

"You're taking this all wrong," Christiane said, pulling into the parking lot of a little Italian restaurant called Luca Lorenzo's that Bruno had liked. She parked the car near the back of the lot, turned off the ignition. She didn't look at Ryland. "I'm not attacking you. This isn't about judgment. I'm only telling you what he wanted to say himself."

"Which is what, exactly?"

"Take it easy. Enjoy life. Find things that give you *real* pleasure, not synthetic substitutes. You're right, he *was* feeling his mortality. It has a way of creeping up on you. I think Bruno was starting to realize the things that are important to have around you when it does."

"I don't think Bruno was starting to realize anything. And I'll tell you something else—he never worked on weekends." This last jab was a cruelty that felt justified.

Christiane's mouth drew into a thin line. "All I'm saying is you're still young, Ryland. You have chances left. Bruno didn't start to wake up until he'd blown every chance he ever got."

"I am awake."

"No," Christiane said. Her smile bore no amusement, no warmth. "You're stoned." Without giving him the chance to answer, she got out of the car and stood in the light rain, waiting for him to follow. Bitterly, he did, and the two of them walked across the slick parking lot and into the restaurant.

Inside, sitting at the table with his family, Ryland was put off by the small-town simplicity of the restaurant's interior—the drab, generic wallpaper, the awful carpeting, the poor lighting. Menus printed on cheap cardstock and shoddily laminated; their edges trimmed unevenly as if scissor-cut by children. Faint Muzak rose from tinny speakers.

The staff were slouched and slovenly, the chairs ancient and creaky and uncomfortable. It was the kind of place Bruno loved; he favored places where he could flaunt his wealth, where everyone was force-fed the astringent awareness that he came from a higher cloth. This was one of the most distinct differences between the two of them—ever since Ryland had started making real money, he liked to be in places where he was surrounded by people of his ilk, where he could blend in among the upper tiers of the social strata. Intermingling among the lower classes only grossed him out.

"Ryland," said his mother. She phrased his name like a bland observation. "We didn't think you'd come."

"Yeah, well," Ryland muttered, and then said nothing else. He ordered a Belvedere on the rocks. The waiter only blinked and asked him what that was, so Ryland sighed and rubbed his temples and asked for a glass of Chianti, instead. "Actually," he amended, "just bring the whole bottle."

"It's awfully early," his father said—quite hypocritically, Ryland thought, given the man's own relationship with alcohol.

Ryland mumbled something about being on California time. He realized too late that this didn't make any sense because it was morning on the West Coast, but no one challenged him. His mother protested when he declined to order food. She fussed that he was "too thin, much too thin." He silenced her with an upheld hand and an expression of exhausted impatience.

He tried to pace his consumption of the wine as the meal progressed, but he'd drunk the entire bottle before anyone else had finished eating. The weak alcohol dulled the idle chatter and the maddening scrape of utensils across plates. No one said much to him —Christiane had already made her case, his parents had given up on him long ago, and his nephews knew from past experiences that he was incapable of indulging the antics of children with the patience other adults could.

Ryland's alienation at the table afforded him the opportunity to observe things he might have otherwise ignored, like how much his parents had aged since he'd last seen them. The deepening lines in his father's face, the receding gums, the burst capillaries crowded around his nose...his mother's ballooning weight, her thinning hair, the cloudiness of her eyes.

It came as something of a shock, seeing them so old—his father, especially. He could see himself reflected through the lens of advancing time in his face, but he could not reconcile the notion that the image of the man on the other side of the table was what waited for him. Old age was not something Ryland had ever been able to envision for himself. He saw nothing fatalistic or tragic about this blind spot in whatever foresight he thought he had for his future; it simply was not something he considered a possibility. Something *else* would happen, be it a medical panacea for aging or some scourge that eradicated mankind—whichever polar extreme came first.

When lunch had concluded—Ryland had attempted to at least pay for his wine, but his father had dismissed him with a summary wave of his hand without looking at him—the family stood outside under the dripping awning, hugging, and saying their goodbyes.

Ryland stood away from the rest of them, not engaging. He felt like an outsider and was comforted by this. He didn't want to be one of them. He'd never wanted to be one of them.

Christiane offered to drive him to his hotel, but he declined. He wanted to get away from all of them as soon as possible. He'd expected her to say something stereotypical in parting, something along the lines of "Think about what I said," or "Try and be good to yourself," but she didn't. She and her sons walked across the parking lot to the Maserati and none of them looked back.

Before taking their own leave, Ryland's parents offered stilted words of farewell to their sole remaining son—his father shook his hand, and his mother hugged him, but there was no warmth there, no sincerity. He was as dead to them as Bruno. Maybe more so.

On the way to the hotel, he had the Uber driver stop at a liquor store, where he bought a fifth of Tanqueray. Ryland tore the seal and took a long swig as he walked through the rain. He continued to drink in the backseat and gave the driver an egregious tip to avoid any impact on his passenger rating.

Ryland blacked out somewhere between the hotel elevator and his room. He regained consciousness the next morning on the plane, already airborne, wearing the wrinkled suit from the day prior. The passenger next to him kept shooting him wary, sideways glances. All Ryland could do was order another drink from the frumpy stewardess and wait for the plane to deposit him back into his life on the other side of the country.

TWENTY-FIVE
QUINCEY

WHEN REBECCA TOLD Arden he couldn't come over because she was planning to drive up to Valencia to visit Quincey, he said, "I could go with you, if you want company." And then, "Who's Quincey?"

"I've mentioned him. He was a friend in high school. There was an accident, and now he's at an assisted living facility. I like to go visit him every couple months or so."

Arden couldn't recall having ever been told about Quincey. He wondered if Rebecca had slept with him.

His phone felt hot in his sweat-slickened hand. A noxious balloon of jealousy inflated in his stomach and floated into his chest. "Well, if you want company..." he said again, trailing off. He could hear her moving through her apartment, gathering up her things, preparing to leave.

"It's not going to be fun, Arden. He's not...he doesn't look good. And the facility, it's...you know, it's depressing."

The word "FUN" appeared in Arden's mind in capital cartoon lettering. It flashed with neon irony. *Fun.* He tried to associate the word some familiar activity. All that came to mind was a dimly remembered snippet of a conversation in a dorm room hazed with pot smoke. He saw himself lying in bed with a naked girl without a name or face. Both of them were high on various hallucinogens. *Are we having fun yet?* he'd asked her. She'd given him a phantom's ethereal smile and said, *Are we ever?*

"You shouldn't have to go there alone, then," Arden said. He thought he could feel the beginnings of a headache creeping into his temples. His walls were beginning to warp and undulate. He carried the phone into the bathroom and muted the speaker so Rebecca wouldn't hear him shaking two Vicodin into his palm.

"What did you say?" Rebecca asked. "Sorry, I was looking for my keys."

Arden dry-swallowed the pills and unmuted himself. "I said you shouldn't have to go alone," he said. He returned to the couch and lit a joint.

"Oh. Well, it's no big deal. I always go alone. I mean, Ianthe went once but she got too bummed out."

Arden didn't ask who Ianthe was. The name sounded familiar. He thought Rebecca might have mentioned her, but the context was lost to him. "I won't get bummed out," was all he could think to say.

"Probably true." He heard her keys jangling, the front door closing. "I mean, you can't *get* bummed out if you're *always* bummed out."

"Hey. I'm not always bummed out." He'd meant to infuse some tenacity into his voice, but it came out flat and dull.

"Whatever you say, babe." Arden's heart lifted at her use of a pet name, something he didn't think she'd done before with him, save for in bed. "Anyway, yeah, whatever. I guess you're sort of on the way." He heard her car door opening, the instrument panel beeping. "I'll pick you up in...I don't know, a half hour? Give or take, depending on traffic."

They hung up. Arden finished the joint and did a little coke before going out to the curb to wait for Rebecca.

When she pulled up, she gave him a quick, distracted peck on the cheek as he buckled himself into the passenger seat. An Eagles playlist was playing low on the stereo. For most of the drive, as they wound their way up northern hills of increasing elevation, she kept skipping through the tracks, humming along, or singing under her breath for a minute or two before thumbing the "NEXT" button on her steering wheel.

Arden floated along on his mildly inebriated cloud. He cast wary glances at the angry, fire-reddened skies to the east. Few words passed between the two of them for the duration of the drive. Some moments, Arden was able to feel content, enjoying Rebecca's proximity and the warmth of the sun through the windows. Others, he felt his mind spinning into fretful paranoia. He attributed Rebecca's relative silence to waning interest in him, and wondered if she was preoccupied with someone else.

The care facility's parking lot, shaded by tall palm trees in need of trimming, was sparsely populated with a small gaggle of dusty sedans and hatchbacks all parked far away from one another. Four identical white vans were parked near the wheelchair ramp leading up to the entrance. The Berkeley bear mascot leaned against one of them. It held an unlit cigarette and stared ahead with its unblinking eyes.

The building itself— "Wild Palms Rehabilitation Sanctuary," as announced by the quaint wooden sign at the mouth of the parking lot—was unimposing but functional and modern. It bore more resemblance to a country club. The sprawling grounds were well-tended and dappled with genial sunlight.

"'Rehabilitation' is a euphemism," Rebecca said when they passed another, smaller sign as they walked toward the front door. "You don't come here to get rehabilitated. You come here to wither away and die slowly."

The interior was a clean and sanitized palette of harsh whites and soft beiges and polished wood paneling. Everything smelled of antiseptic and pine-scented air freshener. Calming spa music floated from unseen speakers. The fresh-faced staff members were young and predominately female, blonde, and sporty. They looked more like tanning salon employees than nurses. Everyone appeared to know Rebecca; they spoke to her with the warmth of old friends, and while they were almost equally polite to Arden, he thought he detected a glint of cold suspicion in their eyes.

They were led out to a serene courtyard with clustered foliage and a trickling fountain fashioned into a weeping angel, her stone hands pressed to her face as water streamed around them, running down her arms and cascading into the pool at her feet. A man in a wheelchair sat facing away from them near a wooden bench shaded by a low fern. "Stay as long as you like," the nurse said to them. She squeezed Rebecca's arm before going inside.

Following Rebecca over to the man in the wheelchair, Arden winced when he saw his face, or what remained of it. A network of faint scars indicated corrective surgery had been attempted, but the worst of the damage had been irreparable. His nose was crooked and mangled, flattened into a porcine and slightly upturned snout. The left eye was fused shut and hung a half an inch lower than the right. One of the scars on his indented forehead cut into his shock of curly black hair, rising to the center of his scalp. When he saw Rebecca, he emitted a short hooting noise and smiled, exposing gums pocked with a small handful of crooked teeth.

Arden had to avert his eyes.

Rebecca sat on the bench and began talking to Quincey as if he were a normal person. As if he understood the things she was saying.

After a beat of hesitation, Arden sat beside her. He listened to her tell Quincey mundane details about her life, her job, her friends. Occasionally, Arden would glance over at him, but the blank expression with the dopey smile and the sole functioning eye that rolled in its socket always made him look away after a few seconds. It wasn't just the disfigurements; the man was like a big, hideous child, and children had always made Arden uncomfortable. There was something about their helplessness and their ravenous need for care and attention that he found embarrassing.

More than that, Arden didn't like the doting and affectionate way Rebecca talked and interacted with Quincey. He wondered again if there'd been something romantic between the two of them before the accident. It wasn't likely she would keep coming out here after all this time for someone who'd simply been a friend. He tried to think if he'd do anything similar for any of his friends if something crippling happened to them, but he didn't have to think for long. He couldn't name more than a handful of people he would count as friends, and the ones he could meant so little to him that he didn't think he'd feel anything at all if something horrible happened to them.

His thoughts turned to Baxter, who he guessed was his oldest and closest friend. He tried to locate a feeling that would indicate he'd care enough to visit him if a Quincey-esque tragedy struck. But the more he searched within himself, the number he felt.

An image of the sex robot flashed through his brain. The numbness became accompanied by a distant nausea.

On the drive back, Arden asked, "So, was it a drunk driving accident, or something?"

Rebecca adjusted her LGR sunglasses and pursed her lips. "No," she said. There was a cold distance in her voice. "It wasn't anything like that."

"Well, I mean...what *was* it?"

She took a deep breath. Arden noticed her hands tightening around the steering wheel. "It's like I told you before. We were mixed up with some bad drugs. Stuff you probably haven't even heard of. We were young and stupid, and things got...out of hand." She swallowed. "That's all that matters. It's not something I like to talk about."

"Right, um. I'm...sorry."

"Don't be. It's fine. Just remember what I said. I'm not signing up to watch you spiral into oblivion. I'm not your mother and I'm not going to tell you what you can and can't do, but there are certain things I won't be a part of."

"Sure. Yeah. I...I get it."

She glanced at him. "Do you?"

"Yeah. I do."

"Okay. Good." She reached over and put her hand on his leg. Squeezed a little, gave him a small smile. "Movie at my place?"

"That sounds good." He looked out the window at the neon green clouds swirling into funnel shapes. They danced around each other, growing limbs and nightmarish faces that glared down at him. Shutting his eyes and leaning back in his seat, Arden thought to himself, *I'm fine. We're fine. Everything is fine and nothing matters.*

TWENTY-SIX
FREE SHIT

"I GET SO exhausted with all the *wealth* in this town," Lyssi was telling Ryland. She stood before her full-length mirror in her bra and panties, teasing her hair, examining her face.

They were at her place for once; Kyle was in Vegas performing at some sort of charity event for which he was being paid handsomely. Ryland reclined on the bed in his underwear, watching Lyssi, listening to her. He'd listened to her a lot over the past few days, having spent Friday night and all of Saturday with her. It was now Sunday morning, he was out of coke, and he was exhausted.

"This whole city is a tribute to capitalism," Lyssi went on. "It fetishizes it in the grossest of ways. I get so sick of it. Kyle and I are going to this party in Calabasas when he gets back tomorrow, and I'm dreading it. All the parties, all the drugs. Everyone with their fancy cars and their designer clothes and their gaudy jewelry. It's disgusting. I grew up with basically nothing. Both my parents are drug addicts. I never imagined I'd be where I am, and sometimes I think I was better off poor. I wish the communist revolution would hurry up and get here already. I hope it comes to LA first."

Ryland breathed in, bit his tongue. He tried to focus on Lyssi's exquisite beauty, the smooth, proportional perfection of the shape of her. The way she made him laugh, the way she made him come. The compliments with which she lathered him. How safe he felt when she ran her fingers through his hair.

She was a kid, he reasoned. She'd grow out of her ridiculous ideology. It wasn't worth a confrontation.

Lyssi turned away from the mirror, facing him. She put her hand on her hip and studied him, her fingers drumming against the fringe along the hem of her panties. "Don't *you* get sick of it?" she asked. A cruel malice flickered in her eyes. The grin she wore had bloodlust in it. "I mean, you're technically the worst kind of rich person. You're not *creating* anything. You're a corporate prostitute. You whore yourself out to Big Business, and you don't care that you're being used as a chess piece as long as they keep stuffing your bank account with the ill-gotten spoils of their sick game."

Ryland shut his eyes. "Lyssi," he said, controlling his breathing, measuring his tone. "Why are you doing this?"

Her evil smile could have cut through glass. "Doing *what*, darling? What is it that I'm *doing*?"

"Why are you picking a fight with me? We've been having such a nice weekend."

She laughed her frayed hyena's cackle. "Oh, have we? That's news to me. You think I don't notice how distant you've been? You think I don't know what it is? Its guys like you, you all have this *thing*. It's this *thing* that makes you incapable of staying satisfied. You're so used to getting new things, *shinier* things, so you get bored too easily. You're getting bored of me."

Despite his efforts to remain calm, Ryland could feel his blood pressure rising. His pulse chugged in his temples. "Lyssi, this is ridiculous. I'm not bored of you. I think the way you romanticize communism is a little immature and it can be irritating, but that doesn't mean—"

"Oh, *I'm* immature? That's good. That's *hilarious*. Enlighten me, *Daddy*. Tell me about all the ways I need to *grow up*."

"It's not *all* the ways, it's just...look, you're very mature. But the whole 'capitalism is evil' thing is where your age betrays you a bit. It's naïve. That's all."

"Oh, God, if only you could hear what a condescending prick you sound like right now."

Ryland massaged his eyes with his thumb and middle finger. "Christ, Lyss, let's not argue about this."

"Too late, boss man. You opened the door, now come on through. Tell me all about how naïve I am, Mr. Cor-po-*rate* Ex-ec-u-*tive*."

Maybe it was the petulant way she called him *boss man*. Maybe it was the goading wickedness in her eyes and in her smile. Maybe it was his faint hangover or the nagging coke withdrawals. Something in Ryland snapped.

He leaned forward on the bed, gritting his teeth and narrowing his eyes and bailing his hands into fists, and he unleashed. "You *kids*," he snarled, a little taken aback by his own savagery. "You all talk about communism like it's some kind of merry fucking carnival, but it's not. It's desolation and depression, and it's the eradication of everything you love. All this *stuff* you have—your clothes, your accessories, your jewelry—all of it, you think you get that in a communist state? Is that *honestly* what you think? How about all your streaming services with your stupid Japanese cartoons? Which, I'm sorry, but tell me how it is you can tolerate subtitles when you're watching nine straight hours of pastel-colored kids' shows about magical eighth graders with gigantic breasts and dead parents, but you can't stomach a hundred minutes of Kurosawa? Never mind, don't fucking answer that."

His eyes fell upon her bookshelf as he rubbed his aching bicep, his chest heaving. "And that Eastridge guy you get off on—you think a guy like him would even *exist* if it weren't for capitalism? Do you think he'd even fucking *bother*? Or your phone, your phone that you're *always* on—you can thank capitalism for that one too, baby doll."

He spread his arms out, wincing at the pain in his left one.

"Everything in this goddamn room, everything in your *life*—it's all from capitalism. You don't know what you're saying when you talk about communism. You're parroting the juvenile blowhards your age who think they have all the answers. Honey, *sweetheart*...you *think* you want communism. That, I believe. You think you want it, but you don't. You just want free shit."

Lyssi could have been a statue. Her regal poise as she stood still, eyes unblinking, the marble quality of her skin that, for all its yielding softness, appeared hard, impenetrable—Ryland had the absurd urge to take a picture of her. Even in her silent, seething rage, even as he steeled himself for her inevitable outburst, she was still the most beautiful thing he'd ever seen.

The outburst didn't come. Not at first, and not in the way he was expecting. After staring him down like an opponent in a duel, she bit her lip and nodded. Her fingers moved a lock of hair from her face. "You think I care," she said in an almost whisper. "You think I care about *stuff*. You think I care about any of it. This is..." She nodded again, as if realizing something. "This is funny to me." The calm in her voice was unsettling, a distant shape lying across a path; it could have been a branch, it could have been a snake.

Ryland wished she'd start yelling.

She pivoted on her heel and strutted into her walk-in closet. A rustling, and then a pair of Prada shoes came flying out, landing on the carpet in front of the bed. They were followed by several more shoes, a number of dresses, some purses, a pair of jeans, a handful of blouses, some more purses, still more shoes—all designer. Lyssi exited the closet, and then the bedroom. When she returned, she held a long, curved chef's knife in her hand.

She's going to kill me, Ryland decided, surprised at how readily he accepted this. He felt no panic. What he did feel wasn't quite relief, but it was close.

Instead of killing him, Lyssi got on her knees and began hacking the clothes apart. Fabric shredded like flesh. Shoe straps came untethered, their bases sawed in half. The dresses fell to ribbons.

Blouses were reduced to strips of tangled string, the jeans to bands of frayed denim. Her face remained calm but there were smudgy black tears running down her cheeks.

It all struck Ryland as theatrical—she possessed dozens of additional outfits—but then she went again into the closet and came out with her jewelry box, which she carried to the window and set on the floor. After unlatching and opening the window, she hurled the jewelry box outside. She pulled the TV off its stand, and it crashed onto the floor with a snap and a spark. She left the bedroom again and came back carrying the Wi-Fi modem. Her arm drew back, and the modem sailed into the wall. It broke into several hunks of plastic and left a small dent.

Turning to Ryland, her eyes streaming, she screamed, "I don't care about any of it. I don't want any of it." She sat down on the floor and sobbed.

Ryland's eyes moved again to the Chandler Eastridge novels on the bookshelf, which she had left untouched. He rejected the impulse to call attention to this.

He got off the bed and went to her, kneeling beside her amid the mess on the floor. She at first flinched from his touch like a small, frightened animal, but then she folded into him. She wrapped her arms around him and wept into his chest. He stroked her hair. "What *do* you want?" he whispered.

She murmured something unintelligible against his skin. He gently drew her away from him and wiped sooty tears from her face with the backs of his fingers. "Tell me what you want," he said.

Her eyes shifted away. They fixed on something distant and unseen. "I want to belong to someone," she said. "I've never belonged to anyone."

Ryland could think of nothing to say to that. He could only hold her.

TWENTY-SEVEN
ALEISTER CROWLEY IS MY SUNBEAM

ARDEN TAGGED along with Rebecca to a party at Luke "The Duke" Viceroy's compound in Calabasas.

Luke was a former MMA fighter in his late twenties who'd amassed most of his enormous following and fortune when he'd transitioned to a career in streaming videos in which he pranked celebrities at various high-end gyms. He was represented by one of Rebecca's colleagues.

"Luke's parties have a reputation," Rebecca told Arden as she pulled her Range Rover into the entrance. A bikini-clad girl about Tess's age opened the gate for them, and Rebecca drove through.

"A reputation for what?" Arden asked.

"It's kind of tough to summarize. You'll see. But...look, there's going to be a lot of drugs."

Arden tensed up. He felt Rebecca's silent judgment as she looked straight ahead and drove up the winding driveway. He'd taken four Xanax before she'd picked him up, and it hadn't been enough. He was on edge. Though he had no tangible reason to believe it, he sensed he was losing Rebecca. Something hadn't been right ever since the trip to see Quincey.

"I mean, doesn't that go without saying?" he asked. "It's a party, so." He looked out the window. They came to a stop in a line of cars at a wide turnabout in front of the chateau-style mansion. "What are you telling me?"

"I'm not telling you anything. I'm just saying, that's all."

Another young girl in a bikini approached their vehicle. This one was ponytailed and wearing a red baseball cap with "VALET" printed across it in white letters.

They got out, and the valet girl handed Rebecca a ticket. Arden gazed around at the extravagant grounds, the tall statue of the naked nymph in the middle of the turnabout, the valet girls bouncing from one car to the next and driving them off to some unseen location. He envisioned the fires arriving here, after they'd taken the city. The chateau would blaze like a funeral pyre. The girls in their bikinis would be reduced to black charcoal. He could almost taste the imagined odor of burning flesh.

Inside, they were greeted by hip hop remixes of dance-y pop tunes, and by Luke Viceroy himself. He was shorter than Arden had pictured—maybe five-eight, tops—and rippled with awkwardly bulging muscles straining against, of all things, an Affliction T-shirt. His sandy mop of hair fell over his ears and partially obscured one eye. Tribal tattoos laced around his tan, vein-corded arms. He was flanked on both sides by another two young girls in bikinis.

"Becca, *babe*, you look good enough to fuckin' eat," he said, grinning, ignoring Arden. He put his hands on Rebecca's hips and drew her to him, kissing her cheek and then the corner of her mouth. "It's been way too fuckin' long. I don't think I've seen you since—"

"It's been a while, yes," Rebecca said, pulling away from him. Her eyes shifted to Arden with unease. "This is Arden," she said. She took Arden's hand and squeezed it—a small gesture that, for a moment, made Arden feel better about everything in the world. "He...um, he just graduated college," she added. Arden at first thought this was a nonsensical thing to say before realizing there wasn't anything else she could say about him.

"College?" Luke said. He sneered at Arden. "Wow. That's pretty fuckin' gay."

"Come on, man," said Arden, exhausted. "You can't say shit like that anymore. It's just...not acceptable."

The two girls giggled. Luke made a face at Rebecca. "Aw, fuck, babe," he said. "He's one of those types?"

"Arden went to Berkeley," Rebecca said. Arden wasn't sure if this was an attempt to change the subject or to explain his response.

"Ah, gotcha," said Luke. "Fuckin' Berkeley. Bunch of prissy fuckin' soyboys, the whole fuckin' lot of them." He grinned at Arden. "No offense, dude."

"Right," said Arden. He heard the double doors open behind him, and he glanced over his shoulder to see a guy enter with what Arden was pretty sure was a Kardashian.

"We'll catch up later," Luke said to Rebecca. He winked. "Head on out back. I think most of the people you'll know are out there." He grinned at Arden again. "Nice to fuckin' meet you, soyboy."

"Whatever," said Arden. Rebecca took his wrist and led him away, appearing to know where she was going. They walked through crowds of people, passing more girls in bikinis carrying around silver trays, some with champagne or martinis, others with lines of coke. A few held wide glass bowls filled with pills of varying sizes, shapes, and colors.

Arden felt a surge of longing at the sight of the drugs, but he was aware of Rebecca watching him from the corner of her eye as she pulled him along through the castle.

They exited onto a wide deck overlooking a huge pool complete with a towering water slide. Also occupying the ample space of the grounds was a go-kart track, a miniature Ferris wheel, a tennis court, and a row of batting cages. It was the kind of property you'd expect an eight-year-old boy to buy.

There were fewer people on the deck, and Rebecca led Arden to where a beautiful but mean-looking blonde girl about her age was standing by herself. She was smoking a cigarette and sipping a cocktail. Rebecca hugged her and introduced her to Arden as Ianthe.

"Oh, right, cool," said Arden. He lit a cigarette and took a flute of champagne from a nearby bikini girl's tray. "Rebecca's told me about you."

Ianthe said nothing. Arden cleared his throat, looked over the balcony. He thought he saw Tess down by the pool, but he couldn't be certain.

"I took him to meet Quincey the other day," Rebecca said.

Scowling, Ianthe said, "God, Rebecca, that's so morbid. I don't know why you keep going up there. It's not even him anymore."

"I don't believe that. He's in there somewhere."

"It's cruel, really, his family keeping him there like that. It's no way to live, and he'll probably outlive all of us."

"It's a nice facility," Arden offered. "He seems to have...a lot of comforts available to him."

"Vegetables don't know what comfort is," Ianthe said. "The most humane thing would be to euthanize him." She glared narrow-eyed at Arden. To Rebecca, she said, "If you took him up there as some sort of scared-straight field trip, it obviously didn't work."

Arden took his Wayfarers out of his shirt pocket and put them on.

"You're probably one of those kids who are super into drug culture, aren't you?" Ianthe said. "Reading Timothy Leary and Aldous Huxley and, I don't know, who's another one...Ken Kesey. Tao fucking *Lin*. Watching videos where teenagers wax philosophic about *the next psychic frontier*, or whatever. Go ahead, tell me about the psychological benefits of psilocybin. Give me a lecture on the medicinal properties of marijuana."

"No," Arden said. "I'm not...I'm not one of those people. I hate those people." He'd known a lot of *those people* in college, had counted many of them among his "friends," if such a word could be used, but he'd found their romanticization of drug use to be juvenile and insipid. He'd never cared about *unlocking the doors of perception*, or any of that hippie bullshit. He hated Pink Floyd and Jefferson Airplane and The Grateful Dead. He just wanted to get high.

"Ianthe," Rebecca said. "Be nice."

"He's so stoned he can barely stand up straight," said Ianthe. "If he'd ever gotten his hands on Captain Howdy, he'd be—"

"Don't talk about it," said Rebecca, her face darkening.

"Who's Captain Howdy?" Arden asked.

"It's your dream come true," Ianthe sneered. "It's your worst nightmare." She turned and walked over to a short statue of a nude angel whose cupped hands had been fashioned into an ashtray, where she deposited the remains of her cigarette.

Returning, she took Rebecca's arm and said, "Come inside for a minute. There's someone I want you to meet." To Arden, she said, "We'll be right back." Rebecca threw Arden an apologetic look as she was pulled away.

After standing around for ten or fifteen minutes, nervously smoking and sipping his champagne, Arden descended the long staircase to the pool area.

He found Tess standing with her hip cocked, looking bored, holding a cigarette and a glass of champagne in one hand. She was dressed in ultra-short denim cutoffs and a bikini top that left less to the imagination than Arden felt comfortable with. Her Versace sunglasses were perched atop her head. Chandler stood next to her. He was talking to a girl with anthracite hair in a miniskirt whom Arden recognized from the book signing, and a doughy, baby-faced blond boy with pale skin in a Lil Wayne T-shirt whom he took to be her boyfriend.

"Arden," Tess said with disinterest. "I thought you might be here. You remember Lyssi."

"Um. Sure."

Lyssi's hungry green eyes appraised him. They searched for something of potential value. Finding nothing, they returned to The Writer.

"This is her boyfriend, Kyle," Tess said, when it became obvious Lyssi wasn't going to introduce him.

"What up, yo," said Kyle, barely glancing at Arden.

"Uh, hey," said Arden. After a few awkward moments, he added, "Yo." He looked at Chandler. "I read *Sickness and Health*," he said.

Chandler raised an eyebrow at him. He appeared to be annoyed that he was being pulled away from whatever he'd been talking about with Lyssi. "I thought you don't read fiction," he said.

"I usually don't."

"Well then." Chandler brought his cigarette to his lips. His eyes were obscured by a pair of Persol sunglasses, but Arden felt he was glaring. "What did you think?"

Arden had tried to find something to hate about it, some crucial flaw in its composition, but it had startled him in how much it had engrossed him. Each sentence had the gleaming smoothness of chrome. The words were so sharp he thought he might cut himself as he turned the pages.

"It was okay," he said.

Chandler's mouth twitched. He turned his attention back to Lyssi.

Tess was looking at Arden with something approaching concern. "Are you okay?" she asked.

"Yeah," Arden said, startled. "Yeah, I'm...great."

"Would you tell me if you weren't?"

Arden didn't know the answer to that. "Totally."

Tess's face was furrowed in consternated skepticism, but she didn't push the issue. "Anyway," she said, "where's Rebecca?"

Arden shrugged. "Inside, somewhere. I don't know."

He pictured her talking to Luke, laughing at the stupid shit he said. He pictured them doing other things. These images he shoved in a mental drawer and locked it, but he couldn't force himself to lose the key. He'd come back to them.

Kyle's head perked up. He looked at Arden and said, "Whoa, slow up. Rebecca as in, like, my publicist? You fuck with her?"

"You could say that," Arden said.

"Man, I gotta *talk* to her, G-skillet. She did me dirty and I'm boutta pop off. Be a homie and go swoop her, dig?"

Arden blinked at him. To Tess, he said, "Why is he talking like that?" Tess shrugged, looked away.

Lyssi touched Kyle's arm and said, "Babe, I told you to let it go."

"Bitch, no way. I'm K-Dolla Money, yo. I'm the rizzle dizzle. No *way* am I gonna *open* for fuckin' *Frisk*. Those fruity old fucks should be opening for *me*. No one listens to that boy band bullshit anymore."

"I like Frisk," Tess said.

"Huge Frisk fan here," Arden said. He hated Frisk.

"Nah, that's *cap*, dawg biscuit. Yeet the fuck out. *Sheesh*."

Arden looked helplessly at Tess. "I have no idea what he's saying."

"Shit, slice. You look like you fuck with a lot of...*shit*, G-homes, I don't even *know*. Hawthorne Heights, or some shit like that."

"Hey," Arden said. "I don't listen to Hawthorne Heights. *Slice*."

"I'm going to get some more champagne," Tess said, rolling her eyes and stalking away. Arden caught both Chandler and Kyle watching her ass as she went.

Muttering to Kyle about how he "really *didn't* listen to Hawthorne Heights," Arden wandered off in the opposite direction of his sister.

He walked the considerable length of the pool, smelling the clean air commingled with the crisp scent of chlorine, catching tidbits of conversations about yachts and Learjets, movie deals and press releases, stocks and cryptocurrency.

He came upon one of the girls bearing a bowl of pills. Before he knew what he was doing, he grabbed a handful of them and pushed them into his mouth. The feeling of them on his tongue, crammed against the insides of his cheeks, had an immediate calming effect. It was not unlike the feeling of his hand inside Rebecca's. But...where *was* Rebecca? What exactly had transpired between her and Luke?

And whom had Ianthe carted her off to meet? Some other guy, someone more suited for her?

He swallowed the pills. The girl grinned at him. He grinned back.

"You can't fuck my pussy," the witch said to him. She began stripping off her black lace blouse. "You'll have to fuck my asshole."

Arden blinked. He tried to remember how he'd gotten here.

He was in a dimly lit bedroom with a four-poster bed and a bearskin rug on the floor near the dark fireplace. The bear's black eyes needled into him. He had only the vaguest recollection of the past however many hours, going from bikini girl to bikini girl, drinking and snorting and swallowing whatever they offered.

He faintly remembered smoking opium with a trio of middle school girls in the billiards room before moving on to smoke hash with a grizzled old hippie who looked like his Uncle Brad. He'd taken Ecstasy in a gargantuan bathroom with someone who might have been Elijah Wood, or possibly Haley Joel Osment—Arden's vision was too blurry by that point to be certain.

At some point, he thought he'd run into Baxter and snorted angel dust with him, but it may have been some other blond surfer. He kept thinking he saw a pale man with black eyes and a ghoulish grin lurking in the shadows, watching him. The Berkeley bear mascot always seemed to be on the edge of his peripheral vision. And then he'd somehow ended up alone in a room with this girl, the witch— she'd introduced herself as that—who'd insisted on reading his fortune in tea leaves.

After she'd stared at the scattered leaves before her for what felt like a long time, she'd said, "I can't figure it out. Do you want to fuck?"

Arden had looked at her shimmering figure and decided she was attractive in a gothic way. She was probably the type of girl who listened to a lot of My Chemical Romance and Bring Me the Horizon. He *would* have fucked her, under different circumstances, but instead he'd told her he was "sort of with someone."

"Where is she now?" the witch had asked, and Arden had told her that she was probably fucking the host.

"Well, that sounds like a pretty good reason to fuck *me*," the witch had said. And that, Arden supposed, was how he'd gotten here.

"Did you hear what I said?" the witch asked. She stepped out of her frilly black skirt and pulled off her fishnet stockings.

"Yeah," Arden said. "Fuck your asshole. Not your pussy." His eyes moved up and down the naked girl before him, his vision swimming. He couldn't tell if she was sixteen or thirty-five. "Why is that, exactly?"

"I'm saving myself for someone."

"For...Jesus?"

The witch snorted. "Fuck, dude, *no*. Aleister Crowley. When I turn twenty-one, I'm going to perform a suicide ritual and meet him in the Valley of Death. There, we shall enact a sacred coupling, and my eternal spirit will give birth to a spawn who will crawl into the earthly realm and bring an end to the reign of man."

"Wow," Arden said. "That's...heavy."

"Indeed," said the witch. She came to him, undressing him with black-tipped fingers.

Arden felt a surge of guilt as he thought of Rebecca. This was somewhat assuaged when he told himself she was doing the same thing with either Luke or the mystery man to whom Ianthe had wanted to introduce her. It was obliterated completely when a fresh wave of euphoria from the many intoxicants coursing through his bloodstream hit his brain. He allowed himself to be pulled onto the bed.

The witch began by sucking his cock. She did this, Arden realized with dismay, with far more ardor and expertise than Rebecca did.

Within thirty seconds he was pushing her away, gasping. He told her he didn't want to come yet. She grinned at him, wiped her lips with her thumb and forefinger. She turned and positioned herself on her hands and knees, spitting on her fingers and massaging the saliva over the puckered ring of her anus, dipping them inside. He moved behind her and tried to remember if he'd ever done this. No, he decided, drawing in a breath as he worked his cock into her asshole, he didn't think he had. He put his hands on her narrow waist as she pushed against him. She whimpered, increasing her tempo. Her ass cheeks slapped against Arden's thighs.

"Tell me when you're gonna come," she whined, panting. No sooner than she said it—it was the pleading in her voice, the soft desperation—he was telling her, "Now, now, now." She un-impaled herself from him and drew him once again into her mouth. Her hands clutched his ass. Arden took hold of her head and pulled it closer, forcing himself deeper into her mouth. She gagged, and he came into her throat. Some of it spurted out her nose. She giggled as she wiped her face on a throw pillow, smearing it with snotty semen and the runny mascara from beneath her watering eyes.

Lying next to her afterward, listening to the walls breathe, Arden asked her, "Why couldn't you read my fortune? You said you couldn't figure it out. Why? Does that happen often?"

The witch blinked her damp, smudgy eyes at him. "It's never happened before," she said. "Not with anyone I've read. But with you, there wasn't anything there. There was just...it was nothing. It was so much *nothing*."

"What does that mean? That I'm going to die?"

She giggled and tapped the tip of his nose with her index finger. "This may sting a bit, but we're all going to die."

"Right, yeah. But, I mean...does it mean I'm going to die *soon*?"

"I don't know. Probably not, but that's not something I specialize in. Hey, do you want to do some shrooms?"

Arden stared up at the rippling ceiling. Its surface roiled like waves. "No," he told her. "I don't do hallucinogens anymore. I had a really bad weekend in college."

He didn't tell her it was already too late by then.

The witch got up and put on her clothes. "I hope things work out with your ladyfriend," she said. "Maybe we'll meet again on another spectral plane." She left, shutting the door behind her. Arden was left alone with the sounds of his organs twisting within him, of his blood swirling in his veins. He shut his eyes. The sleep into which he fell offered little reprieve.

His phone said it was 7:06 AM when he woke. He had three missed calls from Rebecca, one from Tess, and one from a number he didn't recognize. Rebecca had texted twice—*where are you?* and, much later, *have a good time?*

He stood, groaning. His head was filled with wet sand. He had to fight a near-crippling nausea as he struggled into his clothes. The flat surfaces in the room had stopped moving, but he couldn't shake the uneasy sense they might come alive at any moment and ensnare him in a smothering embrace.

The house had gone quiet. He passed a lot of young maids in bikinis cleaning up the wreckage of the night prior, sweeping hallways and scrubbing tabletops and mopping floors. They didn't look at him. He felt like a ghost.

The chilled morning breeze bit Arden's skin when he let himself out of the house and began the long walk down the driveway. He ordered a Lyft as he neared the gate. The same bikini girl who'd let him and Rebecca in the previous day was sitting inside a small hut at the end of the driveway. Her bare feet were kicked up and she was reading *Barely on Fire*. Seeing him approach, she shut the book and got up, pulling open the gate for him.

"Do you ever leave?" Arden asked her. "Do any of you ever leave?" She smiled at him, blinking, like she didn't understand the question. She shut the gate behind him. Arden sat on the curb, smoking, waiting.

TWENTY-EIGHT
TOIL AND TROUBLE

RYLAND WAS on his way home from work, sitting in a traffic jam on Olympic, when his phone rang.

The Caller ID that showed up on his dashboard Bluetooth display read "RESTRICTED." Thinking it might be work related—medical offices would use restricted numbers—he thumbed the button on his steering wheel bearing the green phone icon and said, "Ryland Richter."

"Mr. Richter." A woman's voice, urgent but tinged with traces of exhaustion. "Thank you for taking my call. I apologize for the restricted number." A pause, some rustling in the background. "My name is Dr. April Diver."

Ryland rolled his eyes. He lit a cigarette and cracked his window. Doctors sometimes managed to get a hold of his personal number for the purpose of making an impassioned plea on behalf of their patients, peddling some sob story that was supposed to convince him to reverse the decision on a denied claim. It never worked.

"I'm a psychiatrist," April went on. "I'm calling in regard to a former patient of mine." She spoke carefully, tempering her words. "This is...strictly off the record. I'm not under any professional obligation to contact you. It is, in fact, of *questionable* professionalism that I'm doing so." Ryland heard the snap of a lighter, a drawn breath. "This patient, her name is Gwendolyn Tanner. It's come to my attention she's relocated to California, and that you may be...involved with her."

"I don't know any—"

"It is quite likely she's using an alias," April said. "I could describe her to you, but I suspect that isn't necessary. I suspect you know exactly whom I'm talking about."

Ryland swallowed. A car horn sounded behind him, and he realized traffic was starting to inch forward. He let off the brake, feeling lightheaded as the car began to move. "I'm...I don't understand," he said. "How do you know this? How do you know I'm involved with anyone? What *exactly* do you know?"

More rustling, followed by an exhalation. "That's not important," she said. "What you need to—"

"It's *extremely* important. You can't call me, saying these things, and expect me not to want some specific answers."

"Listen to me. The first and most important thing you need to understand is that roughly half of what she says is a lie. She can be honest and deceitful in the same breath. As such—and I cannot stress this enough—*you cannot believe a single word she says to you.* She'll counterbalance one truth with a fabrication, often in the same sentence. What's fascinating is that she's able to keep track of it all. She never gets confused or forgets what she's told someone. It's like she has a logbook in her head."

"I've had enough of this. I don't want—"

"Mr. Richter, please. What I'm getting to here is that Gwendolyn is dangerous. To herself, and to others. It is crucial that you sever contact immediately and inform me of her whereab—"

Ryland hung up, breathing heavily.

His cigarette had gone out. He tossed it out the window and reached for the pack to retrieve another, only to find it empty. Cursing under his breath, he pulled into an Arco station. The restricted phone number tried calling him twice while he stood in line inside. He sent both calls straight to voicemail. April left a message both times, but he deleted them as he walked out of the gas station, using his teeth to tear the cellophane from the pack of Marlboros.

He stopped several yards short of his car. A homeless woman was standing near the driver door, staring into the window. She was sunburnt and overweight, her age indeterminate, wearing tattered basketball shorts and an oversized "I <3 LA" T-shirt. She looked at Ryland and pressed two fingers to her ear.

"This is Channel 6 Action News live...on the *scene*," she said. Her voice was clear but much too loud. She spoke with the syncopated cadence of a newscaster. "As you can see here, Kurt, the *fires*...are raging out of control *all around me*...and we've got a *two-car collision* in the middle...of the *roadway. Emergency responders*...have *just* arrived, but there appears to be *at least*...two *fatalities.* The *first car* is *on fire*, and the *driver*...seems to have *fled* the *scene* of the crash, leaving behind a *woman*...in the *burning wreckage.* The *driver* of the *second car* was *ejected*...from his *vehicle.* We're going to cut to a *shot* of the *vehicles.* What you're about to *see*...is *graphic.* Viewer *discretion*...is *advised.*"

Ryland took a step forward and made shooing gestures with his hands. "Get out of here," he said. "Seriously, fuck off."

"This is Channel 6 Action News live...on the *scene.* As you can see here, Kurt, the *fires*...are raging—"

"I said fuck off," Ryland barked, raising his voice. He grabbed a squeegee from the compartment beneath the garbage can beside the pump and flicked it in her direction, spraying her with water. She flinched but did not retreat. He took another step closer and jabbed her with the squeegee. "Get the fuck out of here," he said. "I just want to go home."

"—*all around me*...and we've got a *two-car collision* in—"

"*FUCK OFF*," Ryland shouted. He hurled the squeegee at her, harder than he'd intended. She shrieked and scurried backward before turning and fleeing.

Ryland looked around. Several people were watching. One was recording with his cell phone. Ryland gave him the finger before getting into his car and peeling out of the gas station. As he drove away, he glanced in his rearview mirror and saw the homeless woman standing on the sidewalk, pointing at him.

TWENTY-NINE
BEAUTIFUL RUIN

FRIDAY NIGHT, Dan Tana's. Tess pushed her food around her plate. She drank her champagne too fast and kept refilling her glass.

She'd been observing The Writer all evening with more scrutiny than was customary. The way he moved, as if gliding. How he always held himself as though there were a camera pointed at him. His easy smiles, his lilted speech. The eyes hidden behind the sunglasses. The way the light danced upon his gaudy clothes and accessories. That constant *flourish* present in everything he did, said. Affectations, she realized. All of it. Affectations.

"I think I've finally figured you out," she said to him after another long swallow of Dom Perignon. She glared across the table at the dual images of herself reflected in the lenses of his sunglasses.

The Writer took a languid sip of his own champagne. Tess couldn't tell if he was looking at her, or at someone behind her. "You've figured me out," he said. The voice so cool, so at ease. No inflection but poised as a question all the same.

"Yes. I have."

The Writer leaned back. The faintest hint of amusement was

present beneath the surface of his features. "Why do I feel like you're about to pick a fight."

"I'm not." She forced a smile. It felt ghastly, probably looked it. "I've just made some observations and, you know. I've drawn some conclusions."

"*Fasc*inating," he said. He held up his hand, fingers splayed, examining the nails. His mouth twitched in a flicker of admiration. "Please, do en*light*en me."

Tess drew in a slow breath. "Well, I—"

The waitress appeared, asking if they wanted more champagne. Chandler's lips twisted into a lion's grin. He started to respond, but Tess interrupted and snapped, "*No*. We're fine." The waitress flinched and backed away, as if Tess were a rattlesnake, fangs bared and tail flicking.

The Writer regarded Tess with a raised eyebrow, the wry amusement more perceptible.

"You aren't real," Tess said. "Nothing about you is real. You're totally made up. Like a...like a fictional character of your own making."

The Writer stared at her. His face was impassive, impenetrable. He glanced at his watch. "*I* think," he said, "you've had a touch too much to drink."

"*No*. No, I haven't." She had, and she knew it—they both did—but she wasn't anywhere near wasted. A little drunk, yes, but not drunk enough to be written off. She suspected they both knew that, too. Her eyes were focused, her voice clear.

"Your whole personality," she continued, "it's something you created. You have this larger-than-life fantasy of... of what you think you're supposed to be. I think you cribbed pieces—*big* pieces—from *other* fictional characters. Gatsby, for one. A bit of Don Draper from *Mad Men*. And the guy in *Citizen Kane*. A few others, probably. I don't know. And the rest of it...the rest of it is just random things you want to embody. Pieces of an image you want to project."

The Writer raised an eyebrow but didn't say anything.

"I think you probably created this character when you were very young," Tess said. "You never talk about your childhood, and I think that's because you're ashamed. I think you were a normal, nerdy kid who read a lot of books and didn't have a lot of friends. You were bullied, I'm sure. Your inner monologue was probably a chorus of 'One day, I'll show them.' Reduced to your basic elements, you'd have been...what? Fifty percent rage, fifty percent aspiration? Give or take a few percentage points on either side."

"I think that's an oversimplification."

Tess ignored him. "You bided your time through high school, through college. You became a teacher so you could sleep with the kinds of girls who'd never given you the time of day when you were a teenager. So you could flunk the douchey jocks who couldn't formulate an opinion about Shakespeare. And then your first book took off, and you reinvented yourself. Sort of. Because what you made yourself into, that character had always been there, right? Waiting. Waiting for you to have the right amount of money and status to swap him with the old you. And now you've been wearing his skin for so long that you've forgotten it isn't *real*. It's imaginary. You've convinced yourself you're so *unique*, so *original*, but it's all *fake*. *You are fake*." She collapsed against the back of her chair. Her fists were clenched in her lap.

Chandler steepled his fingers. If Tess's tirade had pierced him in any way, it wasn't evident. "No one is original, Tess," he said. "If that's how you choose to define authenticity, well..." He trailed off. "Everyone's personality is an amalgamation of things they've taken from someone else."

"But you *didn't* take it from someone else. You *created* it."

"If that's true, then isn't that the *definition* of originality?"

"No. Because with other people, it happens more...I don't know, it's more *natural*. People are a product of their environment, yeah, and there are...outside influences, sure, but it's *organic*."

"I think you're confusing originality and authenticity," The

Writer said. "You're using them synonymously. They're not the same thing."

"You're not denying anything I've said."

"I guess I'm not seeing where you're going with this."

"Why does it matter?"

The Writer angled his head to the side, smiling. "Yes, precisely. Why *does* it matter? What difference does it make how I became the way I am today? Why is it important to you?"

Tess felt a sudden stinging of tears behind her eyes. She hadn't anticipated them. Frustrated, annoyed, she blinked them back.

"It matters to me because...because if I'm right, then you're just a... a projection reel. There's nothing *true* beneath it all. And if I'm right about *that*...then, well, where do I fit into that?" She flinched at her own words, at how sad they sounded. How weak, how pathetic. Still, she pressed on. "Why would you want to...to marry me if you're nothing more than a robot dressed up to look like something human?"

Chandler looked at his lap. Smiled, looked back up. "Ah," he said. "And so we arrive at the heart of the matter. Don't you suppose you could have led with that?"

Tess said nothing. She hated the flush she felt rising to her face.

"Again," said The Writer, "I must ask why it matters. What does any of this have to do with my inclination to marry you?"

"You're a robot," Tess reiterated. "And robots can't love."

The look The Writer gave her made her feel very young. Stupid. Small. "Tess," he said, his voice angled downward like he was chiding a child. "Come on. Love? Are we really going to talk about love?"

"It's usually something people talk about when they talk about marriage." Her voice was defeated. She'd lost, somehow. She realized she had no idea what victory would have looked like, or if it had even been something attainable here. She only knew she'd not achieved it.

"Okay," The Writer said. "Fine. Tell me, then...do *you* love *me*? If this is the road you want to take, let's take it. Tell me if you love me."

Too quickly, Tess said, "I don't know. I don't know if I love you."

"No, you *do* know. You don't *want* to know, but you do. Let me make it easy for you. The answer is no, Tess. You don't love me. Do you know *why* you don't love me? Of course you don't, so I'll tell you. Love—in the romantic sense, at least, that fairy tale happily-ever-after kind of love you read about in novels and see in movies—*that's* what isn't *real*. To people like me, it's a plot device. It sells books. To other people it's something they chase until they've convinced themselves they've found it, and then one of two things happens. One—the attraction dies, the novelty wears off, they become resistant to one another's pheromones, and the fun goes out of the whole ordeal. So, they break up and start chasing that elusive chemical reaction again. The cycle repeats, ad infinitum. Or, two—they learn to tolerate each other because they wind up in a position where they can't get anything better, and they're terrified of being alone."

The tears had escaped Tess's eyes when she hadn't been paying attention. She didn't wipe them away. It would be a useless gesture. "I don't believe that," she said.

"Yes, you do. Deep down, you do. You just don't want to."

"You're wrong. And...and if you're not, then why should I marry you? If love isn't real, what's the point?"

When Chandler replied, his voice was low, soft, benevolent. "The point is, Tess, I'm the best option you have."

Tess shut her eyes. Pursed her lips, took a long breath through her nostrils. She stood, excusing herself to the restroom, where she used wet paper towels to scrub the black tracks of tears from her face before fixing her makeup. She returned to the table feeling hollow, disembodied.

The Writer had already paid the bill. At Tess's approach, he took a final swallow of champagne and then rose, offering her his arm. She looked at it for a moment, as if she might refuse it. An absurd notion. The illusion of choice. She took the arm, and they left.

Outside, waiting for the valet, a girl walked toward them on the sidewalk. Tess paid her no attention until she stopped several yards away. "Chandler Eastridge," the girl said with a quaver in her voice.

Chandler and Tess both turned to look at her. She wasn't young —maybe late twenties or early thirties. Pale, overweight. She had gnarled, overlapping teeth that jutted forward like those of a piranha. Coke-bottle glasses, greasy brown hair like a swarm of cockroaches. Simple, un-branded clothes off a rack at Walmart, maybe even Goodwill.

"Yes? How can I help you?" The Writer said. The smile came out, his eyebrows arching over the lenses of his sunglasses. His tone was PR-pleasant, but Tess could detect the trace of annoyance seething beneath it. He wanted all his fans to be attractive little sexpots. Girls like this one detracted from the fantasy.

"My name is Delia Johnston," the girl said, her voice still tremulous. She spoke with a slight lisp, likely caused by her jumble of teeth. "All these years...I've been trying to get your attention for all these years, and now I...I just run into you on the street. Part of me always knew it would happen, I guess. I just can't believe it."

Chandler lit a cigarette. Cars trundled by in the trawl of late-evening traffic on Santa Monica. They swept hot air over the curb. "You've been trying to get my attention," The Writer repeated. Thick coils of smoke unspooled from his nostrils before being swept away into the night.

"For years," the girl affirmed. "Twitter, Instagram, Facebook—I comment on *all* your posts, I send you messages, I retweet and repost *everything*. And still, nothing. Not a word from you. Not a single word. And then I go to *all* your book signings, and I bring you samples of my writing, and always you tell me you're going to read them, you'll get back to me. But, again, *nothing*. I'm literally the *greatest* unsung writer of my generation. Nobody pays any attention to me and it's only because I'm not conventionally pretty."

She turned to Tess, sneering, and said, "And then there are girls like *you*. You make me *sick*. You're God's favorites. Everything gets handed to you, and you're too privileged and entitled to appreciate any of it. Of *course* the great Chandler Eastridge would choose someone like you, with your legs and your tits and your face. Your little cocktail dress that shows it all off, that I'm sure *he* bought for you. What do you bring to the table besides a body that's fun for a man to fuck? Do you have *anything* going on in that pretty little head of yours?"

"Easy," The Writer said. "Leave her out of this." He moved Tess behind him, as if the girl posed some sort of threat. It was, Tess thought, a nice gesture, and for a half of a second, she appreciated it as a possible display of his affection for her, but then she realized it was just another element of his chivalrous façade.

"Do you have anything to *say* for yourself?" the girl asked. The exasperation in her voice teetered over a hysterical edge.

Chandler hit his cigarette, looking around, probably wondering where the valet was. Tess was wondering the same thing. "Honey," he said, the condescension prickly and poisonous. "I'm not even *on* social media."

"But...you are, though. You—"

"Do you actually think *I'm* behind those accounts? Is that really what you think? That I sit there on fucking *Twitter* and dick around with hashtags? Honestly. You look a little old for that kind of naivete."

The Writer had people who ran his social media accounts. Interns at the publishing house, or something. Tess had always assumed this was common knowledge.

"That's..." The girl fumbled with what to say next. "Well, what about my manuscripts? I've given you *six* of them."

The Writer looked around again for the valet. He glanced at his watch. Tess kind of admired how pointed he could make his boredom. The way he wielded it like a cudgel. "Honey," he said again, "you don't want to know what I thought of your manuscripts."

The girl recoiled. She took a step back as if pushed. "You *read* them?"

"Of course I read them. I read every manuscript a fan brings to me. Not always all the way through, but I at least look at them."

"And? Tell me what you thought. You have to tell me." Her eyes shone.

"No, I don't. You wouldn't want me to, believe me."

"I do, though. I have to know. Please." She retook the step she'd relinquished.

The Writer brought his cigarette to his lips. He pulled from it while he studied the girl from behind his dark glasses. "You don't have it. There's nothing there. Maybe try pottery."

Tess didn't think she'd ever seen such despair in a person's face before. Maybe in textbook photographs of people in concentration camps during the Holocaust.

The valet showed up right as the girl's dreams died. He offered The Writer a thickly accented apology for the wait. Chandler handed him a twenty and told him not to worry about it. The valet opened the doors for the two of them and then disappeared again.

Chandler pulled away from the curb without so much as a glance in the rearview mirror at the girl they'd left standing there, weeping and alone.

"Why did you do that?" Tess asked.

"Do what," The Writer said. He rolled his window down and flicked ash from the dying remnants of his cigarette.

"Tell that girl you read her stuff," Tess said. "You told me you never read any of the manuscripts your fans bring you. That you have your publicist throw them out."

"I do have her throw them out. No, I don't read them. But that's not the point. I don't have to read them. I certainly don't have to read *hers* to know it's trash. Good writing finds an audience. If she's remained unpublished for this long, it's for a reason."

"You destroyed her," Tess said. She was ashamed of the admiration in her voice. And yet...she couldn't deny she *had* admired the deftness with which he'd broken her. *Maybe try pottery.* Such a casual display of power. Efficient, remorseless. She crossed her legs over the damp heat blooming between them.

"If she was destroyed by what I said, then that's what she needed. A real writer wouldn't be fazed by that. If she takes it to heart, I've saved her a lot of time and energy. One big heartbreak in place of a million smaller ones. What I did to her was a kindness."

As they drove into the hills, it occurred to Tess that her shameful arousal was accompanied by an equally shameful relief. There was consolation, she realized, in the knowledge she wasn't, nor would she ever be, in Delia Johnston's position. Labeling Tess "God's favorite" seemed unfair and untrue, but she couldn't deny the comfort in being the one in the Halston cocktail dress. She had The Writer's attention. She was going home with him. She couldn't be broken by something so trivial as a question of talent. For the first time that night—in *many* nights—she felt as though she'd won something, after all.

In the foyer at The Writer's estate, she moved on him with preda-tory insistence. With the door still open and the keys hanging in the lock, Tess pushed against him. She raked her fingers up the back of his neck and through his hair, pulling on his lower lip with her teeth, sliding her groin over his.

He was surprised but responsive. He whirled her around with a strength and grace which brought pleasant dizziness to her head. She flattened her palms against the cool wall. Spread apart her stiletto-heeled feet. The Writer's hands clasped her breasts, moved down over her hips. The hem of her short dress went up, bunching around her waist; her panties went down, slung between her thighs. Sounds—breathy gasps, the unfastening of the buttons on his pants, the rustle of the leather sliding against his legs...the torn foil of a Magnum wrapper, the crinkling of latex. He entered her, and with him came the image of the girl crying on the sidewalk. Her crumpled face, the desolation swimming in her cartoonish eyes. Just some random girl, some nobody with no prospects and no future—ruined in the blink of an eye.

Toxic ecstasy blossomed in Tess's core. It spread outward to her extremities like a parasitic fungus, tingling in her fingertips and toes. She bucked against The Writer, crying out, and it was almost enough. She disengaged herself from him and turned, pushing him to the floor. Situating herself on top of him, she guided him back inside her. Her ensuing movements were frantic, desperate. The Writer's hands slid over her thighs, winding up her torso, pulling down the top of her dress and taking hold of her sweat-dappled breasts, the nipples stiff against his smooth palms.

Tess shut her eyes, and there was the girl again—sobbing, destroyed. Reduced to nothing. A shuddering sack of lumpy flesh in bargain-basement clothes. Such beautiful ruin, poetic only in her plainness. Tess came, her voice hoarse in her throat as she rode atop The Writer, her hair flying, her hands clutching his lapels as if she might jettison into the air. Chandler—his sunglasses askew, his face grimacing and his back arching, his grip on her breasts tightening to a clench—let out a long moan, and it was over.

They lay gasping together on the floor for a long time before Chandler said, "What was that about?"

"Not you," Tess said.

THIRTY
THE LANKY FELLOWS

AT DINNER one night at La Boheme, Lyssi was returning to the table from her traditional post-meal trip to the restroom. Ryland was on his phone, responding to an email from his boss. There was an odd contempt in Lyssi's eyes when Ryland looked up after returning the phone to his pocket. "What's wrong?" he said.

"Oh, nothing. I guess I just don't get the work obsession. That's all. Can't you go *one* evening without checking your stupid fucking email?"

Ryland winced. "Lyssi," he said, sensing she was edging into one of her volatile moods. "My job is important to me. You know this. This isn't anything new."

"Oh, no, you're absolutely right. It's *not* anything new. I *do* know this about you. But you know what I *don't* know? I don't know what *else* is important to you. I don't know if there even *is* anything else. All you care about is your job, and the money you get from your job, and the fancy things you buy to show off at your job. So, tell me, *please*, because I'm *dying* to know. What else do you care about, Ryland?"

"I care about you."

Normally, something like this would elicit a smile, a batting of her eyelashes. Now, all she did was glower at him. "I'm fucking serious."

"So am I."

"No, listen. Like, tonight, when I was telling you about Chandler Eastridge's new book, your eyes kept glazing over. I could tell you were thinking about work the whole time. You just didn't care because you don't care about anything but work. It makes you so fucking *boring*, honestly."

Slumping forward, already exhausted from what he could see this was going to turn into, Ryland put his elbow on the table and rubbed his eyes with his thumb and forefinger. He ignored a nagging pain in his left arm. "Lyssi, why are you doing this. Look, I'm sorry I wasn't more enthusiastic about the book. But, I mean, come on. You know I'm not much of a reader. Books don't interest me the way they interest you."

"You're not much of an *anything*. *Nothing* interests you. You don't get into movies, or TV shows. You don't even listen to *music*. You drive around in silence like some kind of fucking *psychopath*. Who *does* that? Who doesn't listen to music?"

Ryland leaned back and downed the rest of his scotch. He wished there were more, but now didn't feel like the appropriate time to signal for the waiter.

"Why does this bother you so much? You've never had a problem with it before. And you've never had a problem with the money I make to buy you the things you want."

Lyssi rolled her eyes. "Oh, so now it's about me."

"No, that's not what I'm—"

"What are they going to say about you when you're dead? Have you ever thought about that? 'He was good at his job,' probably. That's what they'll put on your gravestone."

"I don't care what people say when I'm dead. They can put whatever they want on my gravestone."

"See, that's so *boring*. *You're* so boring. Everything *about* you is boring."

"If I'm so boring, why do you spend time with me?" He lowered his voice. "Why do you fuck me, then? Why are you here in the first place?"

Lyssi stood. She slung her Louis Vuitton purse over her shoulder. A purse Ryland had bought her. "You know what," she said, "that's a great fucking question. I'm fucking leaving. I'll get a Lyft home. Don't come after me."

He didn't. He watched her strut out, and then he ordered another scotch. When that was gone, he went into the bathroom and did some coke off the edge of the sink. He ordered yet another drink when he got back to the table. By the time the amber elixir hit his tongue, his head was humming. He almost felt okay.

At home, he'd nearly fallen asleep when he heard a knock at his door. Lyssi threw herself upon him as soon as he opened it. She kissed him and ran her hands over him, apologizing through her tears.

The sex was brief but intense. She bucked and gyrated atop him, her head thrown back, her hands clutching her breasts. Near the end, when she sensed his climax approaching, she whined, "Am I gonna make you come, baby?" Ryland nodded, gritting his teeth, and she dismounted him. "Come on my face, baby. Please. Come all over my face. I know how much you like that." Ryland got up on his knees, groaning. Lyssi knelt before him. Her small hand pumped up and down his cock as she angled it toward her. His ejaculation was profuse. She fingered globs off her cheeks and forehead into her mouth. She sucked it from locks of her hair.

After lying together in spent silence for a long time, Ryland said, "Why do you do it, Lyss?"

"Why do I do what?" she asked. She traced her pointed finger-nails up and down his chest. "Let you come on my face?"

"No. Jesus. Why do you pick fights with me?"

She didn't answer for a while. When she did, her response made Ryland go cold. "Because they tell me to," she said.

"Who? Who tells you to?" He felt himself receding from his voice, falling backward.

"The lanky fellows."

"The...the *what*?"

"The lanky fellows," she repeated. "They're these things that follow me around. They tell me to do things. I don't always listen to them. But, you know. Sometimes they're convincing."

Ryland sat up. "These...these 'lanky fellows,'" he said, shivering a little. He looked down into her eyes. "Are they here now?"

"Oh, yeah, totally." She sat up, and she looked toward the corner of the darkened bedroom. She smiled. She waved. "They're always with me. Wherever I go." Her voice was too calm, too casual.

"What do they...look like?"

"Well, they're *lanky*, for one. I mean, obviously. That's why I call them that." She giggled. "Really tall and super skinny, except they don't *have* skin because they're made of shadows. They like to stay in the darkness. And they have these great, big wings. Like bats." She giggled again. "I mean, *of course* I know they're not *real*. I'm not a *complete* loon. It's just that, you know...sometimes I sort of forget. Sometimes they *seem* so real, and I forget that they're imaginary. That's usually when they can convince me to say things. Do things."

Ryland thought of the call from that psychiatrist. April Something. "Lyssi," he said, "do the...the lanky fellows...do they ever tell you to hurt people? I mean, like...*physically* hurt people?"

"Sure, I mean...yeah, sometimes."

"And do you ever...listen?"

She grinned, kissed his nose. "Only if they deserve it."

THIRTY-ONE
DIGITAL BEAUTY

BAXTER WASN'T sure why he accepted the invitation to the party at his friend's mansion in Sherman Oaks, but he figured it had been the right decision when he saw Tess standing alone on the veranda.

She was dressed in a short, strapless yellow sundress which fluttered around her body as she looked out over the lights sparkling across the dark valley. She wasn't a Porn Girl, but she was close.

Baxter approached her, and she turned. She held a wine glass in her hand. It was nearly empty. He could see by the faraway look in her eyes she'd had several, and he took a long swig of his beer as though he needed to catch up.

"Baxter," she said, sounding bored. "Hey."

"Uh, hey. I didn't expect to see you here."

"I needed to get out." She averted her eyes as if she were ashamed of something beneath this statement.

"Out of where?"

"Nowhere. Just out."

"Oh. Uh. Right on." Baxter scratched the side of his neck. He offered Tess a cigarette. She took it, and he lit it for her.

"Have you talked to Arden recently?" Tess asked.

"I mean, a little, yeah. I've seen him a couple times since he's been back."

"Does he seem different to you?"

Baxter thought about it. "Um. I guess, sort of. He's more... distant? I don't know. Like, he was always kinda spacy, right? But now he's, like, pretty zonked."

"I'm a little worried about him."

Baxter coughed a nervous laugh. "Oh, I wouldn't be. I think he's just been stoned. Or something."

"Yeah. Or something."

An uneasy silence passed between them. Baxter fidgeted, and then said, "You're very beautiful." He cleared his throat. "I always thought so. Like, in a way that doesn't seem real. Sort of, like...digital."

Her smile eased some of the disquiet from her features. Some. Not all of it. "I don't know what that means exactly," she said. "But I guess it sounds nice."

She exhaled smoke. The edge of the wine glass touched her mouth. Its remaining contents vanished. The flash which appeared in her eyes and passed over her face wasn't pleasant. It existed somewhere between mirthful sickness and shameful bliss. Baxter had seen something like it before, with Celeste Ludovica. It wasn't as developed in Tess, didn't have the same necrotic cloud, but it was there. In its infancy. Growing.

He thought of the MechaHooker, alone and waiting for him at the house. Waiting to serve him. Her sole purpose. No baggage, no complications. Only a need to please.

Tess set the empty glass on the low stone wall at the edge of the veranda. "Do you know anyone here?" she asked.

"A few people." He looked over his shoulder at the house. Silhouetted bodies danced to the thump of the music on the other side of the glass wall. Technicolored strobe lights washed over them. "Not too many. I don't know why I came."

"Yeah. I don't know anyone here. My friend who invited me

didn't end up coming."

"That's, um. That's a bummer."

"Yeah."

Baxter hated this. The words so stilted and sterile, so uncomfortable. The conversational equivalent of a trip to the dentist.

This was how his interactions usually went with real women. There was no way around the glaring, unspoken truth—that the small talk was a pretense for sex. As soon as he approached them, he knew that he was a dangling cock to either be stoked or snubbed. The implication simmered beneath the surface of every lame sentence. Threatening to bubble over. Tess knew this. They all knew it. It was a game Baxter couldn't imagine anyone enjoying, but everyone played it.

He thought again of the MechaHooker. Her ignorance of the whole sick charade. Her intentions were always clear.

"Is it true you're dating that author guy?" Baxter asked.

"We're not dating. We're just...we're hanging out."

"Oh, cool. Well, listen, um." Baxter set his half-empty beer next to Tess's barren glass. The moonlight shone on the faint lipstick smudge along its rim. "Do you want to dance?" He dropped the cigarette and crushed it out with the toe of his shoe. He wasn't sure why he was doing this. He had the MechaHooker. He didn't need Real Girls anymore.

Tess appraised him. Her glassy eyes looked so lost, so forlorn. Her shoulder, bare and tan and freckled by the sun, lifted in a lazy shrug. "Sure," she said. "Why not."

Her hand felt small and warm in his as he led her inside.

The music was too loud. The swollen thrum of the bass reverberated with such oppression you could hardly locate the beat. It didn't matter. Tess situated herself in front of him, reaching up to put her arms around his neck and moving her pelvis against his groin in some vague semblance of rhythm. Her hands moved down his back, up over his arms. She fitted one of his legs between hers and clenched it with her thighs. Baxter kept his hands low on her shifting hips.

It felt good, having her pressed snugly into him, the side of her head flat against his chest. Her hair smelled like lavender and cigarettes. Even amid the mass of moving bodies in the dark, the air thick with hot, drunken breath and evaporating sweat, there was a comfort offered by the soft warmth of her body.

A solace that felt like home. That felt safe.

The music increased in tempo. Tess turned, bending slightly at the waist. She gyrated her hips, pushing into him. Baxter felt the stirrings of his arousal and knew she did, too. Perspiration broke out on his forehead that had little to do with the muggy heat. He expected her to tear away from him, but she remained. She was goaded by it. Her movements increased in tenacity. The way she stimulated his growing erection with her moving buttocks, allowing the hem of her dress to ride up, could not have been unintentional.

Baxter wondered if this was in violation of his friendship with Arden. Guys weren't supposed to hook up with their friends' sisters. But he didn't think Arden would care. He didn't think Arden cared about much.

There was a lull in the music as one track merged into the next, the pounding bass slowing to a hushed heartbeat. Baxter took advantage of the decreased volume to lean over and say into Tess's ear, "Do you want to get out of here?"

She turned, nodded. Took his hand. He led her through the crowd toward the front of the house. She stopped him at the drinks table by tugging his hand, and she mixed herself a screwdriver in a red plastic cup before taking his hand again and following him to the front door.

Outside, with the din of the music shuttered behind the barrier of the closed front door, a residual ringing fell over Baxter's hearing. He grimaced as they walked across the lawn and past the line of cars parked along Mulholland. Tess thanked him when he opened the

Mustang's door for her. She settled into the leather seat and took big sips of her drink.

At the darkened house, Tess noticed the still silhouette of the MechaHooker sitting at the dining room table. "Who's that?" she asked.

"That's, um...Megan," said Baxter. "She's my, uh...she's my room-mate." He moved Tess toward the staircase, casting a wary glance at the MechaHooker. Her unmoving shadow looked like something out of a horror movie.

"Why is she sitting in the dark like that?"

"She's, um...you know, pagan," said Baxter.

He kissed Tess tentatively in the bedroom. She responded with more fervor than he'd anticipated. Her arms around his neck, her tongue rolling into his mouth, her pelvis pushing into his. Baxter felt his arousal returning and prayed to something unformulated that he wouldn't lose it.

"You're nervous," Tess said, guiding him to the bed. She pulled off her dress. Baxter let himself look at her for only a moment. Only long enough to take in the image of her in her black lace bra and panties in the darkness, and then he lay back and closed his eyes lest they begin scanning for imperfections that could ruin everything.

"I don't normally do this kind of thing," he said as Tess's hands began moving over him, peeling off his clothes.

"I really don't either," she said. "But. I guess that's what we're all supposed to say. So, you know. You can believe it, or not."

"I believe it," Baxter whispered. He was naked now. His eyes remained squeezed shut. He felt the warmth of her body on top of him. Felt his erection pressed against her thighs.

"We're having fun," Tess said. Her liquor-hot breath was in his face. "It's just fun. There's nothing else to do, anyway."

"Your brother, I don't know if he—"

"Shh," she whispered, putting her finger to his lips. "There's nothing to do but enjoy ourselves." Her voice was like the whisper of wind amid a light rain. Her nails grazing his skin sent pleasant shivers through his taut nerves. The sound and feel of her was a honeyed comfort. Hot chamomile tea on a cold, gray day.

Baxter opened his eyes only after Tess's soft hand had guided him inside her. They both gasped. She smiled down at him, moving slowly.

"You...you told me as I was beautiful," she whispered. Her hand went to his face. Caressed it, her fingertips brushing a lock of hair from over his eye.

Baxter could only nod, his eyes wide.

"You're...kind of beautiful too, in a way." Tess said. She shut her eyes and let her head fall back while she moved atop him.

As Baxter's own hands moved up Tess's stomach and to her breasts, a queasy guilt began to form in his esophagus. He thought of the MechaHooker sitting alone in the dark downstairs. Oblivious.

It was ridiculous to feel beholden to a robot, but even as the word appeared in his head—ROBOT; the composition of the letters so flat and gray, so mechanical—it didn't seem right. That's not what she was to him. And yet, being with Tess gave him something the MechaHooker could not. There was real warmth. Tenderness. A sense of serenity.

He felt protected. Against what, he didn't know; he knew only that it was out there, somewhere, waiting, and he needed shelter from whatever it was. And Tess, this girl he'd known since they'd been children, gave him that shelter. Was it her, specifically? Or was he putting something onto her, pointing various needs in her direction because she'd been able to provide him with a sustainable erection?

When it was over after two-ish minutes—a personal best for Baxter as of late—they lay together in the warm dark. Sticky, entwined. Breaths slow and content. Tess ran her fingertips over the surface of Baxter's skin. The pleasure was immense. Coupled with the sensation of her heat next to him, her leg draped over his, it was perhaps better than the sex itself. He dared not speak lest he disturb the silence, though he wanted to tell her he felt good and at ease, that for the first time in recent memory he felt he had nothing to fear. He fell asleep to the sound of her humming something low and plaintive, her lips vibrating gently against his ear.

He was alone in the bed when he woke near dawn. A sudden panic overtook him as he grasped at the night's memories, fearing they were false images conjured in a dream. But no. It had been real. The sound of her voice, the heat of her skin—these sensations were too fresh and lucid, too crisply poignant to have been dreamt.

He found her downstairs, passed out on the living room floor. She wore only her panties and socks. Two bottles of red wine stood empty on the coffee table.

"Good morning," Baxter said when she stirred. He smiled. "I had a lot of fun last night."

Tess ignored him, looking around. She scowled when she saw the wine bottles. "I shouldn't be here," she said. "This is terrible. I shouldn't have done any of this." She rose to her feet. "Where's your roommate? I think she was...coming on to me? I don't know."

Baxter glanced around the living room, grateful the Mecha-Hooker was nowhere in sight. "Um, yeah," he said. "She's, you know...kind of forward."

"I shouldn't be here," Tess said again, looking distracted. "If you could get my clothes, please. That would be great." There was an edge to her voice. A cruel, biting annoyance, like she couldn't be bothered with him.

"Yeah, um...yeah. Sure." Baxter scratched the back of his head. "I can drive you home if you want."

"No, no, I don't want that. I'll get a Lyft."

"Are you sure? I really don't—"

"My clothes. Please."

Baxter winced. As he retreated from her to the foyer and went up the staircase, she called after him to make sure he got her purse, as well. He brought the items down to her and averted his eyes as she got dressed. Once she was clothed, Tess sat on the edge of the couch, her shoulders hunched around her neck, and took her phone out of her purse to summon a Lyft.

"Um, listen," said Baxter. Tess's eyes flicked up from the phone screen. A dark fire blazed within them, sad and angry. Lost. Defeated. Baxter looked away. He fixed his gaze on the patch of carpet where she'd lain. "If you're worried about what Arden will—"

"No. Jesus. This has nothing to do with Arden. I told you, this was all a mistake. I shouldn't be here."

"Uh, well, you know. It's just...I had, like...I had a really nice time. With you. And I thought—"

"Oh, did you? Did you have a nice time? That's great, I'm so happy for you. Fuck *off*." She shook her head, grunting in disgust. "You know what, I can wait outside. It's no big deal." She rose off the couch and pushed past him. Baxter stood in place, not moving, his mouth hanging open. He listened to the front door open and close. His hand went to his cheek, as if she'd slapped him.

The MechaHooker entered the living room from the dark hallway. She looked at Baxter, blinking.

"I don't know what I was expecting," Baxter said to her. "I don't know what I thought would happen. Or, like, what I wanted to happen. But it wasn't that." He sat on the floor.

"Fill me up with your hot love juice," said the MechaHooker.

"Not now," said Baxter.

THIRTY-TWO
BAD INVESTMENTS

KNOWING Lyssi was at a release party in Long Beach for Kyle's new single—"Cum Gutters," the thing was called—Ryland busied himself working with Katrina on staffing models for a proposed department expansion.

It was after ten when they finished, and Katrina suggested a nightcap at The Edith. Ryland flashed on his first night there with Lyssi. He felt a sting of melancholic longing for how promising the romance had seemed at the time.

He nearly turned Katrina down—he wanted only to go home and lull himself into a stuporous slumber with Valium and gin. But there was a loneliness which compounded with the longing to produce an unpleasant, almost fearful malaise that made solitude unappealing. His guilty attraction to Katrina, as well—with the shape of her legs beneath the suit skirt, the contours of her torso in the tightly fitted blazer, the scent of her Chanel No. 5—led him to accept her invitation.

She smiled—professional, demure, but it ignited a warmth within her hazel eyes glimmering behind the glasses she wore. It made Ryland dizzy. He vowed not to sleep with her as they walked to his car, no matter how distraught he was over the mounting tragedy of his affair with Lyssi .

What he wanted was comfort. A sense of safety. Lyssi was no longer providing that, what with her lanky fellows and her frequent outbursts. There was something pacifying about Katrina. He wanted to cling to it. To burrow beneath it. Use it as respite, a harbor against Lyssi's storm.

But he would not sleep with her.

At the lounge, sipping highballs at a table Ryland was sure was the exact one at which he and Lyssi had sat, Katrina appeared looser, younger. He felt a sick kinship with her when he noticed the relief that passed across her face when she first brought the drink to her lips.

"You don't seem to like spending time at home," Ryland said.

"I could say the same thing about you."

"I don't have a family." Ryland realized how this may have sounded, so he added, "I'm sorry, that wasn't meant as judgment. It's just...work is all I have. The, um...the pathology of that isn't lost on me."

"It's not so pathological." She traced her finger around the rim of her glass, her eyes lowered. "I've never been much of a homebody. When I was younger, I was—don't laugh—I was an aspiring actress. I tried to make that work for a long time. Everything I did was in service of that. Even my kids...they're adopted because I didn't want to wreck my body, to lose years of my life carrying babies around like a goddamn marsupial. It was my husband who wanted them. I never did." She sipped her drink, still not meeting Ryland's eyes.

"The youngest one, he's—she's Jared's pet project. Jared is mainly retired now—he used to direct films, if you want to call them that. But when he walked away from the industry, he got bored. And he lamented not being around much for Arden and Tess—they were both mainly raised by nannies. He wanted the *father experience*, I guess. By this point I'd given up on acting and had gone back to school, gotten a degree. I was working at Blue Cross. So, we adopted *Daffodil*—" she rolled her eyes "—and she keeps Jared busy and entertained. I was hardly involved with the process."

"I didn't, um...I didn't realize it was like that."

"It's not as pitiable as it sounds, really. Everyone gets what they want with this arrangement. Jared gets his second chance at being a dad, and I get to escape the banality of domestic life for a well-paying career that will probably put me in an early grave." Her smile was wan but not without humor.

Her eyes moved to his, gleaming in the warm, dim light of the lounge. "And Arden and Tess, they don't know any different. They do their own thing. I think they're better for it, really. More...you know, *adjusted*. It's funny, Arden's friend called me recently and asked if Arden had turned out how I'd hoped. I didn't know what to say. I never had any specific hopes for my kids. I never believed in heli-copter parenting. They have to make their own mistakes. For that reason—among others, so many others—Daffodil is kind of fucked. Jared has latched onto her like a parasite. It can't be healthy for either of them."

"You're probably right about all of that," Ryland said. "Neither of my parents played a very active role in my upbringing, and I turned out fine." Even as he said this, he felt doubtful. *Am I fine?* he wondered. *Is* fine *the word I would use?*

"Exactly. *You* get it. Jared hassles me about 'not being present' for Daffodil. Really, though, I think I'm doing her a favor. Any amount of distance I maintain will contribute favorably to hi—to *her* development in the long run. Probably not enough to offset whatever damage my husband is doing, but." She took a drink. "Lis-ten, I'm sorry. I'm talking endlessly about myself and my boring family."

"Nothing about you is boring. Not to me."

Ryland cringed as soon as he said it. It was the kind of throw-away line he used on the girls with whom he usually went out, the teenagers and twentysomethings with bigger breasts than brains. The words hung in the air between them, hollow and deflated.

Attempting to recover, he said, "My life has revolved around my job for so long that there isn't anything else. It's interesting to hear about people who have other things going on."

"Is that by design? Do you *like* having a life that revolves around work, or do you *want* something else?"

"It's...all I know. I'm thirty-two, and I've been with the same company for fourteen years. Other people my age—people with *other things going on*—they gawk at me when I tell them that. They go from job to job. They'll work somewhere for a year or two, and then they'll get bored and go work somewhere else doing something completely different. For me, the most stable relationship I've ever had—probably *will* ever have—is with this company."

"There's something admirable in that. It's old-fashioned. Still, I suppose there's something kind of gloomy about it, too. But you'll get to retire early, so there's that."

Ryland emitted a short laugh that sounded like a cough. "Oh, no. I'm not going to retire. I don't even have a 401k."

"Why on *earth* wouldn't you have a 401k? The company matches dollar for dollar up to five percent. You could be sitting on a mountain of gold by the time you hit retirement age. Well before that, even."

Sipping his drink, Ryland said, "I know, I know. I keep hearing that same refrain. I just don't see myself ever getting to that point. The idea of retirement is so far off, so...hypothetical. I'd be putting money away for a future I'm not confident is going to come."

"Why wouldn't it? You're healthy, right? Why wouldn't there be a future for you?"

"Sure, I'm healthy enough, I guess." The image of his brother's casket getting lowered into the damp ground appeared in his mind. Her heard his sister-in-law telling him to "take it easy, enjoy life," that "mortality creeps up on you." He chased her away with a stiff swallow of liquor.

"I'm healthy," he said again, with some defiance, "but something could happen. The world being the way it is, I'm always amazed so many of us can move from one day to the next over and over again without getting killed by something. I mean, Christ, look at the way people drive in this town. And on that note, it's not only *my* future that's questionable—it's *everyone's*. Society is decaying. It's collapsing under its own weight. You know what I'm talking about. I can see it in your eyes. Can you imagine what the world—or America, for that matter—will look like in thirty years? Twenty, even? Ten? I know I can't. Preparing for retirement would be investing in a future I don't believe in. I try not to make bad investments."

"Well. I had no idea you were so cynical."

"I don't think I am. I think I'm practical, at least in respect to my own expectations."

"I guess that's fair, but you don't need to look at it as an investment. It's basically just a savings account."

"I don't save all that much. You'd probably be surprised by how little I keep in my savings at any point in time. I look at money as something to be spent. Money is like coke. You don't *save* coke. It doesn't do you any good just sitting there. There's no fun in that. I want to enjoy the fruits of my labor. I have to turn it into tangible assets." He unclasped his Omega Speedmaster Moonwatch from his wrist and held it in his hand. The soft light danced along its silver surface.

"I paid eleven thousand dollars for this watch," he said. "Whenever I check the time, I'm reminded of how far I've come. I was making twelve dollars an hour as a data entry clerk when I started with this company. I wore a Timex I bought at the drugstore. I think it cost me something like eight bucks." He gazed at the watch with affection before refastening it around his wrist. "I look at this watch, and I know I'm worth something."

His eyes lifted to meet Katrina's. "Putting money away for a future I'm not confident will ever come to pass—that wouldn't give me the same feeling. It wouldn't come close."

Katrina looked surprised by his candor. Ryland was surprised, himself. These were things he admitted to no one. He had enough wherewithal to know how most people responded to the sentiments he was expressing. *Greed*, they called it. *Privilege*, they called it. The latter incensed him. He saw no privilege in himself. He saw hard work which was rewarded.

"I don't normally talk about this kind of thing," Ryland went on, looking away. "I know how it comes across. Guys like me, we're expected to flagellate ourselves. We're not supposed to celebrate our accomplishments—we're supposed to atone for them. And, typically, that's the façade I'll put on. 'I've been very lucky' might as well be my catchphrase. 'Life has been good to me'—that's another one. But I *haven't* been lucky. Life *hasn't* been good to me. Life kicks the shit out of me the same way it does everyone else. The only difference with me is that I've worked my ass off, and I don't feel guilty about reaping the harvest from the seeds I've sown."

"You shouldn't," Katrina said. "The way people stigmatize success now—it isn't right. People shouldn't try and make you feel guilty for hard work."

"It's all part of the decline of western civilization," Ryland said. "This used to be the greatest country in the world, and we've become a nation of pissant pussies." He was on a roll. He was echoing things he'd heard from his fellow executives, but in the moment it felt right. It felt true. "But having a sentiment like that is considered *problematic.* We aren't allowed to be content until we've dismantled everything that made America a world power. We have to burn it all down, and then we'll be expected to dance on the ashes."

Katrina smiled. Bashful, like a schoolgirl. She dropped her eyes, took a small sip of her drink.

"What?" Ryland asked.

Katrina shook her head, still smiling. "I was just thinking," she said, "that you're nothing at all like my husband."

"Well." Ryland cleared his throat. "I should hope not."

Katrina shifted her gaze back up, meeting Ryland's. Something electric passed between them. A white, charged heat that spun and sparked above the table. The air nearly crackled. When Katrina spoke, her voice was a sultry murmur. "You live close by, don't you?"

There wasn't exactly a conscious decision made on Ryland's part. He went through the motions. The bill was paid, the remnants of their drinks chugged. His hand on the small of her back as they left. Resting on her thigh as they drove to his condo. He didn't give any of it much thought. It was instinctive. Like he was typing a long Excel formula he didn't need to focus on, his fingertips moving mindlessly over the keys.

He felt like someone else when he kissed her in the dark bedroom. His body was alien, far away. The clothes fell from him of their own volition. His hands on Katrina's naked skin belonged to an unseen, unknown entity. He was aware of the pleasure when he was inside her, but it was indistinct. Purely biological. Existing on the surface of his body but failing to penetrate any deeper.

He looked into her face as they moved together in the bed, but it was featureless, the visage of a storefront mannequin behind a smudged pane of glass. He knew she was making noises, but he couldn't hear them. The feeling of her strong legs around his waist barely registered.

The numbness shattered when he came, but it was by pain. He felt like he was ejaculating battery acid. He cried out, something Katrina mistook for ecstasy, and she clung to him. She pulled him deeper into her, raking her nails over his back.

She said something when they fell away from each other, and Ryland answered, but he didn't know what was said. They were both speaking in a foreign dialect. At last she turned and nestled into him and drifted to sleep. Ryland lay there for a long time, staring up at the ceiling. He attempted to locate the reason for the black, viscous sadness seeping in from the edges of his perception. He eventually got up and went to the bathroom to do a couple lines of coke, which slowed the advance of the dark slime but didn't stop it.

He took a Percocet for good measure and pulled on sweatpants before walking outside to the pool. He sat looking at the lighted water, smoking cigarettes and thinking, for some reason, of a winter morning in Pennsylvania, when he'd lain in a warm bed with Penny and stared out her window at the new snow that had fallen overnight, sparkling like crystalline gold in the cold sun.

THIRTY-THREE

THROUGH ANOTHER LENS

TESS FOUND herself with nothing to do on a Sunday afternoon, so she wound up at a graduation party for her friend Megg.

She was still feeling queasy about her tryst with Baxter Kent. The memories of that night were hazy and perforated with alcohol-induced amnesia, but she couldn't write it off as a drunken mistake. She knew she'd only gotten wasted after the sex, and that she'd been almost sober when she agreed to go home with him. What disturbed her was she didn't know why, or what she'd been looking for.

The party was at Megg's family's vacation house in Lake Holly-wood Estates. When Tess arrived, Megg told her, "We had to close off the downstairs bathroom. The last Airbnb guest clogged the toilet and, like, *I've* never unclogged a toilet in my life, you know? And my mom's assistant is sick so *none* of us knew what to do. We were like, can we DoorDash a plumber? But it turns out you can't, so we had to seal it off. All the upstairs bathrooms are fine, though."

Tess murmured words of acknowledgment as she followed Megg into the living room. People stood around sipping from cans of White Claw and bottles of Pacifica, dancing to a remix of Bonnie McKee's "I Want It All." Tess went to the drinks table and poured some Grey

Goose into a red plastic cup. She eyed a jug of orange juice before forgoing it, taking the drink outside and lighting a cigarette.

Attractive young people lounged in the pool, floating on inflatable rafts. Others stood talking beneath the canvas awning stretched over the back door, their voices lost in the din of the music, their sunglasses on and their faces blank.

Tess walked around the length of the pool to the edge of the backyard. The cement dropped off into a steep incline dotted with sagebrush that led down to the Hollywood Reservoir some seventy or so feet beneath her. She sipped her drink and smoked her cigarette. The breeze played at her hair. A row of mansions on the other side of the ravine shone hot and white in the stark sunlight.

A voice saying her name caused her to tense up. She turned. The girl standing a few feet away looked familiar, but Tess couldn't put a name to the face. She was pretty enough, with long red hair and glasses, and a subtle bloom of freckles dappled across her nose and cheeks. She wore a cheap pink bikini.

"Jasmine Yates," the girl said, sensing Tess's failure to recognize her. "We went to high school together?" She said this as if it had been ages ago.

"Right, of course." Tess supposed she might have had a few classes with Jasmine, but her awareness of her had been tangential at best. Jasmine and her younger brother—Connor or Connell, or something—were part of the poor kids crew. Tess and her friends hardly regarded those of their ilk as real people, much less deigned to associate with them. She was surprised to see Jasmine here.

"How have you been?" Jasmine asked. "Since graduation, I mean." She looked nervous. A slight blush had risen to her neck and face.

Tess hit her cigarette. Shrugged. "You know," she said. "Just kind of existing. Trying to figure out what I want to do with my life."

"Oh, I'm sure you'll do something extraordinary." Jasmine's gray eyes shone behind her glasses. "I always knew you'd turn out to, you know, *be* somebody." She looked at the water, blushing some more.

"I mean, I *worshipped* you all through school. I guess it was sort of a crush. You've always been so beautiful. So majestic. I wanted to *be* you."

"That makes one of us," Tess muttered, gulping down a big swig of her vodka. "Um. What have you...been doing?"

"Working, mostly. I have a job at the Petco in Hollywood? It's not great but, you know. And I do some babysitting on the side, which I really love. All the kids are wonderful."

Tess made a conscious effort not to scowl. Adjusting her sunglasses, she said, "That's...super." She cleared her throat. "Are you going to college in the fall?"

Jasmine's eyes flicked to Tess's face before falling away. "No," she said with quiet guilt. "My mom can't afford it. I could get student loans, or whatever, but I don't want all that debt. Plus, my mom has some health problems, so I need to be around for her, you know?"

"Right, sure," Tess said. "That's...good of you." She inclined her head and studied Jasmine over the lenses of her sunglasses. The lines of her neck, the soft angles of her face. The slender white calves. Even in her obvious anxiety, she had an easy, relaxed posture, a comfortable fluidity that embodied peace and calm. The rare times her eyes met Tess's, they reminded her of lazy Saturday afternoons in bed while gentle rain pattered outside.

Tess thought again of Baxter. Something became clear to her. A nameless desire with an empty stomach and probing tendrils.

"So," said Tess, realigning her focus, "you had a crush on me?"

They wound up in one of the spare bedrooms on the second floor. Kissing lazily, pulling at each other's clothes. "Temperature" by Sean Paul was playing downstairs. The sound of the beat penetrated the closed door. Tess kept her sunglasses on while Jasmine went down on her.

"I'm sorry," Jasmine kept saying, nervous and giggling. "I've never done this before. I don't really know what I'm doing."

"Shh," Tess told her. "Just do what you'd want done to you. There you go. Like that. Just like that."

They spent twenty or so minutes doing various things to one another in the bed. Jasmine came twice. Tess didn't come at all. She felt detached. Not in sync with her own body. Jasmine was drenched in perspiration by the end of it. Tess's skin was dry save for the sweat which had rubbed from Jasmine's body onto hers.

They lay together for a while afterward. Neither of them said anything. Tess kept thinking about the tragic hopelessness of Jasmine's life. No money, no prospects. A sick mother. A babysitting gig, a job at fucking Petco.

I don't want to end up like her, Tess kept thinking. *I can't.*

And she wouldn't, she knew that—not to Jasmine's extent, at least. Jasmine was an extreme case.

Nevertheless, Tess's future was limited. The idea of striking out on her own, doing something without aid...it was absurd. She didn't even know how to check the oil in her car, or how insurance or taxes worked.

I'm the best option you have, The Writer had told her. It sickened her to think he could be right. There had to be something more. Her whole life in the hands of a male benefactor. It was an affront to women everywhere.

She glanced at Jasmine. Jasmine could only hope to land herself in a similar situation. Tess wondered if Jasmine would have the same reservations. Likely not—she'd probably swoon at the idea of being swept off by some ultra-rich Prince Charming, but it was impossible to know for certain. Tess couldn't begin to fathom how poor people looked at life.

She did not want to find out.

As Tess got out of bed and began to get dressed, Jasmine sat up and said, "Can I get your number? We should do this again sometime."

Tess flinched. She thought of the hopeful pleading in Baxter's eyes and saw it now in Jasmine's. "Um. I don't think that's such a good idea. I mean, this was, like, fun. You know? I had fun. It's just not something I do all the time."

Blushing and lowering her eyes, Jasmine said, "It's not some- thing I *ever* do. So, like, we don't *have* to do it again. But we could, you know, hang out?"

Tess gave her a smile she hoped wasn't too cold. "Take care of yourself," she said, and left the bedroom, re-closing the door behind her. She pushed past people in the hallway and made her way down the stairs, letting out a relieved breath once she was out the front door and walking to her car. She put on a Calliope Laing playlist and idly skipped through the tracks every thirty seconds or so, soundless tears running black tracks down her face the whole way home.

THIRTY-FOUR
THE LOST WEEK

AFTER HIS RUN-IN with the witch at the party, Arden embarked on what he supposed could have been called a *bender*. He hadn't set out to do so and he didn't look at it as such until he'd come out of it. He felt these caveats were important, but he understood both of them probably applied to most benders.

It started when he realized he wouldn't be able to face Rebecca. The last text she'd sent him—*have a good time?*—was a glowing blight on his screen whenever he had the inclination to text her. He thought about deleting it, but it wouldn't have done any good. Those four little words. They held all the disappointment she knew she didn't need to express. Arden could almost see her sad eyes staring up at him whenever he looked at his phone.

He somehow ended up at 4100 Bar in Silver Lake the afternoon after the party, by then already spinning out on too much coke after having gone a little overboard when the Lyft had dropped him off at home.

He sat in a booth outside, nursing a martini and chewing Xanax that had little effect. A long procession of soldiers in red uniforms marched along the sidewalk, led by the Berkeley bear mascot in its scarlet-smeared jersey. Arden paid them no attention. His eyes kept moving to a billboard on Sunset advertising a new antidepressant called Invigora. *Feel something again*, it proclaimed in blue letters beneath a blonde woman frozen in a moment of laughter.

Things got progressively hazier. He didn't regain his sense of time and place until much later, when he was in the middle of having sex with an unfamiliar blonde girl. She kept asking him why he was crying.

At a party in his neighborhood thrown by someone who called himself Oregano, and with whom Arden had apparently gone to high school, he had sex with Oregano's fifty-something mother while her husband was downstairs doing body shots off teenage girls. In bed, Oregano's mother kept transforming into various farm animals—a horse, a cow, a pig, a barn owl. Arden was dismayed this didn't cause him to lose his erection.

There were many instances like those over the course of that lost, liquor-soaked week. Strange girls in strange beds, everything foggy, the edges of various flat surfaces bleeding into empty space like clouds of paint in water. People were always asking him what was wrong, why he looked like that. He stopped taking his sunglasses off no matter the time of day or where he was.

Prowling Pasadena one night toward the end of the binge, he caught a glimpse of himself in the black mirror of a vintage store window. Pale, haggard, somewhat hunched. Almost shockingly thin. His hair hanging over one eye. The skin stretched tight over his face like a Halloween mask. The cigarette burning between his spindly fingers looked enormous. His clothes hung from him like drapery.

When, he wondered, had he become so gaunt? He'd always been thin, but never like this. He watched as the ghoul in the window lifted the cigarette to its lips. Sucked on it like it contained sustenance. *That's not me*, he thought. *Whatever it is, it isn't me.*

He woke relatively clearheaded for the first time in days on Sunday afternoon, though he had no recollection of the past twenty-four hours. He was lying on the couch in his parents' pool house. The walls gasped the breaths of dying things.

Rubbing his temples, he sat up and lit a cigarette. He checked for texts or calls from Rebecca. There were none. Unwelcome images surged into his brain—Rebecca getting railed from behind by Luke Viceroy, Rebecca sitting astride the mangled shape of Quincey in his pathetic wheelchair, Rebecca gagging on some faceless pop star's cock. He suppressed a wave of nausea.

The door opened, and Tess came in. "Oh," she said, taking her sunglasses off and regarding Arden with bored pity.

"What?" Arden said. His voice was thick.

"I'm, uh, going to this thing Megg is having. A pool party, I guess. I was going to see if you wanted to come, but. Yeah. You don't look like you're in any shape to go anywhere."

"Yeah, well." Arden took a deep drag from the cigarette. He struggled not to choke on the smoke.

"Where have you been? You went AWOL at that party last weekend, and I haven't seen you since."

"Are you my keeper now, or something? Is this something Dad put you up to?"

Tess didn't appear to be fazed by his hostility. "No," she said. "No, it's just...you don't look good, Arden." She paused. Her eyes searched for something in his face. Whatever it was, they didn't find it. "Are you...you know, like, okay?"

"Yeah." He dropped his eyes. He couldn't look at her. "Yeah. I'm fine."

"Well, you know. If you ever want to, like....*talk*. About....I don't know, whatever. I just hope that you know you can. You can talk to me."

"What, because all of a sudden we're the type of siblings who talk about shit?" He glanced at her, saw the flicker of hurt in her face. Looking away again, he watched the ripples moving through the fabric of the carpet, like winds sweeping across desert sands.

"No, I guess we aren't," Tess said with dreamy sadness. "Anyway. I'll see you later."

"Yeah."

Tess left and closed the door behind her. Arden put the cigarette out and leaned back on the couch. He picked up the TV remote and pressed the power button. A rerun of *The Hills* was on. He turned the sound off and let the images moving across the screen lull him to sleep.

THIRTY-FIVE
ASHES, ASHES

MONDAY MORNING BROUGHT with it a sense of something wrong. Ryland moved about the quiet stillness of his condo, getting ready and trying not to prod at the unfamiliar knot of anxiety worrying itself in the pit of his stomach.

Lyssi. She was the cause of it. He hadn't heard from her all weekend. His texts went undelivered. He woke up to a notification on Saturday that she'd "stopped sharing her location with him."

This, he reasoned, was justification for a small amount of worry, but not the gnawing dread. It bordered on panic. A harried restlessness which refused to be soothed, even with three Xanax and two shots of Belvedere.

He was running behind. He'd normally be at the office by now. Time passed out of synchronization with the clock as he moved from room to room, unfocused, displaced. Three times he made it out the door but had to turn back when he'd realized he'd forgotten something—tie, belt, wallet. He kept checking his phone. Nothing.

She's gone, a voice kept whispering. It wasn't his voice, but it was close. *You've lost her. What have you done?*

"Nothing," he muttered, locking his door on the way out and

patting his pockets to make sure he had everything. "I didn't do anything."

His brother appeared at the end of the hall. The skin on his ample flesh had begun to rot. "Nothing? Come on, little bro. How about that tall glass of MILF you brought home Friday night? Was that nothing?" He laughed. It was a fetid sound, putrid with soggy decay.

"It was," Ryland said. "It *was* nothing. And she couldn't know. How could she know?"

"Take it from me, Ry-Ry. Bitches *always* know. Don't ask me how. Never figured it out myself. It's like they're all connected." He tapped his temple. His finger left a smeared indentation. "Some kind of fuckin' cerebral network, man. They're all linked up. Like the fuckin' Matrix."

"You're insane."

That laugh again. If maggots could laugh, that was how they'd sound. "Right, yeah. You're talking to your dead brother, but sure, man, *I'm* the crazy one."

Ryland pushed past him.

Time slipped away from him again in the parking garage. He stood blinking at his Mercedes, refusing to see it. Untold minutes slid by him. He'd shut his eyes and hold them closed, telling himself it would be different when he opened them, but it was worse.

Remember, don't ever betray me. If you betray me, I'll kill you. But first I'll make you wish you were dead.

Bruno materialized beside him. He shook his head, his gray lips turned down. "Man, that's a shame. Bitches, man. Fuckin' *bitches*. I blame that cunt Carrie Underwood. That goddamn song. You remember my Escalade? Christy did a real number on it the first time she caught me cheating. *This*, though..." He shook his head, let out a puff of befouled breath. "*This* is something else." He looked around. "You got cameras in this joint?"

"No," Ryland said, barely hearing himself. He moved in a slow circle around the car, unable to believe it. Both the headlights and taillights were smashed. The bumper had somehow been torn off and lay amid shards of shattered glass on the concrete. Puckered dents covered the car's entire body.

Both the front and rear windshields were intact, but all four of the windows were blown out. Inside, the seatbelts had been cut and lay coiled in the passenger seat like sleeping snakes. Deep gashes had been slashed in the leather upholstery. And everywhere—across the hood, along all the doors, etched into the roof and the fenders and the trunk—she'd carved "Lyssi" hundreds of times in neat, cursive letters, dotting each *i* with a little heart.

"How do you suppose she did that?" Bruno asked, bending to inspect one of the occurrences of her name. "Not a key. Must have been an X-Acto knife, or something. You almost have to admire the craftsmanship." He stood, placing his yellow-nailed hands on his broad hips. "She left your tires alone, though. More than I can say for Christy. She slashed three of 'em. Knew insurance wouldn't cover it that way."

"She wanted it to be drivable," Ryland muttered. "She wants people to see. She wants people to know what I did." He ran his hands through his hair. "I just...I don't get it. How could she have known?"

"I'm telling you, man. The fuckin' Matrix."

"And she has a *boyfriend*. She goes home to him *every night*. What I did wasn't betrayal."

"Careful, there, boy-o. You're applying logic to a situation with a woman. They're not logical creatures, remember. They're made up of emotion and irrationality. From a sensibility perspective, they aren't all that bright. They have smaller brains. That's just science."

Ryland lit a cigarette, his hands and mouth performing the comfortable, familiar motions independent of his brain. He turned away from the car, unable to look at it any longer.

Don't ever betray me.

He hadn't. He *hadn't*.

Walking out of the parking garage in a daze, he took his phone out of his pocket to hail a Lyft to the office and noticed he had four missed calls from his boss. The list of PATRICK STANLEYs on his call log glared at him like accusations.

"She wouldn't," he said aloud, staring at his phone. "No way."

"You sure about that?" Bruno asked. "You've got a beat-to-shit Maybach back there that begs to differ. You're obviously not dealing with a normal bitch. But you know that, don't you? You always knew that. Was her pussy that good? Was she *really* worth it? Are you chill with losing your livelihood over some loony slag?"

"I'm not going to lose my livelihood," Ryland said. He wished his voice had more conviction. "I'm almost an hour late. I'm sure Pat was just calling to see where I'm at."

He looked beside him, hoping to see something reassuring in his dead brother's face, but Bruno was gone.

When he got to the office, he knew it was over as soon as the elevator doors opened on his floor. Margot, the receptionist, looked up from her computer and her face contorted into a grotesque mask of disgust. Ryland lowered his eyes and walked by her, moving past the rows of cubicles. Everyone who saw him gave him that same look.

Lyssi, goddammit, what the fuck did you do.

He shut himself in his office and collapsed, trembling, into his desk chair. With frantic hands he unlocked his top drawer and took out his bottle of Valium. He popped two of them into his mouth and chewed them down. The bitter taste of the tablets was a small comfort.

Within minutes of turning on his computer, an IM popped up from PATRICK STANLEY – VICE PRESIDENT. The sternly professional profile photo appeared now to signify hateful contempt.

Please meet me in Florence's office, the message said.

Florence Nixon, vice president of HR. A hateful woman who bore more than a passing resemblance to a toad in stature, countenance, and comportment. If she was involved, it truly was the end.

To bolster himself, he did two quick bumps before logging out of his computer for what he knew would be the last time. He expected to feel something profound, but there was only a stupefied numbness, like he'd been slapped.

Lyssi, Lyssi, Lyssi. What did you do.

Pat and two other VPs were already waiting for him in Florence's office, sitting in chairs against the wall. Their faces were inscrutable. Florence sat behind her desk, drumming her stubby fingers on a closed manila folder in front of her.

"Shut the door, have a seat," she told Ryland as he entered the office. He closed the door behind him and moved to the chair before her desk, sinking into it. He felt like he had left his body and was hovering near the ceiling, watching the scene unfold below.

"You shouldn't have come in," Pat said. "I tried calling you."

"I'm sorry," said Ryland. There was nothing else he could say.

Florence opened the folder, scowling at its contents. "You know why you're here, I presume?" she asked.

Ryland didn't answer.

"Elysium Rhodes," Florence said, and from her greasy lips Lyssi's name sounded like something ugly, something profane. "The pages I have before me are screenshots of text exchanges you allegedly had with her."

For a moment, Ryland was confused. They couldn't have obtained his phone records. It was impossible. But, of course, they hadn't. Ryland knew what Florence was going to say before the words left her mouth.

"Lyssi emailed these to everyone in the company." She slid the folder across the desk. Ryland stared at it for a few long seconds before picking up the pages.

I need to be inside you.

I can't wait to come all over your perfect tits.

I'm gonna fuck your tight little pussy till you scream my name.

I wish your mouth were on my cock right now.

I want to lick coke off your cunt.

All things he had indeed texted her. She'd changed his contact name from "Ry <3" to "Ryland Richter," followed by his phone number. Her responses pictured in the screenshots were fabricated. The images had been doctored.

Plz stop texting me

i'm begging u just leave me alone

ur disgusting. I don't want anything to do with u

GO AWAY

He could probably prove the pictures had been altered. And if it ever went to court, he was certain he could get a lawyer to obtain Lyssi's real responses, which had been enthusiastic and libidinous. It didn't matter. It wouldn't go to court. Lyssi knew that. She knew what she'd been doing.

"Apparently she sent them to several news outlets, as well," Pat said, shutting his eyes and pushing his fingers into his temples. "The press has been hounding us all morning."

I'll make you wish you were dead. I'll take everything from you.

"You'll be suspended pending an official investigation," Florence said. "We'll need to—"

"Ryland," Pat interrupted. "Tell me it's bullshit. Be straight with me. Tell me this girl is a lunatic and you didn't text her this stuff."

Ryland kept staring at the words on the pages. There were many things he could say in response to Pat. "Oh, she's definitely a lunatic," he could tell him. He could tell him about her lanky fellows, her whispered threats, her violent mood swings.

"It's not what you think," was also something he could say, explaining that the affair had been consensual, the messages reciprocated.

He could say all these things, but there was nothing he could say to absolve himself of incrimination. They'd find the drugs and liquor in his desk, too. They'd find them before anything else, and since such an infraction was a terminable offense in and of itself, they might not bother to go forward with the investigation.

Given the apparent scope of Lyssi's corporate carpet bombing, the board would demand swift and resolute action. Even if the circumstances were different, even if Lyssi *had* been nothing more than a deranged lunatic and Ryland had never touched her, never texted her, it wouldn't matter. They couldn't keep in him a high-profile position; not after something like this. He'd be quietly moved behind the scenes, possibly given a token consulting job until they could find a way to eliminate the position.

But, of course, the circumstances *weren't* different. He *had* touched her, *had* texted her. In a way, she *was* a deranged lunatic, but she was so much more than that, too. And thus, it didn't matter. Nothing mattered. It was over.

Florence picked up the handset on her desk and pressed a button on its cradle. "He's ready," she said before hanging the phone up. To Ryland, she said, "Security will have to escort you out. A formality. You understand."

Ryland's head dipped in a capitulatory nod. "Can I get a few things from my office?" he asked, thinking he might at least remove the contraband from his desk.

"You know that's against protocol."

Pat rolled his eyes. "Come on, Florence. Let the man at least get his stuff before you make him walk the plank."

Florence didn't look at Pat. "There are policies," she said. She glowered at Ryland. "They must be followed. Any personal items will be FedExed to your home address."

She knows, Ryland thought. He could see it in the mischievous twinkle in her eye, the way her lips quivered, resisting the urge to pull into a smug smirk. It didn't matter now if he got his things. He had drugs at home.

The office door opened, and two security guards entered. Ryland looked at them, unable to recognize their faces. He saw security guards around the building but never paid them any mind. They could have been anybody. He could have passed these same two men in the halls every day for the last several years, and he'd have no idea. He didn't regard them as real people, and here they were. His executioners.

"I'll call you," Pat said as Ryland got to his feet. When Florence shot the VP a disapproving look, Pat amended, "I mean, ah, we'll be in touch."

Ryland kept his head down and his gaze lowered as he was walked out. He felt eyes on him. Everyone's eyes, everyone looking.

"Come on, man, at least go out with your head held high," Bruno said from behind him. "Throw those shoulders back. Don't let the bastards get you down, and all that happy horse shit."

"It doesn't matter," Ryland muttered.

"What was that?" the security guard to his left barked.

"Nothing," Ryland said. "It was nothing."

Not yet wanting to return to his condo, where the reality of the situation would somehow feel heavier, Ryland walked in the hot sun for a time, sweating and smoking cigarettes, ignoring the constant vibrating of his cell phone in his pocket. He eventually stopped in front of a nondescript bar he didn't recognize.

The white plastic placard hanging inside the door was turned to "OPEN." He went inside, squinting against the spots dotting his vision as the bar's dark interior enveloped him. The bartender was the only other person there, a spooky guy with alabaster skin and black eyes who looked familiar in a way Ryland couldn't put his finger on. He was reading a Chandler Eastridge paperback. Placebo's cover of "Running Up That Hill" played low over the sound system.

Ryland stalked over to the bartender and ordered a Johnnie Walker, which he gulped down as soon as the glass was in his hand. He started to order another before pausing and then saying, "Actually, just...just give me the whole bottle." The bartender grinned at him in a way that made Ryland shiver. He handed him the bottle when Ryland slid his AmEx card over the counter. "Don't bother me," Ryland said. "Please. Just read your book and I'll leave you alone."

The bartender kept grinning at him, and Ryland carried the bottle and his tumbler to a booth in the back.

Glancing at his phone, he saw he had a number of missed calls, text messages, and voicemails. Most were from Pat and Katrina. A few of the calls were from numbers he didn't recognize, and one was from Penny. Penny had left a voicemail, as well. Ryland pondered this as he sipped his scotch. He hadn't heard from Penny since his ill-fated visit to her apartment.

His thumb hovered over the "play" button on the voicemail screen, but he elected to delete it without listening to it. He'd call her back, he told himself. Then he deleted the rest of the voicemails from Pat, Katrina, and the unknown numbers, and finally did the same to the text messages. A small but noticeable weight lifted for the time being. He knew it was there, floating above him, and that it would soon descend upon his shoulders once again, but for now he could drink in peace.

Not without reluctance, he gave some thought to his current state of affairs. He had enough money in the bank to survive somewhat comfortably for six months or so. Longer if he liquidated some stocks, and longer still if he were able to cut back on his spending.

But he knew himself; the sudden excess of free time—something he'd never had before—stretched before him like a red, gaping maw. The only way across it would be with a proportional increase in drug and alcohol consumption. He'd have to fire his housekeeper and cancel all his memberships in an attempt to offset the inevitable spike in his expenses. He tried to remember the last time he'd cleaned or done laundry. He wasn't even sure he owned a dustpan.

Finding new employment would be tricky. Recruiters constantly sent him messages via LinkedIn, but those would dry up as soon as word of the accusations spread. Not to mention he hadn't applied or interviewed for a job since he'd been a teenager. Every promotion he'd received had been offered to him; many had been all but forced upon him. He had some friendly contacts at several other insurance companies, but none so friendly that they'd be willing to ignore allegations of gross sexual impropriety. He didn't know where to start. The future had never been something to which he lent much thought. It had never seemed real.

Grimacing, he refilled his glass and knocked half of it back, rubbing a throbbing twinge in his left arm. He decided there was nothing to be done at the moment. The only thing to do was to drink.

He thrashed awake on his couch around eight PM, fully dressed, his head throbbing. He had no recollection of getting home. His most recent memory was of sitting alone in the empty bar, locked in the cycle of draining and refilling his glass.

He found a fresh baggie of coke in his pants pocket, which brightened his spirits somewhat. Pouring some on the glass coffee table, he did a few lines and then went to his bathroom to take a Valium and a couple Vicodin.

All the lights in the condo were off. The air conditioning was on. Standing in the dark hallway, shivering, he felt like he wasn't alone. He went from room to room, switching on lights, each time expecting to see Lyssi standing in a corner, wielding a butcher knife.

I'll kill you; she'd promised him. *But first I'll make you wish you were dead.*

Did he wish he were dead? He was too numb for such dramatic notions.

He'd once been jumped by a group of jocks in high school over some unfortunate business about a girl. They'd beaten him so savagely that for hours afterward there had been no pain at all. It had been as though they'd bludgeoned all the sensation from his body. That's what he felt like now. The pain would come later, but now there was only a hollow, empty deadness accompanied by a faint tingling, as if his whole body had gone to sleep.

The last room he checked was his bedroom. When he turned the lights on, his gaze fell upon the stuffed animals. He scowled at them. They scowled back. Their black eyes taunted him with their aloof knowingness.

He went to the kitchen and came back with a garbage bag. One by one, he deposited the awful creatures into the bag. He tried not to think about the delighted expression Lyssi had worn whenever she presented him with a new one.

When he lifted one of the last of them—a purple rabbit with a wide, freakish grin—he stopped. It was too heavy for something made of stuffing and fabric. Its head lolled backward.

Ryland pressed his fingers to its face and felt something hard beneath the surface. Turning the thing over in his hands, he saw a tiny white zipper sewn along the base of its head. He unzipped it and reached inside, pulling out a tangle of wires and a heavy black box with "SHIFUKU" printed in white, italicized letters across the top. On the front of the box were the rabbit's eyes.

"Not eyes," Bruno's voice said from behind him. Ryland turned. Bruno lounged in the bed, green and decaying, smoking a cigarette. "*Lenses*. They're lenses, Ry-Ry. But you know that. Maybe you'd have known it *sooner* if you weren't so fucked up all the time."

Ryland let the rabbit fall from his hands. Its empty sockets stared up at him from its deflated head. He looked at the black box. The video camera.

He supposed he should feel shock, revulsion, debasement. There was nothing. The damage was done. Knowing how she'd done it didn't make any difference.

"I don't know, man," said Bruno. "*I'd* be a teensy bit pissed off, me. This proves that crazy bitch didn't just suddenly go off the deep end. She was *plotting*. It's like she always knew you were going to fuck up. She was biding her time till she caught you."

"I didn't fuck up," Ryland said. "I didn't do anything wrong."

"Come on, little bro. The whole thing was wrong from the start if you want to get technical with it. That's just facts. No moral judgment, of course. I'm speaking purely from a place of rationality. You always knew that girl was a psycho, and you went and got yourself caught in her trap all the same."

Ryland's phone began to vibrate in his pocket. For once, without thinking, or even glancing at the Caller ID, he moved his thumb across the screen and lifted it to his ear. "Hello," he said, without inflection. His brother had vanished.

"Yes, hi. Is this Ryland Richter?" A woman's voice, lightly accented. Hard, blunt, but infused with a subtle tone of solemnity.

He thought of his boss telling him Lyssi had sent the emails to several news outlets. Clenching his free hand into a fist and gritting his teeth, he said, "Who's asking."

"Yes, of course. Apologies. My name is Dr. Joshi. I'm an ER physician at St. Christopher Charity Hospital in Desert Hot Springs." She paused. Again, she asked, "Am I speaking with Ryland Richter?"

"Uh, yeah. Yeah. This is Ryland."

"Great. Good evening, Mr. Richter. I apologize for the somewhat late call. Now, I—"

"You said you're in Desert Hot Springs?" Ryland began to pace.

"Yes, that's correct."

"What happened to her? Penny. It's about Penny, right? Is she..." He couldn't bring himself to say it. "Did she..." He coughed into his fist. Sat on the edge of the bed.

"I'm afraid there's been an accident. Her landlord informed the authorities that you're the emergency contact listed on her lease."

"An accident," Ryland repeated. The word tasted bitter. It ground against his teeth on its way out. "What kind of accident."

"It appears she fell from her fourth-floor balcony. She's suffered some extensive—"

"She fell," Ryland said. He looked at the floor. Shut his eyes, shook his head. "She didn't fall."

The other line was silent for a moment. "I'm sorry, Mr. Richter, but...beg pardon?"

"She jumped. That's what you're telling me. She jumped."

The doctor cleared her throat. "To my knowledge, the police

haven't officially ruled whether it was accidental or intentional, so."

"Right. Okay."

Clearing her throat again, she said, "Now, ah, in addition to—" Ryland heard papers rustling "—numerous bone fractures, primarily in her legs and spine, she's suffered extensive cranial damage. The surgeons have done what they can to relieve the pressure on her skull, but there's...Mr. Richter, I'm sorry, but there's a chance she may not make it through the night."

Ryland kneaded his throbbing arm, cradling the phone between his ear and shoulder. "What hospital did you say you were with again?"

"St. Christopher Charity Hospital, but Mr. Richter, I would advise—"

"I'm on my way there now."

"Mr. *Richter*, I would advise against that. The hospital is being evacuated in the morning due to the proximity of the fires."

"You said she won't make it to the morning."

"There's a *chance* of that, yes, but Mr. Richter, I can't guarantee you'll even be permitted to see her. Our visiting hours—"

"Fuck your visiting hours," Ryland said, and hung up the phone.

Bruno was standing in the bedroom doorway, sipping a glass of scotch. The whisky seeped from worm-eaten holes in his neck, spilling over the collar of his Hugo Boss shirt. "She tried to call you, little bro," he said. "I know I don't gotta tell you that, but still. She *tried* to *call* you. Sound familiar? People close to you try and call you, and you keep telling yourself you'll call them back, but you never do. And then? And then they die. Kind of a toxic trait of yours. You should maybe answer your phone more often."

"She's not dead," Ryland said.

"Good as, from the sounds of it. And now you're gonna...what? Drive your beat-to-shit car through the towering inferno to go read her last rites to her? You sure picked an inconvenient time to start giving a shit."

"I always gave a shit," Ryland said, and pushed past his brother.

THIRTY-SIX
BREAKING DOWN

BAXTER WOKE at noon on Monday and wanted to see the ocean.

More than that, he wanted to take the MechaHooker to see the ocean. He knew her algorithms would process the sight of it the same way they processed an empty room, and he wasn't sure how she would act around crowds of people, but for some reason, the idea of standing hand-in-hand with her at the end of the pier while the sea breeze swept into their faces seemed like a good one.

His father would be home in a few days, and he still hadn't decided how he was going to handle that situation. He'd always felt like he did his best thinking near the water. It would be appropriate to have the object of the dilemma at hand along with him.

Traffic was light on the 10 most of the way there. The whole time, the MechaHooker stared placidly forward, her hands laid flat on her thighs. At a stoplight on PCH, Baxter reached over and put his hand on her knee, forgetting it was one of her 294 erogenous zones. She began to gasp, moaning, "Fuck, fuck, I need you inside me *now*."

Baxter paid forty dollars for parking in a garage near the Santa Monica pier. He felt a twinge of pride when the attendant leered lecherously at the MechaHooker.

She crossed the busy intersection with him without incident, her hand clasped in his, staring straight ahead. On the boardwalk, Baxter steered her around families of pale, overfed tourists. They all looked bewildered and lost with their simple, sloping faces screwed up in slack-jawed wonder, clutching their hot dogs and cotton candy in meaty hands and pointing at surfacing dolphins in the distance.

At the end of the pier, Baxter put one hand on the railing and slipped his other arm around the MechaHooker's waist. She shuddered and smiled but didn't say anything. The sea breeze filled Baxter's nostrils. Sunlight glinted off the hulls of distant sailboats. Pelicans circled overhead, periodically dropping in sleek dives into the waves.

Baxter glanced at the MechaHooker. The wind lifted her hair away from her perfect face. *I can't give her up*, Baxter thought. *No matter what happens, I can't give her back to him. She's the only thing that matters.*

"You make me so happy," he told her, pulling her closer.

"You make my cunt so fucking wet," she replied.

A nearby tourist with a strip of sunscreen on his nose and a Kansas City Chiefs T-shirt straining against the bulge of his beer belly gave Baxter and the MechaHooker a horrified look. The man's son, who was maybe four or five but weighed about as much as a twelve-year-old, looked up at his father and said, "Daddy, what's a cunt? Why is that lady's cunt wet?" He began to cry. "Do we need to help her?"

"We should maybe head down to the beach," Baxter murmured to the MechaHooker, avoiding the tourist's indignant glare.

"Put your fat cock in my asshole," said the MechaHooker.

The tourist gasped and covered his son's ears, leading him away and muttering, "Goddamn Californian *freaks*. Place is a moral wasteland. No respect."

Down on the beach, they sat in a spot on the sand away from anyone else. Baxter stretched out and laid his head in the MechaHooker's lap. He thought he saw a pale man grinning at him in the distance, but then he became obscured by a roving mob of over-weight beachgoers. When they'd moved past, the man was gone.

Remembering the sensation of Tess's nails on his scalp, Baxter said, "Hey, um, MechaHooker? Would you...could you, like, run your fingers through my hair?"

She was silent for several moments. Baxter imagined the computers in her head cross-referencing various responses with one another, applying different algorithms as lines of code rained down in a constant stream. Finally, she said, "I want to feel your gigantic dick spasm inside my tight, wet pussy." Her hands did not move.

Baxter sighed. Maybe, he figured, with a future software update.

It was late in the afternoon when they got back to the house. Baxter led the MechaHooker upstairs, and if he'd been having any gnawing misgivings about her less-human qualities on the drive home, they were eradicated once he was inside her again. When he was done, he snuggled against her and went to sleep for a long time.

The sun had set when he woke. At first, he didn't sense anything was wrong. He stretched and yawned, hit his bong a couple times, and got up to retrieve his cigarettes from his discarded shorts. Upon turning toward the bed, he froze.

The MechaHooker wasn't moving.

Not that she was particularly active when he wasn't fucking her, but the rigid manner in which she lay flat on the bed as she stared up at the ceiling wasn't normal.

"Hey, MechaHooker," he said, panic edging into his voice and making it crack on the last syllable. "Hey, wake up." Nothing. He dropped the pack of cigarettes and leapt into the bed, poking and prodding her, smacking her face, shouting in her ear. He seized her shoulders and shook her. Still nothing. When he slipped two fingers into her vagina, it remained dry and loose; under ordinary circumstances, it would slicken and tighten around them.

After another few minutes of futile shouting and jostling, he called Dimitri.

"I have no idea how it happened," Baxter said after he'd explained the problem in a mad rush. "I mean, I took her to the beach, but—"

"You took robot to the beach?" Dimitri said. He chuckled. "I do not know why you would do this. Did you take it in water?"

"No, no, of course not. But...I mean, we were on the sand, and...I don't know, is sand bad for robots?"

"Hard to say. I have never taken robot to the beach."

"Well, what's wrong with her? How do I fix her?"

"Hard to say," Dimitri said again. "I cannot tell without seeing for myself, and even then..." He trailed off. "Is there tech support number?"

"No. I've read the whole manual a few times now. There's no phone number anywhere in it."

"Mm. Sounds like you are in shit luck, my friend."

"You have to help me. You have to. I'll do anything. I'll give you anything you want."

"I cannot come to you. The fires are all around me. I—"

"I'll come to you. Don't worry about that."

"You cannot come, either. You will never make it. Many people are evacuating. *I* am fine, of course. House is like bunker. But to *get* here, through the fires...this is impossible."

"I'll make it. I'll figure it out. Please, help me. I'll give you anything you want, seriously. Anything. Name it."

Silence, and then, "Mm. Will you let me take it for, ah...test drive?"

Baxter's stomach clenched, flipped over. "Come on, man. She's... you know, she's my..." He couldn't figure out how to finish the sentence. "Please. Anything but *that*."

"Is that, or no deal."

Baxter sat on the edge of the bed, running his hand through his hair. He looked at the frozen body of the MechaHooker. The thing which had become his *every*thing, reduced to a lifeless sex doll. "Fine," he said through gritted teeth. "You can have *one* round with her. Just one. And only after you've fixed her."

"Well, yes. No point in having go at her if she cannot be fixed, no?"

"I'll leave right now."

"Remember, I gave you warning. Probably is not good idea at all. If you get killed by fires, I will not feel least bit badly."

"I'll make it," Baxter said. "See you soon."

Once he'd hung up, he got dressed and then drew the Mecha-Hooker into his arms. She was very light. Carrying her was easier than he'd imagined it would be. "Hang on," he whispered as he buckled her into the passenger seat of his Mustang. "Just hang on. I'm not gonna lose you. I can't lose you."

He was weeping as he pulled out of the driveway.

THIRTY-SEVEN
SOMEBODY ELSE

THE WIND BUFFETED Ryland through the blown-out windows as he drove. After he'd cleared the broken glass from the driver's seat, he'd pressed the ignition button, and the car's motor had purred to life. He'd expected nothing different.

She wanted it to be drivable, he'd told Bruno. *She wants people to see.*

Eastbound traffic was almost nonexistent. The farther outside the city, the scarcer other cars became.

The red-orange glow on the horizon loomed like something otherworldly, until the flames themselves became visible. They shimmered and danced in the dark. Molten yellow embers swirled across the roadway in gusts, sometimes spinning into hellish cyclones. The smell of smoke and soot filled Ryland's car.

"I think this is probably the most dangerous thing you've done for another person," Bruno said from the back seat, raising his voice over the wind. "We should call Mom. Have her put it in your baby book. It might restore some of her faith in you as a human being. Man, I can't *tell* you how disgusted she is with you these days. Her and Dad both, but especially her."

"Shut up," said Ryland. His hands tightened on the wheel. "It doesn't matter." He glanced at the GPS. Fifteen more minutes. Almost there.

"Hey, man, I defended you. I told them you were just living your life. Had to find your own path. Didn't matter, though. They've got it in their mind you're some sort of monster."

"It doesn't matter," Ryland said again.

"*Speaking* of things that don't matter, what exactly is your plan for when you get there? What do you think is gonna happen? Are you gonna be her Prince Charming, wake her up with true love's kiss? And then she'll melt when she sees you, swear off the drugs, and the two of you'll ride off into Happily Ever Afterland?"

The freeway had narrowed into a wide two-lane road. Raging fires dotted the landscape on either side. The closest ones were fewer than a hundred feet from the asphalt on which Ryland drove. There were no other cars now. Many of the buildings he passed were burned black and misshapen. Ryland thought he saw a man standing on the side of the road, smiling with a freakish, glaring white grin which was much too large for his face, but when he passed him and looked in the rearview mirror, no one was there.

"I don't have a plan," he said, shaken by the nightmarish phantasm. "There's no fantasy. I just have to see her."

"Why, though? Why do you have to see her? You stopped caring about that poor girl years ago. All you're doing is trying to ease whatever shriveled lump of a conscience you have left. It's not gonna work, Ry-Ry. You're too far gone."

"You don't know anything. You're not real."

"Little bro, I'm the only real thing you've got left."

There were hardly any cars in the ER parking lot when he arrived at the hospital. The heat that smothered him when he got out of his car was an enormous, oppressive force. Like something alive and angry. The noxious odor of smoke shoved its black hand down his throat and brought tears to his eyes. He put his arm over his mouth and nose and jogged inside.

A pretty blonde nurse with a name badge identifying her as

WENDY ST. JOHN stood behind the reception desk. She held the phone to her ear and spoke to someone about evacuation plans. When she hung up, Ryland told her he was there to see a patient. He gave her Penny's name.

"I'm sorry," Wendy said. "You shouldn't be here." She had a compassionate air about her that seeped into her voice, her face. "Visiting hours are over, and the fires...we're in the middle of—"

"I know," Ryland said. "I know all that. But...please. She doesn't have anyone else."

Wendy started to say something else but stopped. Ryland had the sense she detected something in his face. Maybe the pained desperation in his eyes made her realize something. She gave him a small, sad smile. Glancing around, she consulted an iPad on the counter, tapped the screen a few times, and scrolled for a few moments. She looked up and said, "Follow me."

She led him down several stark white halls and to a door with the number 15 printed beside it in black numerals. "She's in there," she said. "Listen, you can't stay long, and the staff may give you some trouble if they see you."

"I'll be quick," Ryland assured her. He thanked her and went inside.

Penny was almost unrecognizable. She was thinner than when he'd last seen her, and her skin was a grayish-green color. Her head had been shaved and was wrapped in bandages. A ventilator was strapped to her face. Some kind of brace enclosed her wiry torso, and both her legs were suspended in casts with metal rods sticking out of them.

"Christ, Pen," Ryland breathed, collapsing into the chair beside her bed. He put his elbows on his knees and bowed his head, running his hands through his hair. "Goddammit."

He sat there listening to the ventilator and the chirping of the monitors. It was difficult to look at her. He didn't think he'd ever seen someone look so small. So broken. He tried to reconcile the image of her now with the one in his memory, the one where she'd been smiling and happy, vibrant. Glowing. She wasn't there anymore. She hadn't been for a long time.

"I don't totally know why I came here," he said. "I don't know what I thought I'd say. It's not like you can hear me." He leaned back in the chair. Shut his eyes.

"It seemed like the thing to do, you know? The *only* thing to do. But now I'm here and...and I don't even know if you'd want me here if you had a say in the matter." He paused. "I know I'm probably the worst thing that could have happened to you. I told myself I was doing you a favor by ending things. I think I even believed it. But the truth is, Penny...the truth is I wasn't thinking about you. After a certain point, I just stopped thinking about you."

He opened his eyes, looked at the shattered person before him. "I loved you. I did. I remember that. I remember that I was a person who loved you. But...but somewhere down the line I stopped being that person, and when I look back, it's like it's somebody else. It's like we were both somebody else." He took a deep, shuddering breath and pulled his cigarettes from his jacket pocket. Then, remembering he was in a hospital, he put them back. "Maybe I should apologize. Maybe that's what I thought I was going to do, coming here. But now...now I don't know if that would be right. I can't apologize for something someone else did. Or, I don't know, *didn't* do." A dull pain began to throb in his left arm. He rubbed at it with thoughtless, kneading fingers.

"And now my life is in shambles. Blown to pieces. I've never felt so hopeless before. And I remember the way you used to make me feel, back when I was someone different. I remember how no matter what was going on, you could make everything better. I think about that, and I...I wish..." He felt tears on his face. Swallowed a burgeoning sob. "I wish I could still be that person. I wish you and I had never stopped being the people we were, because I think every-thing was a lot better back then. I feel cold and alone in ways I don't think I've ever felt before, and I know that nothing is going to make it better, because you're gone and I am, too."

Wiping his face with the cuff of his sleeve, he stood and put his hand over Penny's wrist. It felt cold and brittle beneath his palm. He gave it a squeeze, and his fingers touched something coarse and dry. Puzzled, he gently turned her arm over. There was some kind of small wound on her inner wrist, caked with dried blood and beginning to scab over. Ryland bent closer and squinted at it.

Much as it had been when he'd discovered his ruined car in the parking garage, his brain at first refused to register what he was seeing. The wound was tiny, barely noticeable. At first glance, it was nothing more than a minor abrasion, something that could have been incurred in her fall. Looking closer, it became something else.

Letters. Letters forming a name.

Lyssi. Etched into her skin in careful cursive, the *i* dotted with a tiny heart.

He remained bent in paralysis for a long time. His thoughts came in roaring waves that crashed into one another and fell apart. It didn't make sense. It was impossible. Even if Lyssi had managed to track down Penny, how could she have made it out here? She didn't drive, and no Uber driver in his right mind would take her into this burning hellscape. And for Lyssi to gain access to Penny's apartment, incapacitate her long enough to *carve her name into her skin*, and then somehow have the strength to drag her to the balcony and hoist her over the railing...there was no rational explanation for it. And yet... she *had*. Somehow, she had done it.

I'll take everything from you.

Ryland stood, dizzy and disoriented. He wanted to do something, but he knew there was nothing to be done. It was over. Everything. All he could do was stagger from the room and make his way out of the hospital. He'd hoped to see Wendy again—to thank her, and perhaps to say something about the name on Penny's wrist—but the waiting room was empty, and no one was at the reception desk. It didn't matter. It wouldn't have solved anything.

By the time he was walking out into the scalding night, he was no longer certain of what he thought he'd seen. The blatant impossibility of the scenario made him question his memory of the crimson letters engraved in Penny's frail wrist. He'd imagined it, he told himself, thinking of the vision of the grinning man on the side of the road. It hadn't happened.

He'd expected to see Bruno waiting for him in the parking lot, leaning against his car, ready to make some snide comment. But Bruno wasn't there. No one was there.

When he slid behind the wheel, he lit a cigarette and wiped more tears from his face. The fires howled and raged all around him. He put the car in drive and nudged the accelerator, gripping the steering wheel with quaking hands. The pain in his left arm was flaring. He ignored it. *I have to get home*, he thought. *I just have to get home.* There was nothing else to do. Nowhere else to go.

His phone vibrated in the passenger seat as he was pulling toward the exit from the parking lot onto the road. "LYSSI" appeared on the screen. He stared at it, the car ambling forward.

His brother's words suddenly echoed in his head: *You should maybe answer your phone more often.*

He swallowed. His eyes were glued to the name on the screen. The name that was scrawled all over his ruined car. Seeing that name demolished the fragile certainty that he'd merely imagined it carved into his dying ex's flesh. A surge of emotions rushed through him— fury, sadness, hate, longing. She'd fulfilled her promise to ruin his life, and now she was...what? Calling to gloat? To tearfully apologize, beg for him to come back?

There was only one way to find out.

You should maybe answer your phone more often.

As the Mercedes crept over the speed bump and onto the road, Ryland leaned into the passenger seat and picked up the phone.

THIRTY-EIGHT
AN EXHIBIT IN THE MUSEUM OF A SLAUGHTERHOUSE

BAXTER KEPT his eyes locked on the road. He tried to ignore the fires blazing all around him. The Mustang's top was rolled up and all the windows were closed, but the smell of smoke poured in through the vents. He had to keep wiping his watering eyes with the heel of his hand.

He looked at his GPS app. Thirty-five minutes. Thirty-five minutes, and then Dimitri would bring the MechaHooker back to life. They would laugh about the whole thing, barricaded in Dimitri's "bunker" of a house. Maybe smoke some angel dust.

He just had to make it there.

Thirty-five minutes.

Thirty-four.

More worrisome than the fires was the potential Dimitri might not be able to fix her. He might take one look at her and announce there was nothing he could do. If that happened...Baxter couldn't think about it. He supposed it was possible she'd malfunctioned through no fault of his own—she was, after all, a prototype—but if *he* had broken her by taking her to the beach, he wouldn't be able to live with himself.

The freeway became a two-lane road with the fires closing in from either side. Houses stood charred and black, some of them still smoldering. An abandoned pickup truck blazed in an otherwise empty convenience store parking lot as fiery whirlwinds twirled around it. A coyote engulfed in flame dashed across a lawn of burning Astroturf.

As he was passing a sign for an upcoming hospital, Baxter saw a tall, pale man standing by the edge of the road. The man grinned at him with an evil smile that stretched all the way from one side of his face to the other. His clothes and hair were on fire, but he wasn't moving.

Baxter whipped his head around after driving by the grinning man, but when he looked out the rear windshield, no one was out there. By the time his eyes were back on the road, it was too late. He didn't even have time to hit the brakes.

The Mustang struck the Mercedes in the driver-side door right as the latter car had entered the roadway, before it had even committed to the left turn. Glass exploded. The airbags popped. Metal ground against metal. Twisting, shrieking. The sound was a cacophony of violence. Someone was screaming. Baxter realized it was him.

And then, it was over. An eerie quiet settled in, disturbed only by the crackling of the fires and the sound of liquid spewing onto the asphalt.

Baxter sat in dazed stillness for several minutes, breathing into the airbag. When he felt he could move, he unbuckled himself and fumbled for the door handle. It was stuck. He pushed his weight against it, and the door broke from the car and clattered onto the road. He wrested himself out of the vehicle and stood in the road. The pulverized Mercedes lay several yards away. Steam billowed from under its mangled hood. On wobbly legs, he approached it.

The first thing he noticed was that the name *Lyssi* had been carved into the paint of the Mercedes hundreds of times. All the *i*'s dotted with little hearts. He thought to himself, *That's impossible. A collision couldn't do that.*

The next thing he noticed was that the airbags hadn't gone off, and the car was empty.

With mounting dread permeating his shock, he walked around the Mercedes to the other side. Jagged pebbles of glass crunched beneath his sneakers.

He stood looking at the eviscerated body lying in the road for a long time. His brain kept trying to insist it wasn't seeing the image his eyes were sending it. He hadn't known it was possible for a person to look like that. It couldn't be real. But when reality set in, it came in a great tidal wave. He had to put his hands on his knees and bend down to let out a torrent of vomit which kept coming and felt like it would never stop.

When his stomach was emptied, he straightened and turned toward his Mustang.

He blinked. His brain again refused to acknowledge the image before him.

The oil leaking from the car had ignited, swallowing the Mustang in flame.

The MechaHooker, he thought, remembering she was in the passenger seat. He'd forgotten to check on her in the midst of his confusion, and now she was cooking within the burning vehicle.

He made it half of a step toward the car before the gas tank detonated. The resultant explosion lifted him from his feet and sent him sprawling.

Baxter remained lying motionless in the road, staring up at the smoke curling into the dark sky. He didn't stir until he felt a hand on his arm. A pretty blonde woman in nurse's scrubs was speaking to him. The words were lost, replaced by a shrill ringing. She helped him to his feet. He looked around; a crowd of doctors and nurses had come out of the hospital and was surrounding him. Some of their mouths were moving. The blonde nurse kept saying things to him and then watching his face with an expectant expression; Baxter realized she was asking him questions. He could only shake his head.

As several doctors came over and began to fuss over him, Baxter looked at the exploded car belching thick black smoke. His eyes burned with tears.

"I loved her," he said. His mouth formed the words, and he knew he'd said them despite his inability to hear them. "I loved her. She was everything. She was the only thing that mattered."

He stood watching the Mustang burn for several more moments, and then he pulled away from the doctors and the nurse. He began staggering in the direction of the fires in the hills on the other side of the road. They jumped and flickered across the sloping landscape like some infernal ocean. He had to go to them. There was nothing else to do. Nowhere else to go.

A hand closed around his arm. He yanked it away and walked faster. The hills swam in molten waves before him.

When someone tried to grab his arm again, he broke into a run.

THIRTY-NINE
SUCH SWEET TRAGEDY

TESS WOKE on Monday morning from a fitful sleep plagued with nightmares about Jasmine Yates.

In her dreams, Tess had been Jasmine's mother. Pitiful, penniless. Afflicted with some skin disease. Maggots bred and squirmed in the open sores on her flesh. Cockroaches and silverfish skittered across the walls and floors of her moldy studio apartment. Jasmine kept appearing, licking Tess's wounds. The final image from the dreams was one of Jasmine kneeling before Tess, spreading her emaciated legs, and going down on her. Right before Jasmine's lips touched Tess's vulva, her tongue turned into a rattlesnake that slithered up inside Tess and sank its fangs into her uterus.

After showering, she came downstairs to find her father sitting on the couch with his laptop open on his knees. He had a glass of bourbon in one hand and a cigar in the other.

Glancing at the clock, Tess said, "A little early for that, isn't it?"

Jared didn't answer her. He didn't look up from the screen. As Tess drew nearer, she heard the sounds coming from the video playing on the laptop. She frowned. "Dad," she said. "Jesus. Are you watching porn?"

Jared's eyes lifted and met his daughter's. Tess flinched. There was something wretched in his gaze. His face hard and unmoving, he patted the seat next to him on the couch. Tess hesitated, then crossed the living room and sat beside him.

It took her a moment to realize what she was looking at. The video on the screen was of a large, dark bedroom. The footage was cast in the greenish glow of night vision. A man and woman were having sex in the bed. Tess didn't recognize the man, but after a few seconds, she realized the woman was her mother.

"Oh," she said. "Oh." She looked away. "Jesus, Dad. What is this? Where did you get it?"

"It was emailed to me this morning," Jared said. "It came from an anonymous Gmail account. Kagomethinlife, I think it was. Some Japanese cartoon character for an avatar." He sipped his drink. Scowled at the screen. "I always suspected. That she was having affairs, I mean. It was just, you know. It was pretty easy to ignore. Ignorance, bliss. That whole thing."

"There's no point in watching it," Tess said. She closed the laptop and set it on the coffee table.

"No. No, of course not. You're right. I've already watched it I don't know how many times. I don't know why."

"Are you...okay?"

Jared puffed on his cigar. "You know," he said, "we used to...we were in love. It was just so long ago. That's the thing, I suppose. Love doesn't last. Love always runs out. You just have to hope one or both of you die before it does."

"Wow. Yikes."

He gave her a sad smile. "Don't go looking for love, Tessie. It's a fool's errand. Find someone you can tolerate. It's better if you can keep your emotions out of it. If you can avoid getting attached. It hurts less that way." He swallowed the rest of his bourbon and rose to his feet.

"I have to go get Daffodil up and ready. I told her I'd take her to the beach today." He paused. Looked uncertainly at Tess. "Do you, um. Do you want to come?"

Tess shook her head. She stared at the closed laptop. "No, thank you. There's something else I have to do."

She felt an odd, detached calm as she drove, taking the 110 to the 101 and then winding up into the hills above Silver Lake. She was on the right track. Finally, she had taken hold of her life, set it on a defined course. The future was less nebulous, more pronounced. *This is the right call*, she thought. She recalled the images of Nightmare Jasmine's snake tongue slithering inside her. *I'm doing the right thing. It's the only thing to do.*

Tess keyed in the code to The Writer's gate and parked behind his Bentley in the driveway. The sprinklers were on. One of the gardeners was trimming the hedges on the far side of the lawn. He turned and watched her, staring from beneath the wide brim of his straw hat.

The front door started to swing open right as she was reaching for it. Her fingertips grazed the brass handle before it pulled away from her. She put on what she thought was her best smile. But when the door opened all the way, the smile froze on her face, petrified and cold. Vacant. She stood staring, unable to even blink.

"Oh, my," said the girl standing in the foyer. Lyssi, Tess remembered. The adoring fan. Her hair was disheveled. Skin glazed with sweat. Blouse askew and only partially buttoned.

"Um, hey," Lyssi said. "Tess, right?" Her mouth became an awkward, embarrassed smile, but there was no embarrassment in her eyes. Her eyes were cruel and wild, alight with deviant delight. "Listen, I was just leaving."

"Lyssi, doll?" The Writer's voice called from farther inside. He came into the foyer, looking down at his shirt as he buttoned it. There was a small, dark, wet spot on the front of his underwear. "Don't forget to—" He glanced up and stopped speaking when he saw Tess. Barely missing a beat, he smiled and said, "Well. Tess. This is unexpected."

Tess said nothing. The smile remained frozen on her face. Stretched and painful.

"My Uber is going to be here any minute," Lyssi said. She looked over her shoulder at The Writer. "Thanks for..." She glanced at Tess. Her evil eyes smoldered. "Well, I had a really good time." She giggled. "You've got my number." She giggled again. To Tess, she said, "Great seeing you. You look amazing, as usual." She gave Tess's hand a little squeeze before moving past her and skipping down the driveway like a schoolgirl.

The Writer stood in the foyer. He took his cigarettes out of his shirt pocket and lit one, eyeing Tess. "Well," he said. He exhaled smoke. "Are you going to stand there grinning like a loon, or are you going to come in?"

Tess said nothing. She didn't move.

"For God's sake, Tess," The Writer said. He rolled his eyes and came to the door, taking Tess's hand and pulling her inside. He shut the door behind her and led her to the living room. Tess sat in an armchair. She pulled her knees to her chest. The smile had gone from her face, she realized.

The Writer stood watching her. He leaned against the wall, smoking his cigarette. "I get the feeling," he said, "that you're upset about something."

Tess could only stare straight ahead. She couldn't look at him.

"Come on," he said. "You're not *actually* going to make a big deal out of this."

Tess took a deep breath. "I came here," she said in a weak, quavering voice, "to tell you my answer is yes. To tell you I would marry you."

"Fantastic. That's great news. Certainly nothing to be *upset* about. It's something to celebrate. As a matter of fact, I'll go open a bottle of—"

"Stop it," Tess shouted. She looked at him but her vision swam. It occurred to her she was crying, which didn't make sense. She shouldn't be crying. She shouldn't be so affected.

It's better if you can keep your emotions out of it, her father had told her. *If you can avoid getting attached*. That's why she was here. Her emotions *weren't* in it. She *wasn't* attached. At least, that's what she'd thought. But everything had gotten confused and muddled and she didn't understand why or how.

"Stop...what?" The Writer asked.

"Playing dumb. Acting oblivious. Acting like...like...like you don't know exactly what the fuck you've done."

"Ah," said The Writer. Tess couldn't bring herself to wipe her eyes and thus couldn't make out the features of his face, but she knew he was looking at her in that amused, condescending way of his. She could feel it on her skin. "And what is it, exactly, that you believe I've done?"

"You ruined it. You ruined everything. You blew it all up."

"Is that what you think? Because...why? Make me understand. En*light*en me. Tell me how my having sex with some dumb fan has any bearing on anything. Come on, Tess. She's not even a real person."

"She's...not even a real person," Tess repeated.

"No. Of course not. Fucking somebody like her isn't any different than masturbation."

"Wow. Jesus Christ."

"Oh, please. You know what I'm talking about. Civilians. Peasants. They don't count. They don't have a purpose in life if they're not serving us in some way." Tess felt his eyes scorching into her. "And, what? Are you going to tell me you've not fucked anyone else the entire time we've been involved with one another?"

"Yes," she said. She was unsure of her reason for the lie even as it crossed her lips. It changed nothing. "Yes, that's what I'm going to tell you."

"Mm. Well. I don't know *why*. If that's true, you've rather egregiously misinterpreted the parameters of our relationship."

Tess shut her eyes. The tears rolled down her cheeks. She was ashamed of them. "It would seem that way," she said.

"It doesn't have to be like this. You're making this into something it's not." He paused. She could sense him considering something. Could picture the awful gears in his head turning. "Are you menstruating?" he asked. The smirk was detectable in his tone. "Is that where this is coming from?"

Tess stood. "I'm leaving," she said. "Goodbye, Chandler." As she passed him, he took hold of her arm. She jerked it away. "Don't. Touch me."

Once she'd left The Writer's compound, she parked by the curb a few blocks down. Tess folded her arms over the steering wheel, buried her face in them, and cried for a long time. Hating herself for it. It was absurd. She hadn't thought she'd cared. It didn't make sense.

When there was nothing left, she wiped her face and blew her nose with a Starbucks napkin she found in her center console. Lighting a cigarette, she put her sunglasses on and drove home. There was nothing else to do. Nowhere else to go.

Neither her father's nor her brother's car was in the driveway. The house was empty. She poured herself a glass of wine and decided she didn't want it. Without giving much thought to what she was doing, she went out the back door and let herself into the pool house. The rank odor of weed and cigarette smoke struck her like a backhanded slap across the face.

In the bathroom, she looked at her reflection in the medicine cabinet mirror. Her makeup was a smudged and smeary mess. When she took her sunglasses off and set them on the sink, the eyes that looked back at her were washed out and empty.

Tess opened the medicine cabinet, looking at Arden's collection of pharmaceuticals. She took out the bottle of Valium and shook two tablets into her palm, tossing them into her mouth and dry swallowing. After a moment, she took two more. Then another three. She blacked out for a few seconds, and then the bottle was empty. She moved on to the Vicodin and swallowed everything in that bottle, as well, and then she did the same with the Percocet, and finally the Xanax.

She put the bottles back, closed the medicine cabinet, and walked outside, where she stripped to her bra and panties and stood at the edge of the pool, looking at her shadow shimmering over the still water.

You know, The Writer had told her, *if you were to die young, you'd look so beautiful in a casket. Like such sweet tragedy.*

She lowered herself into the pool. The water enveloped her in a cool embrace.

It felt like coming home.

FORTY
AN ALIBI FOR DESPAIR

IT WAS late morning when Arden woke on Monday. He looked for a long time at the bong sitting on the floor beside the couch, but didn't touch it.

After showering, he took his Lexapro and Cymbalta, his Lamictal and Neurontin, but he left the rest of the pills in the medicine cabinet. He wanted a clear head. He thought about doing a line or two and decided against it.

The house was empty and quiet. His car was the only one in the driveway. Behind the wheel of his Jaguar, he lit a cigarette and keyed Rebecca's address into the GPS.

As he drove, half-listening to the white noise of antidepressant advertisements on the radio, he tried to think of what he was going to say. Heartfelt speeches weren't his thing. He wondered if they ever had been in his other, unremembered life. Before something inside him had changed. Broken.

It would sound better, he decided, if it wasn't rehearsed. It would be more sincere that way. *From the heart*. The sickly earnestness of it made him frown. He told himself this was a necessary thing. Something he had to do, no matter how ridiculous.

He parked on Tamarind and got out of his car, smoking and looking up at Rebecca's apartment building. The Berkeley bear mascot stood on a third-floor balcony jutting from the building next to Rebecca's. It waved at him, and then it removed its giant, stuffed head. Beneath it was the visage of a pale man with black eyes and a too-wide grin crammed with too many teeth. Arden blinked and looked away. He did feel unnerved, but not as much as he knew he ought to be.

Farther down the street, a group of red-clad soldiers ambled around a parked Humvee, drinking beer out of cans. They stared at Arden with disinterest. He ignored them as best he could, just as he ignored the relentless pounding of his heart. *It doesn't matter*, he tried to tell himself. *Whatever she says, it won't make a difference. Life will go on all the same. The universe won't even blink.* He wanted to believe it, but he didn't. It was as though everything in existence, terrestrial and otherwise, was watching him. He began to perspire, his skin hot, like he was standing beneath a spotlight on an auditorium stage.

Dropping his cigarette and crushing it beneath his toe, he walked across the street and went up the stairs to Rebecca's apartment. As he was raising his fist to knock, the door opened.

Arden stared, his fist frozen in the air. Luke Viceroy stared back at him. He was wearing a Gucci baseball cap and a red Supreme T-shirt stained with sweat. The zipper on his Bermuda shorts was open.

"Oh," said Luke. "Hey, dude." He flashed a smile that was somewhere at the midpoint between snide and affable. "Weren't you at my party? Like, a week ago, I think? You came with Rebecca?"

Arden lowered his hand. He could only nod.

"Yeah, bro, I remember. The fuckin' soyboy, right?" He snickered and then glanced over his shoulder into the apartment. Lowering his voice, he said to Arden, "If you're here for what I think you're here for, well..." He snickered again. "I hope you like sloppy seconds." He clapped Arden on the shoulder and pushed past him, jogging down the stairs.

Arden stood blinking, unable to move. Rebecca appeared in the doorway, holding a cigarette, wearing her Versace bathrobe. Her hair was wild. "Arden," she said, frowning. She didn't invite him in. Instead, she came outside, shutting the door behind her. Something inside Arden stretched and broke at the sound of the door closing. He stared at it, feeling cold.

"What are you doing here?" Rebecca asked. She flicked her cigarette. Arden searched her face for something approaching compassion or concern. There was nothing. Only unaffected blankness.

"I..." Arden began. He felt dizzy. Put his hand on the railing to steady himself. "I just wanted to tell you...I wanted to...I..."

Rebecca rolled her eyes. "Jesus. What are you on today? Vicodin? Valium? Xanax? All of the above? God, Arden, you're unbelievable."

"No," Arden croaked. "No, I'm...I'm not on anything. Really. I'm totally sober."

"Uh huh." Her face began to shift. A prism of kaleidoscopic colors broke from it.

Arden turned away, gripping the railing. A tear fell from his face and exploded into a million pink shards that scattered along the ground below. Another one followed and shattered. "You should get some help, Arden," Rebecca said. Her voice was frigid. Devoid of emotion. "You're a goddamn mess. You have been since I met you."

"*What happened*," Arden whispered, looking at the broken fragments of his tears glittering like pink crystals in the sun.

"What?" Rebecca said, annoyed. "I didn't hear you."

Arden looked at her. Her face had gone back to normal, but it was cast in a shadow of disgusted disapproval. He could see himself reflected in her eyes. Pathetic. Pleading. "I asked what happened," he said. "I...I don't know what happened."

Rebecca dragged from her cigarette. "I know you don't, Arden."

"I really thought...it was supposed to be you. I thought you could..." He took a breath. Rubbed his eyes. Ran his hands through his hair. "I thought you could save me."

Rebecca's gaze was hard and cutting. "I was never going to save you," she said. "No one is ever going to save you." She flicked her cigarette over the railing, went inside, and closed the door. Arden heard the lock click.

Arden slid into a slumped sitting position against the railing, his head lowered. Pink tears shattered in his lap. He kept expecting Rebecca to come outside and scream at him to get out of here, to leave and never come back. He was almost hoping she would. But she didn't. The door remained closed.

When he had no tears left, he struggled to his feet. The broken fragments crunched under the soles of his sneakers. Clutching the railing, he moved slowly down the stairs and across the street to his car. "Burn Me to Ash" by Calliope Laing came over the speakers when he pressed the ignition button.

He turned the radio off.

As he pulled out of the parking space, he glanced up the street to where the soldiers in red had been, but they were gone.

Lighting a cigarette, he put his sunglasses on and drove home. There was nothing else to do. Nowhere else to go.

It will hurt, his Aunt Judy had told him. *It always does when it's real.*

His father still wasn't home when Arden got back, but Tess's Audi was parked in the driveway. He went through the house and out the back door, planning to take a cocktail of pills, smoke a bowl or two, and then pass out, succumbing to the sweet oblivion of unconsciousness. He stopped on his way to the pool house. What he saw first was the pile of his sister's clothes. They twisted and pulsed on the concrete.

He saw his sister next. She was floating on top of the water.

Arden moved to the edge of the water and looked down at Tess. The image of her body shimmered like a mirage.

He stripped to his underwear and lowered himself into the pool. There was a sudden urge to sink to the bottom, remain there, to open his mouth and let the water fill his lungs. Let it take him. Take him away. The voice of the water screamed at him to stay. But then he hoisted Tess in his arms. He paddled to the shallow end, carried her up the steps, and laid her on a chaise longue. Her skin was cold. Her eyes were open. He closed them.

Retrieving his cigarettes and lighter from his discarded jeans, he lit one and sat in the chair beside Tess. He didn't look at her. Instead, he looked at the sky. He listened to the water dripping from Tess's body. Overhead, the clouds danced and jeered. Sirens wailed somewhere in the distance. The sound had an apocalyptic finality to it. Arden closed his eyes.

He thought he could smell smoke.

ACKNOWLEDGMENTS

Many people aided me in this book's development—Sadie Hartmann, Katie Alice Greer, Autumn Christian, Marissa D., Breanna P., Lauren P., Nicole Eigener, JP, Sasha Kiyoka, Tracy Applegate, Jeremy Wagner, Steve Wands, Anna Kubik, Kristy Baptist, and Jarod Barbee all made particularly large contributions to the process. They have my utmost gratitude.

ALSO BY CHANDLER MORRISON

#thighgap

Human-Shaped Fiends

Along the Path of Torment

Dead Inside

Until the Sun

Hate to Feel

Just to See Hell

ABOUT THE AUTHOR

Chandler Morrison is the author of seven previous books, including *#thighgap* and *Dead Inside*. His short fiction has appeared in numerous anthologies and literary journals. He lives in Los Angeles.